A THEFT OF MAGIC

THE FAY OF SKYE - BOOK TWO

CARA MCKINNON

Stars and Stone Books

Editing by Literally Yours Editing
Copyediting by Symantha Reagor
Cover Design by Stars and Stone Books
Images © Can Stock Photo Inc. / rbv

Stars and Stone Books
Printed in the United States of America
Digital Edition 1.2
Print Edition 2

Digital ISBN: 978-0-9977081-3-4
Print ISBN: 978-0-9989514-3-0

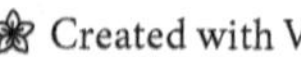 Created with Vellum

For Mandi.

Finally, for reasons.

On the heels of the nightmare came the alarm from the wards.

Someone was trying to break into the house.

Sorcha Fay leapt from bed. She threw on her boots and her coat and scried the wards for the source of the alarm. The beach. She was halfway downstairs and headed for the back door before she even thought to be afraid.

Indignation and anger were the foremost of her emotions. She couldn't wait to confront whoever had been messing with her wards. This time, they were caught, and she'd prepared a few extra surprises in case they tried to escape.

Oh, she hoped they tried to escape. She might not be as quick on her feet with offensive spells as her cousins, but with plenty of time, Sorcha was perfectly capable of mounting an effective attack.

Or perhaps this was more accurately a defense—because she would defend Fay House to her dying breath. But with luck her dying breath would not come tonight.

She hurried down the cliff path to the beach, but stopped

when her feet skidded against the small loose stones, making a terrible racket. She should be more wary. After all, whoever this was had tampered with her wards many times already, and she hadn't been able to track the source or trap the intruder before tonight. There was a not insignificant chance that even her skillful and malicious traps would be avoided or dealt with. She couldn't ignore the danger completely.

She used the salt spray, mist, and moonlight to weave a glamour. It would hide her until she could take stock of the situation, and she could take her time and place her steps more carefully the rest of the way.

The beach was a mix of sand and stone, and her boots made soft crunching sounds on the pebbles that she couldn't avoid without spending more time and magic, and she was impatient to confront her trespasser.

Assuming the intruder was still in the trap.

She came around a jut of cliffwall. A boat sat on the beach, beyond the water's edge. A few steps beyond the waves, at the base of the cliff, stood a man. Sorcha swallowed, hard.

He'd tried to use magic to escape, because her incineration spell had been activated in addition to the binding ward. It had worked exactly as she'd imagined, burning off his clothing and any items he'd been carrying. She'd meant the spell to leave intruders vulnerable, and bereft of any magical tokens they'd planned to use against her, but she hadn't been expecting her adversary to be so…male.

The moon was a hint shy of full, already sinking toward the west in the bright summer sky. Its pale glow and the never-quite-dark of a Scottish summer night illuminated the man's perfectly formed flesh, like a sculpture brought to life. He was tall and lean, with defined musculature but no bulk. He reminded her of a greyhound, with a powerful chest and shoulders but a trim waist and hips. Her gaze shied away from what was clearly visible between those hips and fled upward to his face.

Here, she stared—riveted. He was beautiful. She couldn't tell the shade of his eyes in the moonlight, but he had a long, straight nose and a thin, wide mouth. His cheekbones cast shadows onto the smooth planes of his face, and his jaw was angled and sharply defined. His hair was dark and much longer than was the fashion. He probably kept it pulled back, away from his face, but her spell would have destroyed any thong or tie. It whipped back from his face in the sea breeze, and when he swung his head as far as the ward would allow, a few strands tangled under his chin.

Something inside her belly burned. It was not fair that she would be attracted to this man. He'd invaded her sacred space, had come for a purpose that could not be good, and she was lusting after him as though he were an eligible lad from the village.

Sorcha clamped on her inconvenient desires and crept closer.

He was cursing in several languages. She recognized French and English, and that last was probably Irish because it sounded like Gàidhlig, but the pronunciation was off. His hand made an aborted gesture, probably another attempt at casting a spell-net, and when the ward reacted he suggested that it do something with itself that it did not have the proper appendages or orifices to accomplish.

In short, he looked delectable and dangerous, and Sorcha had no wish to confront him here in the open. So she drew down a few threads of the ward and rewove them, forming a new pattern.

"What in the hells?" the man shouted, as his feet dragged against the pebbled shore. This was going to be the tricky part. She'd had to sacrifice the extra protections to gain momentum, and she hoped he didn't realize that before she could maneuver him back into the little cave in the cliffs behind him.

Fortunately, he was too preoccupied fighting the motion to recognize that if he'd stopped and tried to rip the ward apart, he would have succeeded. She nudged him into the cave and quickly attached the ward to the stones around the entrance. Once she was satisfied with the new configuration, she tied it into the larger house ward so it would be sustained without her feeding it energy.

Only then did she let go, and drop her glamour.

RONAN MCCARRICK'S NIGHT HAD STARTED BADLY AND GONE straight to the hells. First he'd argued with Bart, the captain of his flagship, about the wisdom of going on this mission alone. He'd reminded his friend and smuggling-partner with more force than he'd intended who owned what and who called what shots. He'd then set off for the little cove nestled along the coastline of Skye.

He'd managed to muscle the longboat to shore over a choppy sea, while his ship disappeared into the night, headed south to finish its run. They would be back in a few days, depending on how the voyage went and how quickly they could dispose of their cargo. But he was on his own, and by the time he stumbled onto the beach his chest and shoulder muscles spasmed like fury.

Bart's prophecy coming true did not help his mood improve. The spell had sprung from nowhere. He'd strained against the threads of magic that had captured him, but though he could still move his upper body slightly, his legs had been immobilized.

Who the hells put such potent wards on a beach? With the wind and tide, the net would have to be renewed every day. Only an idiot or someone truly paranoid would go to such lengths to protect a stretch of sand and stone.

Annoyed, he'd flexed his fingers and prepared his typical counter-ward spell-net. But the moment he drew power into the first thread, the world burst into blinding light. He was bathed in heat, and then suddenly plunged into cold. It took a few moments for his vision to return, and when it did, the reason for the temperature spikes—and his now-pebbled flesh—became apparent. The ward had a countermeasure, which had incinerated his clothing.

Fecking hells.

Now he was naked, sore, and trapped on a frigid Scottish beach on a relatively deserted portion of Skye. He hoped whoever set the ward came to admire their handiwork. He intended to give them a scalding piece of his mind.

What sort of monster strips a man bare?

That was when it occurred to him that he'd had something rather important in his pocket. The damned letter to the Seeress, who would be unlikely to believe a random Irish stranger appearing on her beach in the middle of the night.

Bloody fecking hells.

He cursed until he could almost see the words hanging in the air, but it didn't improve his mood. How the feck was he supposed to escape this?

This was all Evie's fault. Damn her for running off and joining the Fay School and then luring him to help them with promises of the duchess's deep pockets. If she hadn't been like a sister to him, he would curse Evie to the dark god. As it was, he sent a fervent wish into the universe that every mug of ale she drank for a month went inexplicably flat.

Something pushed him away from the waves and toward the cliff. He flexed and wriggled as far as the ward would allow, but the pressure against his body was inexorable. His bare feet scraped through the sand and pebbles, and his curses were half in frustration and half in pain.

Darkness surrounded him. A cave, barely taller than he was, and not very deep or wide. He could see the back of the cave in the light of the moon, which had fallen far enough into the western sky to cast its illumination full in his face when he turned around.

The pressure ceased, and he stumbled forward against a force that was no longer pushing him. He fell. Inside the cave, the sand piled into deep mounds, with none of the pebbles from outside. It didn't exactly cushion his fall, but when he rubbed his knees, he was thankful that he had only minor abrasions and not jagged cuts.

The direct light of the moon illuminated the walls of the cave. Carvings and drawings surrounded him as though he'd wandered inside a standing stone.

He pushed to his feet and strode for the cave mouth. Another wall of force blocked his exit. He was tempted to try and break through with more magic, but he'd learned his lesson, and instead balled his hands into fists. He finally remembered to open his Sight, something he ought to have done the moment he landed on the beach. Then he'd not have gotten caught in the damned wards at all.

The ward was intricate and far too well-constructed for him to easily dismantle. The carvings on the walls glowed and hummed with magical energy, helping to feed the damned thing. He slammed one fist against his hip in frustration.

Beyond the barrier, shadow and mist swirled away to reveal a woman.

She was very short, with blond hair so pale it was indistinguishable from the moonlight. It was loose around her shoulders, and she wore a dark fitted coat, half-unbuttoned, over what looked like a nightgown. Was this his tormentor, then?

He couldn't distinguish her features. The moon at her back transformed her into a silhouette, limned by light. The sky wasn't truly dark, but it wasn't daylight either. Beneath the cliff there were too many shadows to see her clearly. She drew a symbol on the ward-wall, and though he hadn't missed the sound of wind and waves, it was a shock to have them return. How had she done that? He hadn't even seen the threads of the weave shift, and it still felt solid under his hand. If this was the Seeress of Skye, someone had lied about her proficiency with magic. She was bloody good.

"Who are you?" she demanded. "What have you been doing to my wards?"

What had *he* done to *her* wards? Better question, what had her wards done to him? He stared at her, and words temporarily deserted him. Then he folded his arms over his stomach and leaned as close as the ward would allow.

"The name's Ronan McCarrick, and I didn't do a thing to your wards before they scorched every stitch off me."

Her head moved, her shadowed face tilting downward. Was she truly ogling his body? Now, of all times?

"See something you like?" The words were mocking and half-growled with anger.

Her head jerked back up, and her silver hair swished around her shoulders. "I'm sorry," she whispered. Then she collected herself and pulled her shoulders back. "But I'm not sorry for trapping you. I knew you wouldn't suspect there were additional protections this time. How did you manage to tamper with the wards and leave no trace of your magic before?"

"Before? I've never been on this cursed isle, and I've certainly never tangled with your wards."

"Why should I believe you? Someone's been doing it, and here you are."

"I'm here because the bloody Duchess of Fay sent me."

"Ha. Why would she send you, and not come herself?"

"What do I know about why the quality do anything?" Never mind that his father was a viscount. That tie had been broken a long time ago. "I presume you're the one I'm meant to contact. The Seeress of Skye." The note had been addressed to Sorcha Fay, but Evie had told him everyone called her the Seeress.

She neither confirmed nor denied her identity, but he didn't have any doubts. "It's easy enough to prove your story." She lifted her chin, revealing the pale skin of her forehead. "I'll send her a telegram."

"That wouldn't be wise." He tried again to meet her gaze, but her eyes were too deeply in shadow. "She sent me because she doesn't want anyone to realize what she's planning."

"And what, exactly, is she planning according to you?"

"I've not a clue. I'm merely the courier."

"Courier implies that you brought something."

"I did. Your spell burned it."

"Oh." She seemed taken aback, even chagrined. Well, and why shouldn't she be?

"So no, I can't prove anything I say is true. All I know is, I was told to bring back the Druid Wand of Triple Wood and Le Fay's Diadem."

She produced a guffaw incongruous with her diminutive height. "Those are two of the most powerful artifacts in the family collection. Do you really expect me to let you waltz off with them?"

"I imagine that was why she sent the note." He tapped on the ward-wall to remind her of her spell. "The one that burned."

"Yes. Well." She coughed. "Then you understand why I won't take you at your word."

He shrugged, as though this were of no importance to him. As if she didn't have him trapped in a cold bloody cave on the coast of a bloody Scottish island.

"I have other methods of contacting the duchess. I'll try that in the morning, and then I'll decide what to do with you."

"In the morning?" He practically sputtered the words. "You're going to leave me here all night in my altogether?"

She inclined her head toward the cliffs, and the moonlight caught her face in profile. The sight impacted him like a punch to the gut. She wasn't the most beautiful woman he'd ever seen, but something about the way her forehead curved to a pert little nose and an expressive mouth with plump, delectable lips, made his blood heat. She worried at her lower lip with her teeth, and he clamped his mouth shut against a groan.

No fecking way was he going to be attracted to this Scots harpy. Well, perhaps he couldn't stop the attraction, but he could damned well refuse to entertain the images that clamored for attention in his brain. Like the vision of her silver hair sliding over his skin, her perfect little mouth open in a moan as he buried his cock in her hot, wet cunny.

No, he wasn't going to picture that. He focused on the cold, and the damp, and his anger.

"I'll bring you clothes, and something to sleep on," she said, and now he was thinking about pushing her onto a blanket in the soft sand. Feck it!

"Your munificence knows no bounds." He sketched her a mocking bow and formed his speech with the upper-crust English accent he'd learned at school, diverting her attention from the fact that his cock had begun to stiffen.

"Even if you are the one who has been toying with my

wards, you've not done any actual harm yet. I wouldn't have you freeze your arse off on my account."

"You could stay here and warm it for me." Now why in the hells had he said that? If there were any gods paying attention, she would assume he'd meant the words to mock her, not as the absolutely sincere invitation they were. He pictured her gripping his arse-cheeks as he spread her legs wide and plunged into her. His cock was almost fully erect now. Damn the thing.

But she—thank you whatever deity had been listening—took offense and stalked off. As she walked away, her face and form entered the light for the first time. She was as short as Evie. But where Evie was wand-slim and sylph-like, Sorcha was the image of an ancient fertility goddess. She was round, and soft, with voluptuous breasts and lush, wide hips that would cradle him as he thrust inside her. Before he could stop it, he had his fist around his cock.

She disappeared from view, and he dragged his hand down the shaft from the head to his bollocks, stretching the foreskin away to reveal the glistening wet crown beneath.

It took depressingly few pumps before he came, ejaculating against the stones of the cave. He leaned back against the opposite wall.

What the hells was the matter with him? He'd never been so aroused by a woman that he'd had to pleasure himself moments after first meeting her. And even with the need temporarily sated, he suspected he would be hard and lusting for her when he saw her again.

She'd better make good on that offer of clothes, or the next time she came to visit her effect on him would be all too visible.

Bloody fecking hells.

2

Sorcha stumbled a half dozen times on the path to the house. Every nerve in her body sang and danced, a mix of exhilaration, apprehension, and desire. She couldn't trust him, but her body didn't much seem to care.

And neither, apparently, had his. She wasn't so naïve that she couldn't identify an erect cock, even if she'd yet to choose someone to have intercourse with. But she'd certainly done her share of kissing and under-the-clothes fondling, and on one memorable occasion, she and Duncan Grant had experimented with a much more intimate variety of kisses.

She'd never been tempted to take her explorations further with any of the young men on the Isle. So why could she not stop thinking about her interloper and probable thief bearing her to the sand and burying that lovely, hard cock inside of her cunny?

Stop it, Sorcha. You need to find a way to contact Etta or Muireall and discover if this man is telling the truth.

The heavy oak doors, shipped to the island by Darach Fay in honor of his namesake in the 1500s, swung open at her approach. No one knew which distant ancestor had put that spell in place, probably because no one had admitted to it at the time, and while she usually appreciated that the doors of the house were open to anyone of Fay blood, tonight the motion startled her.

She leapt backward and put a hand over her pounding heart. She sucked air into her lungs and forced it back again. Her pulse raced, wild and erratic. She had to control herself. Now. No one was in the house except her. She'd neutralized the threat to the wards.

Except, what if she hadn't? What if Ronan was telling the truth, and someone else was still a threat? Someone with the capability of bypassing all her defenses?

Cold fingers of fear slipped down her spine.

He had to be lying.

She slammed the door shut and pounded up the main staircase to the second floor, where the Fay library was housed. Inside the library were several cabinets full of minor magical artifacts. Many of them had more value as display pieces than sorcerous tools, but at least one must be useful in her current situation.

She burst into the library almost before the spell could activate, and braced herself for the sound of the door closing behind her. It clicked, and she stood still for a moment in the moon-washed room. She'd always loved sitting in the seats built into the fourteen-foot-high windows, reading and watching the waves foam against the cliffs. Tonight, the man trapped in the cove kept stealing into her thoughts. At least the cave was well above the tide line. Unless a massive storm surge pulled the tide unnaturally high, he'd stay dry.

But not warm. The memory of his delectable and naked flesh clamored for attention, but she squashed it and strode to the first cabinet. Inside was a Hermetic Tablet, which her mother had once jokingly called the "As Above, So Below Stone." It worked on the principle that things in a small scale corresponded to things in a big scale. Whatever you drew on the tablet could become full-sized in reality. The spell was limited, but she could use it to draw into existence a few necessities for Ronan.

There were three areas delineated on the tablet. The first was for where you wanted the effect to take place. Sorcha sketched in the cave. The second was for what you wanted to appear. She drew the objects she wanted (and thank the goddess the tablet worked on symbolic likeness because she was no artist). The third was for how long they should remain corporeal, with the minimum of one hour and the maximum of a week. A week would drain a lot of energy, and the stone couldn't be used for anything else until the first set of things disappeared, so she drew a circle with twenty-four spokes radiating from the center. A circle with one spoke drawn to the center would have been one hour. Hers represented a whole day. If she didn't have things sorted by tomorrow night, she would add a day to the tablet.

Holding the stone up to the moonlight, she spoke the words of its incantation. The tablet vibrated in her grip, making her teeth snap together, and then magic pulsed toward the sea.

Sorcha put the tablet back and continued searching the cabinets. It was too dark in here, so she summoned a few fairy lights and left them to hang in the air above her. Her mother had installed electric lighting in the house before her death, but Sorcha didn't like the flat, too-bright glare of the bulbs or the stink and noise of the generator in the electrical shed.

Electricity consumed gasoline, the bulbs burned out quickly, and both items cost real money to replace. Fairy-lights were reliable, and only cost her in magical energy.

She found what she needed in the third cabinet.

The mirror was tiny, half-again the size of her palm, but it was infused with a spell that could make contact with any other mirror within a five-hundred-mile radius. Glasgow was less than three hundred miles away, so she ought to be able to reach Etta or Muireall.

Timing would be important. If she remembered this artifact's limitations correctly, it worked for a short burst of time, and then required a ritual to renew its energy. She would have to check The Catalogue to be certain. *The Catalogue of Clan Fay Arcana and Articles of Magic Origin or Usage* was a multi-volume work compiled by Machara Fay, mother of Lilias, in the 1780s. Sorcha had spent most of her life caring for the objects enumerated on its pages.

She found the reference quickly, but the information provided was not heartening. The mirror would work for a half-hour at most, but probably much less time because it hadn't been recharged in a while. She would need to do a ritual at the full moon to bring it to complete potency, but that was still a few days away, and she needed to contact Etta or Muireall quickly.

But not tonight. The hour was too late to catch them getting ready for bed, so her best chance would be when they dressed in the morning.

She ought to go to bed, but she would have trouble falling back to sleep. She was too full of nervous energy, and still had too many questions without answers. Meditation wouldn't do the trick, either, not with a real, live intruder cooling his heels in her cave. Would he be searching for a way to circumvent her wards? She would be if she were trapped in there. He wouldn't find one.

She trudged back down the hall, through the family wing, and into her bedroom, her earlier unease tamped by weariness. The mirror gleamed with reflected fairy-light when she placed it on her bedside table. She took off her coat and boots, dismissed the lights, and sat in her own window seat overlooking the sea.

Would Ronan approve of her offerings? Would bend his pride enough to eat the food, or to wrap himself in the blankets? Would he think of her as the spelled-clothes brushed his skin?

Her hands stole up to cup her breasts, and she thumbed her erect nipples through the thin fabric of her nightgown. She had to conquer this fascination before she saw him again. So she deliberately conjured his image, standing there on the beach, with his sleek muscles bared to salt, wind, and sky.

He could have been a selkie—like his name implied—and she the human woman who stole his skin and trapped him in human form.

Her fantasy followed the legend. The powerful selkie, with his water magic and deep ocean wisdom, was drawn to the woman on the shore, to the alien glow that radiated from her spirit. She was light and moon and air, and he was dark, and cold, and wave.

They embraced and awoke a new magic, together.

Sorcha's fingers stroked her nipples faster, as she imagined Ronan's mouth suckling her. One hand slid over her belly to the cleft between her legs. She caressed herself through the fabric of her nightgown, picturing his large, powerful hands instead of her small but capable ones. She shuddered as a fingertip grazed her clitoris.

The light touch wasn't enough. Sorcha dragged the skirt of her gown to her waist and sank a finger into her wet core, dragging the slickness up to the engorged and sensitive nub at the top of her sex. Ronan's tongue would lave her there, dragging against the tiny hood with quick, determined strokes. Then he would rise, push her legs apart, and glide inside her tight, slippery cunny.

Her finger moved faster, pleasure building and cresting, and then burst like a waterskin, flowing from her core and down her shaking limbs. She ached with emptiness.

She wanted—no, needed—his cock, to fill her, to pump into her again and again and then spend deep in her womb. She longed to cling to his shuddering body as he came, to hear his shout at the moment of climax, to cradle him when he slumped into repletion after.

Sorcha collapsed back against her pillows.

Despite the lovely burst of pleasure and the beautiful fantasy, she hadn't mastered her craving. She'd only primed the well.

SHE HAD A VISION BEFORE DAWN. IT WASN'T THE FIRST SHE'D had like this. She'd been seeing little pieces of a person's life, and as she'd now watched him mature from a child to a young man, and finally to an adult, she had to assume that she'd been viewing the past.

That was what made them different from her usual visions, which were almost always of the future. She had an intense feeling the boy who'd grown up in these visions was a man *now*.

She'd started a new vision journal to document these odd glimpses, but so far had not gleaned anything that would tell her his name. She pulled the journal from her bedside table's drawer and grabbed a pencil.

The blond man was in a jungle, surrounded by a mix of mostly fair-skinned Europeans and a few dark-skinned Africans. I don't know why, but I think this is somewhere in the southern region of Africa. He's telling a balding white man with a mustache that he's an idiot and that nothing good will come of his actions. After that, I get the impression of violence and death.

She put the pencil back into its stitched leather loop and closed the journal. The words were clean, rational, and almost detached. But the jagged edges of each letter proved that her body was still shaking from the residual anger, most of it from his powerlessness to stop what was coming.

Who was this man? She'd seen him as a child, running wild in a hilly area dotted with lakes and rivers. He'd been part of a group of boys that were well-dressed and had ample free time—if she could judge by the pranks and antics she'd seen. A farmer's child would be needed to tend livestock, do chores, and help in the fields. He was gentry at the least.

He'd been the undisputed leader of his friends, with a keen wit, sly humor, and deeply-rooted sense of honor and justice. He did not allow his cohorts to torment animals or smaller boys, and she'd even once seen him intervene when one of the group teased a girl.

Later, she'd seen him stand rigid beneath a strap wielded by a merciless instructor at a boarding school, and seen another adult give implicit permission for a group of older boys to give him a thorough and calculated beating.

Now, as a man, he retained his rigid sense of honor and a need for justice, but his wit had been transmuted to a razor-edge intelligence, and his humor had been beaten out of him.

She traced a fingertip over the leather binding of the journal. *Who are you?* She asked again. *And why do I see visions of you?*

THE SOUND OF WAVES LULLED RONAN TO SLEEP, EVEN THOUGH he'd intended to stay alert and wary until his jailor returned. When he woke, the horizon had shifted from night-black to dawn-grey. The sky was pale blue, with smudges of grey and white clouds drifting in from the west. There'd be rain before noon.

He sat up in the nest of blankets and tugged on a pair of perfectly-sized boots. They matched the perfectly-sized clothes he now wore. She'd somehow managed to make provisions appear inside the warded cave, and he was begrudgingly impressed. He had two blankets, a pillow, the clothes and boots, a hamper full of food and water, a small lamp that glowed with a fairy light, and even a book.

He'd let out an involuntary chuckle when the items had popped into existence in the sand, and he saw the book sitting on top of the neat pile. She might be suspicious of his intentions and unwilling to release him, but she wasn't cruel or without compassion. She hadn't considered sanitation, but he had dug a hole in the sand and then filled it back in, so that wasn't too terrible.

So why did he want to fling himself at the shimmering barrier until it broke, or he did?

He would break first. He'd tested the wards last night, and they were some of the best he'd ever seen. He'd robbed bank vaults with less elaborate and impenetrable shields. The only thing he'd found to match them was the ward on the main treasure room in Trinity College, where the most powerful magic artifacts in Ireland were held. He'd gotten through that not by magic, but by human error. He and his crew had infiltrated the security force, and their mole had gotten access to the keystones. A judiciously-phrased edit in the runes created a gap that they'd exploited.

Those tactics wouldn't work this time. He didn't suppose the Seeress would give him access to her keystones.

The Trinity College job reminded him of Evie. It was her fault he'd gotten into this mess. He ought to have refused her 'lucrative opportunity' and gone right back to his shipping schedule. But beyond the money, she'd asked it as a favor, and there were few things in the world he wouldn't do for her.

Damn her eyes.

The sound of a foot scuffling across the rocky beach drew his attention to the mouth of the cave. Where his adopted sister was slim as a whip and topped by flame-red hair, Sorcha Fay was all soft curves, crowned by pale moonlight hair.

Ronan stood. She wore a dress instead of a nightgown, and the afternoon sunlight revealed her heartbreaking beauty. He'd had only an impression of her in the dark, and that had been enough to give him a cockstand. By the light of day, she aroused and allured, but the desire was mixed with a tenderness that he did not expect and refused to accept.

Her body was even lusher than he'd imagined after that glimpse last night, with generous hips and a rounded belly, a nipped-in waist, and soft, voluptuous breasts. He craved the scrape of her hardened nipples against his palms.

But more arresting than even her body was her face— heart-shaped, with the most vivid blue eyes he'd ever seen. They were like a summer sky in Ireland, when the morning showers have been swept away and puffy white clouds dance through the deep azure. Her eyebrows and eyelashes were almost transparent, the blond was so white. Her mouth was soft and pink, the lower lip fuller and plumper than the upper. He wanted to take that mouth with his, wanted to part those lips and slide his tongue into her. Wanted to see that bow drawn wide around the head of his cock.

Thank the gods for the breeches that restrained his fresh erection.

"Have you come to torment the prisoner?"

A tinge of pink washed her cheeks. Her skin was so pale that even hints of her emotions would show within her flesh.

"I have no wish to torment you, sir. But I also do not yet

have confirmation of your identity or what you're doing here."

"So I'm stuck here indefinitely?" He tensed, and any hint of arousal fled. He'd managed one night and a morning, but too much longer in this small space and he'd go mad.

"Not indefinitely. I was able to briefly contact the duchess, and she began to tell me about a plan she had, but our communications cut off when the...object I was using drained its energy. It can't be refreshed until the full moon, and that's a few days away. But she wasn't surprised that I had company, so you might be telling the truth."

"Might be." That was better than accusations of ward-tampering. But it wasn't a promise to set him free. "What do you plan to do with me until you're sure?"

She bit her lower lip, and his stupid body decided to react, despite his fear of continued confinement. Some parts of him definitely had no sense of self-preservation.

"If you'll agree to certain...accommodations, I'll let you out of there."

"And what would those be?" He couldn't let her know that he'd agree to nearly anything, so he made the words a drawl and leaned against the wall of the cave with as much noncha-lance as he could muster. The currently half-hard and non-self-respecting object in his trousers wondered if she would accept his body in trade.

"You agree to stay on Skye, and within the bounds of Clan Fay property, until I discover the truth from the duchess. You agree to wear a set of magic-dampening jewelry that will keep you from casting spells. And, most impor-tantly, you agree to do as I say."

The first was reasonable, as he'd no intention of leaving until he got what he came for. Of course, each day beyond what he'd planned would be a fifty-pound increase in what he intended to bill the duchess. The second was understandable, but the restriction would chafe. He didn't like feeling vulnerable, and his magic had always given him an edge against opponents. Still, he'd agree, and tack on a hefty fee for inconvenience.

But the last? Impossible. Desperation be damned. "I'll not be dancing to your tune, Seeress."

"If you cannot abide by those terms, you cannot go free."

Damn her. And she was too smart to allow him to lie. She probably intended to make the promise magically-binding.

"What if I can't do something you order me to do? Or if I know that following your orders will make a big mess?"

She shrugged. The movement made her breasts jiggle, and what little control he had on his desire slipped. He forced his breathing to steady. He knew better than to let his body stand in the way of a negotiation. He tried to ignore the fact that he'd never been this tempted before, or this aroused by a fully-clothed woman with whom he should be spitting mad.

"I won't put a compulsion on you to follow my orders, just not to disobey me."

"Bloody hells. You realize it's illegal to use coercion magic on people, don't you?"

"And it's illegal to tamper with wards and trespass on private property."

"How many times do I have to tell you? I was invited, and I didn't lay a finger on your fecking wards!"

Her delectable lips thinned to a firm line as she weighed his outburst. But she wasn't going to believe him. If only he could explain that to his very-aroused body.

"I can't take the risk that you're lying." She held up a small bag and retrieved a few shiny objects from within. "I'm the protector of the House. I won't betray the clan's trust in me." The shiny objects were two cuff-style bracelets and a torque necklace. He couldn't read the runic writing from here, but he recognized a few of the larger knot symbols. They were all meant for containment and control. He shuddered at the image of them rubbing his skin and trapping his magic.

"If I agree, you'll free me? And you'll talk to the duchess as soon as possible?"

Her clear gaze met his. He stared into the sky-blue depths of her soul and found Truth. She would not lie. Conceal, perhaps, but not lie outright. It was not her nature.

How he knew that, was not clear, but it was unassailable. This woman was his opposite, and he could trust that anything she told him was true.

How very odd, for a man who spent his life reveling in deceit, to meet his match in a woman who could not deceive.

He held out his wrists. "I'll do it."

3

S orcha exhaled a painful breath. She'd been afraid he
would say no, and she was at least partially convinced
that he was exactly who he said he was. She hated making
him stay in the cave.

If only she'd been able to maintain the mirror spell a few
moments longer. She'd managed to reach Etta, the Duchess
of Fay, but only after hours of brief attempts every fifteen
minutes. By the time they were both in the same reflection at
the same time, the spell was nearly depleted. She'd explained
the situation in a few terse words, but although Etta started
to say something about a plan, the spell died. Sorcha stared at
her reflection, left without answers. Again.

Since Etta had not been able to tell her whom she'd sent,
anything about his appearance, or what he was supposed to
retrieve, she couldn't trust that Ronan wasn't her intruder.
He might have intercepted the real courier and be pretending
now. Hence her precautions.

She placed the cuffs and torque against the ward-wall.
They were all meant to perform similar functions, so she
tweaked the ward slightly to make it match the jewelry. The

three pieces merged with the ward and she nudged them through. They fell on the other side.

Ronan contemplated them where they lay. "I'm to put these on myself?"

She refused to reward his impudence with a reply. He knew exactly why she would not be placing the cuffs on him. It would be a terrible mistake to lower the ward for any reason, and a much bigger error to go through before he put the restraints in place.

He contained whatever disappointment he may have felt that she did not rise to his verbal riposte, and stared at the copper objects in the sand. The copper was inlaid with iron and nickel to form the runes and symbols of the spells. If they had been normal jewelry, the years would have corroded the copper to a dull green and the iron to rust-red. But they were not normal, and the magic imbued within kept their surfaces as shiny as the day they were forged.

He picked them up, and Sorcha relaxed. He would now be compelled to put them on.

The first cuff closed over his left wrist and the second over his right. He slid the torque around his neck, which was corded with tension as his hands moved without his volition. She couldn't meet his eyes. She hadn't wanted to compel him, but he was too canny and might have cast an illusion to make it appear that he'd complied.

Now that the items were in place, they were spelled so that a piece of them would remain in contact with his flesh until she took them off. He wouldn't be able to remove them on his own, as he discovered when he tried to lift the torque. He tugged at it, but only one side would lift at a time.

Satisfied that he was now neutralized, she dispelled the ward on the cave entrance.

Immediately, he leapt forward, pressed her against the

cliff under the open sky, and wrapped his hands around her throat.

For a moment, her heart stuttered in her chest. But his hands did not close in a painful grip. He growled. His fingers tensed against her neck, but he couldn't choke her, even though she sensed his intent was to intimidate, not actually hurt.

"You'll find that you can do no harm to me," she said, her voice pitched low, as she might speak to a frightened animal. "The cuffs prevent it."

"I thought they were supposed to dampen my magic." He'd stopped trying to squeeze, but his thumbs were still under her chin, his fingers trapping her hair against her skin.

"It would hardly suit my purpose to take away your magic but not also neutralize you physically. And in any case, you need me. I'm the only one who can take those off of you."

"Damn you." He leaned to her, and he had to come quite a distance as he was at least a foot taller. When his nose grazed hers, he stopped. "You're supposed to be a great seeress. Can't you tell the truth about me?"

Heat rose and flushed through her cheeks. She hated being called the Seeress of Skye, but it was true that her intuition rarely failed her. Except right now her entire existence had contracted to the pressure of his thumb, absently stroking the hollow of her throat. Her physical response to him drowned anything her magical senses might be trying to say.

"It doesn't always work that way," she hedged. "And someone has been trying to penetrate my wards. I can't trust you." She reached up and put her hands over his. "Even if I'd like to."

He allowed her to shift his hands to her shoulders, but he didn't take them off her body. She tried not to think about how much closer they now were to her breasts.

"How typical for the Irishman to pay for what someone else has done."

"What does your being Irish have to do with coming to my house and interfering with my wards?"

"Nothing at all. But it has something to do with this." His fingers gripped her shoulders, and he kissed her.

Perhaps if she'd been a sheltered London miss, she'd have been overwhelmed by this different, sensual assault. But she was a Scots woman who understood the power of pleasure, and—more than that—she was a woman who wanted him.

Sorcha kissed him back, pushing her tongue along the seam of his lips and inside his mouth. He stilled at her aggressive act, but then groaned and met her tongue with his. They dueled in the space created by their fused lips, teasing and arousing. His hands moved, no longer threatening violence, sliding up her jaw and over her ears to cup the back of her head.

She put her arms around his waist, caressing the trim muscles as she went, and then over his hips to his sweet, round arse. Her fingers curled around the tight muscle, and she pulled him against her. His erection pressed into her belly, hard and insistent.

The contact shocked him from his lust-fueled haze, and he pulled away from her. In the sunlight, his irises were dark grey, flecked with blue and brown and green, or at least what she could see of them now. His pupils were dilated with pleasure.

She waited while he fought the desire. Her own still burned, bright and clear as a lighthouse flame, and all she wanted to do was follow it to the safety it promised. But she couldn't be certain that he was who he claimed to be, and if he was, there was someone else who'd been tampering with her wards. She wasn't safe.

Once he'd regained control, he said, "So, clever girl, what's next?"

"You come to the house with me and put on clothes that aren't formed entirely of magic, and then we eat supper."

For a moment, the surprise in his expression made her breath wheeze with suppressed laughter. Did he think she would order him to do something unpleasant, or that he'd have to take the oaths she'd required? The oaths were bound into the cuffs and torque. A group of similar items in Clan Fay's collection had once been used to keep rival clan mages hostage. Once she'd activated their latent spells, there was no need for him to speak the oaths aloud.

"I *am* a mite hungry. You forgot to send luncheon."

She refused to respond to that blatant attempt at shame. She'd been busy trying to contact Etta all morning, and he ought to have had enough food in the spell-basket to last him the full twenty-four hours she'd inscribed on the tablet. It wasn't her fault if he'd already managed to eat everything.

"I'll show you the way."

Inside the house, she left him alone in a guest room with clothes she'd gathered earlier. They were castoffs from a generation or so back in the Fay clan, but menswear hadn't changed much in the last fifty years, especially of the casual sort, so she didn't anticipate complaints.

After a few minutes, he emerged into the hallway, now dressed in dark trousers that were too snug around the thigh and dragged at the hem. The shirt was too small across his chest and shoulders as well, and the waistcoat barely buttoned.

"Do you know any tailoring spells?" His tone mocked her, but she actually did know a spell that could take in garments. Unfortunately, it wouldn't work with clothes that were too small. The spell couldn't create new cloth to let out the seams.

Rather than inform him of this currently-useless knowledge, she ignored the question and started to the kitchen and scullery.

She had a small staff that helped with cleaning, cooking, and general maintenance, but after one of the men had been injured last month during another incident of ward-tampering, she'd sent them and most of her livestock away to Kinlochfay Village. Ronan would have to accept his new role as co-chef and co-scullery maid in the Fay House kitchens.

Sorcha pushed open the door and breathed in the divine scent of bread baking. Mrs. Mackinstrie—her cook and housekeeper—had taught her to make the loaves when she was a girl, and for a moment, the loneliness squeezed her heart. She'd been isolated here her entire life, but the last few weeks alone had been especially hard.

At the brick oven, she checked behind the door. Four loaves nestled on the shelves. They'd browned perfectly, so she grabbed a peel from the wall beside the oven and shoveled them onto the counter to cool.

"That smells incredible." Ronan crowded her beside the bread. "Spell-food fills your belly, but it isn't really satisfying once the spell wears off."

"No, I suppose not." She slipped around him and opened a stone door into a spelled cold-pantry. She'd heard that non-magic families used ice or chambers built into springs, but Clan Fay had been keeping their food fresh with magic for over a thousand years.

Ronan followed her into the small space, and she tried not to tense at his proximity. If he noticed her reaction to him, he'd take advantage of the little power afforded him.

Her magical intuition and her experiences with men told her she mustn't allow him to sense her desire. Let him believe that she'd been teasing him on the beach—that she was cold and unaffected.

"There are meats and cheeses in here, as well as what remains of the fruits and vegetables from last fall's harvest."

"There's not much left, considering that it's only now planting season."

"We canned much of it, and that's in the dry pantry. This is what we preserved with magic or froze to keep fresh."

"Who is 'we?' Do you have a cook?"

"Sometimes." She hesitated, then told a half-truth. "I thought it better that you and I not be disturbed until I understand why you're here." What she'd really done was leave a message in a spot outside the property this morning. A member of the staff would be there around noon today, expecting to meet her, and would see it instead. The note said she wouldn't be coming to Kinlochfay for a few days, but everything was fine and not to worry about her.

"No disturbances, but also no assistance should I prove…troublesome."

"Will you?"

"No." He answered too quickly, and a surge of intuition told her he already had something planned, but not what or when he'd act. If only she could read his mind. Some Seers had nearly telepathic abilities to read people, but hers was based on hunches and an understanding of human nature. Except for the recent dreams of the blond boy—now man— her real visions were only ever of the future. And all her visions came not at her will, but at the whim of fate.

She wasn't much of a Seeress, despite her hated nickname. The villagers knew not to use it. Ronan had referred to the nickname but hadn't used her real name yet.

Had she even introduced herself? She supposed he already knew who she was, but it was rude not to have said something.

"I'm Sorcha, by the way."

He paused in the act of reaching for a wheel of cheese and pivoted so he could settle his gaze on her. "Not Miss Fay?"

"We've never been formal in this house. My cousins have titles, but my branch of the family doesn't. And it's silly to call me by my last name. I'm just Sorcha."

"When a woman invites me to call her by her first name, it's usually an invitation for quite a bit more."

Her skin tingled and heat spread from her core. She wanted it to be an invitation to everything. But she mustn't let her craving show. If she didn't stop this flirtation now, she'd find herself in far too deep. He was a man of experience, and she a relative innocent.

But he didn't know that. She had a hunch that he would back off if she acted like a strumpet. Her intuition about him was a mess, but most men were taken aback when women didn't fit nicely into their categories of virtue. She pretended a cool sophistication that she did not feel and chose wicked, scandalous words.

"Perhaps, if you prove to be who you say you are, we can give it a go. I've never fucked an Irishman." She'd never had intercourse with any man, so it wasn't a lie. Merely an implication of a falsehood.

As predicted, her callousness made him retreat. She told herself that was for the best. After all, even if he were a courier sent by Etta, he'd be gone as soon as he collected whatever the duchess needed. And she'd never see him again.

When she slept with a man for the first time, she wanted it to be special, for it to mean something. She didn't want a quick coupling and a pat on the arse before saying goodbye forever. She wished her heart would stop trying to convince her that Ronan would be different, that he would stay. She did not doubt that he wouldn't.

~

THE LITTLE WITCH HAD SURPRISED HIM AGAIN. ON THE BEACH, her kiss had been a gale wind, transforming him to a swirling gyre of need. His cock had been all-too-content to be pressed against her soft, round belly, but that pulse of pleasure had finally broken through to his good sense.

She had him captive. He'd tried to use sex as a tool, to earn her sympathy by making her want him, but she'd twisted that all around until he was the one so aroused he couldn't take a steady breath.

And even then, he'd believed that the passion was real. Hadn't he already decided that she couldn't lie, not in any fundamental way? Her kiss had not been a lie. She'd wanted him. But she could apparently extinguish her desire when it wasn't convenient.

He'd only meant to tease, to perhaps steal a few more kisses. Her crude remark had punctured his burgeoning desire.

Who'd have suspected a cold-hearted jade lurked beneath that seemingly earnest exterior?

And who'd have suspected that it would hurt so much to have her treat their connection the same way he and his former lovers always had. He hadn't realized he'd grown bored with easy sex—the kind that engaged his body but not his heart—until she'd slipped her tongue into his mouth and twisted him round like a whirlwind.

He shouldn't be disappointed to learn that the perfect woman—resilient, sexy, magically talented, and capable of besting him—was also cold and cynical inside. He should have expected it. Hadn't he been telling himself that he didn't have the luxury of believing in softer things? He had two causes in life. The first was an independent Ireland. The second was keeping Evie safe. He would do, and had done, terrible things to achieve both of those ends. He'd stolen, cheated, lied, and killed, and he would do it all again.

His brief dream of Sorcha was a wisp, and he did not believe in children's faerie stories. Real fay were malicious little bastards. Life was hard, and there were no happy endings.

She followed him out of the cold storage room, and they prepared a meal in silence.

Then she licked her thumb, and he thought, *Feck it. She may be a cold-hearted bitch, but I want to be inside her more than I want to draw my next breath.*

He took her hand and put the thumb between his lips.

She dragged in a shuddering breath, and any impression of ice shattered. She glowed for him—his very own candle—and gasped when he lightly stroked the pad with his tongue. He nipped the end with his teeth and then let go.

"Why wait?" he asked. "We don't have to trust each other, or even like each other, to fuck each other."

There. He'd flung the gauntlet at her feet, and even used her pronunciation of fuck to do it. Now the choice was hers.

Sorcha froze. Whatever distance she'd managed to create with her cutting remarks had contracted around her, and he was too big and too close and too much of everything she wanted. Except that he wasn't.

Maybe on the surface, he was the embodiment of her most torrid fantasies. Maybe he had wit, and strength, and good humor. But that didn't make him the man she had been waiting for. Her desires were too sharp and dazzling for her to be certain exactly what kind of man he was.

Her thumb glistened, wet from his mouth, and she made herself casually, haughtily, raise it to her lips. She licked, and through a force of will she hadn't suspected she possessed, she held his gaze as her tongue flicked the pad and nail.

"Tempting," she murmured. His gaze was hot, his grey eyes drenched with desire, but she wanted to be more than desired. She dropped her hand. The words that flooded out were bitter and absolutely true. "But I prefer not to worry that my lover is plotting how to use me to best advantage. Or trying to soften me into removing his restraints. As I said, perhaps later."

She deliberately turned her back on him, lifted her plate, and left the kitchen. In the doorway, she paused but did not look back. "We've another night and day until the full moon. Make yourself comfortable in the house. Anything you shouldn't grope is already warded."

She climbed the steps and went into the library. The spell that opened for a Fay would remain closed for him unless she invited him in. She'd be safe here, and alone.

The tablet was back in its place in the cabinet, and late afternoon sunlight flooded the seaward windows. Usually, Sorcha craved the light, but today she feared what it might reveal.

So she slipped into one of the shadowy alcoves along the inner wall and plopped onto a thick cushioned bench with the plate in her lap. She had chores to do, and danger surrounded her, but she needed a moment to breathe. The food tasted of him—of the brine-water flavor of his magic—so she put the plate aside.

Whether or not Ronan was the one responsible for tampering with the wards, he was still very much a danger to her. He made her feel things, made her want things, that she'd long ago promised herself to share only with someone she could respect, someone who would cherish her. Her mother had been a hedonist, interested in pleasure for pleasure's sake, and while Sorcha respected her mother's right to choose those things, Sorcha herself wanted pleasure with affection. No, if she were to be honest, she wanted pleasure with love.

Affection she had found among the village lads. She genuinely liked the boys, now men, with whom she had kissed and cuddled and experimented. They genuinely liked her. But she'd never fallen in love, and neither had they. At least, not with her. All four of her amorous partners were now married to other lasses, and she wished them well.

What she feared with Ronan was not her own heart. That seemed willing to toss itself at his feet. What she feared was that he would not pick up that heart and hold it close. She feared that he would use her, and trample on her, and leave her bloody and torn. Not because he sought to harm her, but because he didn't care one way or another.

Ronan's callous disregard would be far more painful than if he was her villain. If he meant her ill, she would hurt for what might have been, but she wouldn't carry the sorrow for long. And where she'd always been able to tell the truth of a man, all she could see with Ronan was how much she wanted him.

Was it wrong for her to wish for him to be her enemy, rather than the alternative? To hope he might hate her, rather than feel nothing for her at all?

4

———————

As the afternoon wore on, Ronan mapped the house, or at least the parts where doors would open to him. Two small wings bracketed the main building, with a central tower that probably was once the only structure, guarding Loch Fay. One of the wings was topped by an additional level made entirely of glass, but he couldn't see inside as it had been tinted, either by magic or mundane means.

Taken as a whole, Fay House was not a large home by English manor standards, but it could have comfortably housed several dozen guests and family members as well as upward of fifty staff.

And yet she lived here alone.

Who was this woman, the Seeress of Skye? She fascinated him with her contradictions, and he longed to grasp her secrets even more for how well she eluded him.

An hour or so after he completed his survey, he started again, this time with his Sight open, examining the spell matrices that crisscrossed the building and grounds. He had to stop after a quarter of an hour when his head began to pound. There were so many layers that the spells could have made a second set of walls and floors.

During his explorations, he caught frequent glimpses of his jailor. Her attempts at subtle stalking amused him. The woman's magic blazed like a lighthouse. Unless she wrapped herself in a glamour, he was going to sense when she came near.

The sun set late that night, the nearly-full moon already well above the eastern horizon when it finally made its descent on the far side of the Isle of Canna. He decided to poke at his warden and reveal that he was aware of her stalking.

He pretended to begin another circuit of the house, but instead of continuing on the route he'd already established, he took a side exit from a room and doubled back. She halted in a big casting chamber, and he sauntered in, unseen.

He'd stopped in here earlier to examine the space. Few buildings had entire rooms devoted to magic, and of those, fewer still were as elaborately designed and constructed as this one. It was the central section of a cross-shaped series of linked chambers, all of them on leylines, and the chamber itself sat at the nexus point where the lines met.

The floors, walls, and ceiling were inlaid with many different kinds of materials to provide extraction-points for spells that required a physical focus or a particular kind of magical energy. Earlier, he'd pretended to examine the precious metals and crystals, while really keeping his attention on Sorcha, who'd hovered in the doorway and waited for him to move on. The polished metal embedded in the wall provided an excellent mirror in which he could observe her.

She'd waited while he watched her, her fingers dancing nervously across the fabric of her dress. She kept the rest of her body relaxed and ready to move when he did, but those fluttering fingertips gave away her discomfort.

From that distance, her hair had been a single pale cloud, drifting around her face. She'd made an attempt to pin it back, but he remembered the silky softness of it against his hands, and he imagined that it slipped free from the confines of its pins regularly. He wanted to pull all of it free, to tangle his fingers in it, and draw her mouth to his.

Warmth had filled his chest, and then he'd chilled when he shifted his arm and the cuff rubbed his wrist. He'd hurried from the chamber, and she'd followed.

Watching her now, he opened his Sight and marveled at the way the magic in the room flowed around her, twining with her voluptuous form in a caress that made him catch his breath in envy. Damn her for being so much of what he wanted, and damned him for wanting her even though she'd chained his magic and spurned his desire.

Then whirled, and saw him standing behind her.

"Oh!" Her cheeks flushed with embarrassment. It pleased him to make her color. She ought to be ashamed of what she'd done, trapping a man with magic and holding him against his will.

"Have you enjoyed following me about all day?" he asked, walking toward her with nonchalant steps. He wasn't a massive man—though taller than average—but she was so much shorter that he loomed over her with ease.

Despite her mortification, she didn't shrink under his glower, but glared back at him. "No, actually. I have a thousand things that need doing with my staff gone, and the wards keep tangling, and I'd rather not have to follow you about to assure myself you're not up to mischief."

"You said I should make myself comfortable." He raised his wrists and put them right under her nose. "And doesn't your pretty jewelry tell you what I'm about?"

She stared at him rather than the cuffs, even though the metal was so close his fingers nearly brushed her chin. "It's not that specific. I suppose I could add something to the spells…" she lifted a hand, and he took a hasty step back.

If he hadn't had his Sight open, he wouldn't have been able to see the magic clinging to her fingertips, and wouldn't have immediately assumed the worst. "No. You've done enough to take away my liberty. I won't agree to more limits."

She didn't put her hand down. Instead, she covered the cuff with her fingers. She hadn't cast any spells, but her magic surged through him like a lance, its brilliance heating him through to his core.

Gods, he'd never felt magic like hers, had never comprehended that magic could mingle in this way. With the exception of Evie, everyone he'd ever known had hoarded their gifts, afraid to let anyone else in on their personal tricks and illusions. Sorcha shared magic as though it was simply another piece of her that touched him, like her fingers or her lips.

"I don't believe the limits I've imposed are awful. I can't trust you, and you know why. When I have confirmation that you are who you say you are, I'll let you go." And she truly was sorry about it; her remorse filled her magic. Unless it was a trick.

But gods, he didn't want it to be a trick. He wanted to believe that she wasn't the cold jade that had spurned him in the kitchen. He wanted the passionate gale that had swept over him on the beach.

So he closed the distance between them and took her mouth. He'd expected at least a moment of hesitation, and then the devouring need that she'd revealed beside the cliff. Instead, she gave him no resistance at all, opening her mouth to him and surrendering with so much sweetness that his entire body vibrated with a craving more consuming than anything he'd ever known.

He had her on the floor in moments, her lush hips cradling him, his cock hard against her cleft though still separated from her heated flesh by far too many clothes. Magic flowed through their twined bodies where they lay on the leyline, and he was overwhelmed by the summer-night scent of her, by the flavor of mulberries that burst in his mouth with every deep, drugging kiss.

She arched against him, and he slid his lips down her throat. She wore a high-collared fitted blouse, but the fabric was thin, and there was no corset beneath to restrain her lovely form. He growled his approval at the sight of her nipples, hard and peaked under the cotton. She cried out when he closed his mouth over one and lapped at it with his tongue. Her hips bucked, and he groaned, lifting his head away from her breast.

Her lips were wet and parted, and she panted, her chest rising and falling in quick movements that made her nipple lift and chafe against his throat. He shifted, meaning to tease both breasts at the same time with his thumbs, but one of his cuffs jangled against the stone.

Instead of returning to her breasts, he pushed himself away, out of the stream of magic, and onto the cold stone floor. It wasn't bitterness or anger that pulled him away, but the knowledge that she would not have restrained him if she felt she had a choice. She was alone and afraid, and despite all of that, somehow wanted him.

He couldn't take what she offered. She had no idea who he was or the things he'd done.

Sorcha sat up, her eyes still glazed with passion, her blouse mussed and her nipple clearly visible through the wet white fabric. He forced his gaze to his wrists. "I think you're right," he said, and he deliberately chose words that would push her away. "I prefer not to worry that my lover is plotting how to use me to best advantage, too."

He refused to meet her gaze, but a shock of hurt spiked through the places where their magic still twisted together. He declined to acknowledge that he'd started this, that she had not done anything except surrender to him so completely that he'd lost all control and common sense. Better to upset her, and stop whatever this was before it went too far. She wasn't a jade, and he wasn't so far gone that he would take advantage of her warmth because he had a glacier for a heart.

His hands shook as he pushed to his feet. He kept his back to her, afraid to glimpse everything he wanted but must not have.

"I'll keep to my room tonight," he promised. "And tomorrow, I'll examine your wards. Maybe if I can help you put them to rights, you'll believe that I had nothing to do with disrupting them in the first place."

He left the casting chamber and refused to look back. Because if he saw her again and she still wanted him, he'd take everything she'd offered. That would damn his soul and hers.

SORCHA SAT ON THE FLOOR OF THE CASTING CHAMBER, TRYING to decide what had happened. He'd been angry with her. She'd sensed that clearly, or thought she had. She'd tried to make him realize that it wasn't him, but everything going on right now, that made her so suspicious.

She'd spent the entire afternoon following him, annoyed as he wandered the house and got into trouble. It hadn't been difficult to build a wall around her desires and her heart when he kept her from her duties. She'd even growled at one point that she wanted to be left alone to decipher what was happening to her wards.

Then he'd stroked her, and she never wanted to be alone again. He'd tasted her, and the wall proved to be made of air and less substantial than moonlight. She'd given in to him with almost terrifying ease.

But it had been a move in the game to him, a way to pay her back for spurning him in the kitchen. He could have had her, right here on this floor, and she would have given him everything he asked, would have begged him to take her. She had to stop letting her loins dictate her actions and listen to her magic.

She hugged her arms around her chest and her wrist brushed the wet spot over her breast where he'd suckled her. Her nipple was still sensitive, even to the accidental rub, and a tiny shudder rippled through her, settling between her legs in aching, empty heat.

The vision struck her then, a vivid counterpoint to what had *not* happened.

The blond man had his back to her and was quite naked. Two arms twined around him, and two legs were spread wide on either side of his rhythmically-thrusting arse. A female voice moaned, and the man grunted, thrusting one last time. He pulled away, revealing a mostly-naked woman. Her chemise bunched beneath full breasts with rosy, taut nipples, and its hem was raked up to her flat waist.

"This is the last time," the man said, rolling away from her and gathering his clothes.

"But you said—"

"The last time, Rebecca. You won't see me again. You won't send for me, and you won't make any scenes."

The woman stared at him with something between anguish and horror. "Please...I can do better."

He gave the woman a cold stare, and tears streamed from her eyes.

Sorcha reeled from the force of the vision, throwing back her arms to catch herself. Of all the things she'd seen of the boy, then man, over the last several months, she'd never seen anything like that. Not only the sex, although that had been an unwanted image, but the cruelty he'd shown. She'd seen him be ruthless in a fight—whatever school he'd gone to had refashioned him into a very skilled warrior—but never casually cruel. He'd had too much honor for that.

I don't even want to know who you are anymore, she thought. *I want these visions to stop.* But she'd never been able to make any of her visions stop, had never been able to induce the trance-state that most Seers used to access the future plane.

I'm a fraud. I can't protect the House, and I can't protect my heart. Maybe it's time to admit my failure to Etta.

No. Not yet. Ronan wanted to help her fix the wards. If he was who he said he was, then she could come to Etta with a problem solved. And if he wasn't? She would still have a problem solved.

She would wait until after the full moon.

5

Sorcha avoided Ronan the next morning. When they had been forced to occupy the same room at the same time, they managed only stilted conversation, barely shy of sniping. Ronan couldn't decide if this was an improvement or an infinitely more subtle torment.

Her scent was everywhere, and her magic suffused the house. He could still sense her, magic and woman, but he couldn't embrace either, and denial was driving him mad.

He pushed at the bounds of his restraints, walking the property and discovering its edges by the places where he could no longer lift a booted foot to move forward. He didn't run into a physical wall, but rather an impediment in his mind.

That impediment ran through grazing pastures and up a steep hill, then down again to the rocky coast, and around to the cove where he'd landed his longboat. The boat was still there, drawn beyond the tide line, empty and waiting. But he could not make himself climb inside or push it toward the lapping waves. Nothing that could lead to his escape by water.

He could wade into the surf, perhaps because it was bitterly cold and he had no desire to remain in its freezing embrace. He would not be swimming away from here, even without a compulsion.

No, he was well and truly trapped. And since she'd cut off contact with the village and the few servants who typically helped her run the house, he had no way of reaching anyone in the outside world. He couldn't telegram his Dublin offices and have them send his ship back post-haste. He couldn't telegram Evie and tell her that her friends were insane and to send help.

All he could do was expose the source of Sorcha's ward problems.

Tonight was the full moon, so she would be busy refreshing spells and renewing the keystones. He ought to take advantage of her distraction to make an attempt at escape, but he didn't. Instead, he opened his Sight and made a complete circuit of the house and grounds, marveling at the wards and their structure, and noting anything that felt odd or different from most wards he'd tampered with over the years.

Traditionally, wards were cast using a keystone, which was settled into a central location. Then daughter-stones were created from the original keystone and placed around the area to be warded. But this type of ward had to be frequently renewed and was weakest during the dark of the moon.

So in the late middle ages, an enterprising witch had created overlapping wards, using a linked system of keystones. Each stone would be placed during a different portion of the lunar cycle so that one was always at the height of its strength. They still needed to be renewed, but only at the full moon, and then the energy was slowly released to each stone in sequence. Only the inner-most layer was vulnerable each month.

The Fay House wards, while utilizing multiple keystones, were still synced to a single segment of the lunar cycle, the full moon. He did another quick circuit to verify what he suspected, and this time he noticed a deeper level, that was a hairsbreadth off from the others. This layer felt…wrong. Without his magic, he couldn't do more than inspect it, but he was certain if he could probe the strands of the spell-net, they would warp and tangle.

Something was very wrong here. From the intricate and sophisticated ward-work she'd done the night of his capture, there was no possible way that Sorcha Fay would leave her entire ward network so ill-kempt.

He needed to talk to her, and he couldn't let her hide in the house anymore.

So he walked to the first door that refused to open and shouted, "Your wards are fecked to the hells and back! I can't touch them, but I have eyes. It's no wonder someone was able to tamper with them."

He waited, and sure enough, a door opened farther down the hall.

She wore a dress the same color as a carnelian ring his great-granny had left him in her will. The only thing he'd ever gotten from the McCarrick family other than pain.

On Sorcha, the deep red-brown made her pale skin warm with color. It was also loose, flowing around her ample form with no corset or bustle, almost more shift than dress. As she moved, the fabric clung to her hips and waist, outlining her thighs and knees with every step.

His heart beat faster, and he had to swallow or drool. He swallowed.

"What are you talking about?" Her tone was cold, almost accusatory. But he could handle antagonism.

"I've done two circuits of the wards. They're all matched,

with the weak spots aligning. There's probably been an open door in your wards for an hour or so one day a month for a long time. And the interior ward is a few breaths away from tangling with the others and tearing the whole net down."

"That's not possible. I checked them last night, and they were fine."

"Check them now."

She marched away, and he followed. They walked the same path he'd followed, and Sorcha swore in fluent Gaelic. It was close enough to Irish that he caught the more interesting bits.

"I wasn't aware that female genitalia could fly. And why is it seven middens? Were eight too many?"

"*Rach a h-Irt.*"

He grinned. He would very much like to kiss her arse.

She lifted her hands and casted another elaborate spell-net, similar to the ones she'd tossed around on the beach. Her deft motions mingled murmured spoken spells with the woven strands. She was, beyond a doubt, the most accomplished witch he'd ever met.

"How did this happen?" she muttered. The spell-net settled into the interior ward, and the worst tangles straightened. But even as he watched, the edges frayed. "I have to go to the keystones." Sweat beaded her brow, and she swiped at it before it dripped down into her eyes. "If you'll accept a compulsion not to lay a finger on anything while you're there, you may come with me."

At the moment, he'd have agreed to almost anything to examine the keystones. He was as caught in the mystery now as she was. He wanted to discover what had happened, and he wanted to help her fix it.

The irony of his desire to repair wards rather than circumvent them was not lost on him. But there it was. He wanted to help his little Seeress.

When had she become 'his' anything?

She hadn't, and that was that.

But he nodded, and didn't even much mind when the compulsion settled over him.

DAMN, DAMN, DAMN. SORCHA STOOD AT THE HEART OF THE warding chamber, inside the triangle formed by the three keystones, beside the heartstone that had anchored the original ward. There was something very wrong.

Not only did the wards not match the carving on the stones, but they also seemed to be reaching back into the stones, as though someone had placed new keystones outside of the grounds and those stones were trying to rewrite these.

"When you walked the grounds this morning, did you see anything that could have been a keystone? Or probably five keystones?"

He missed a step when she mentioned his perambulations, but she wasn't blind or stupid. She'd been avoiding interacting with him after what happened in the casting chamber, but that didn't mean she wasn't keeping tabs on him.

"I don't remember anything. But I didn't want to examine what was beyond the grounds. I assumed that was part of the compulsion."

"No. It keeps you from walking across the edge of the property. If you had trouble looking over the border, there's another spell. Fucking hells."

"What are you going to do?"

"I'm going to have to craft two new keystones to strengthen the matrix here, and to write a repulsion into the entire ward system to keep this from happening again."

"That sounds complicated."

"Aye. I can't do it by myself." She frowned. She was going to have to trust him, going to have to follow what her heart was telling her rather than the warnings of her head.

To his credit, he didn't crow or lift his chin at her in superiority. He simply waited for her to admit the truth.

"I'm going to need your help."

He held out his wrists, with only a hint of an expectant smile.

"Yes. Those. But not the torque." Without the cuffs, he'd be able to cast spell-nets, but the torque would restrain his spoken magic. He'd not be able to do anything large or complex that required a spoken spell.

She had to trust him enough for the cuffs, but she couldn't afford to be wrong. That would be catastrophic. What if he was the one who'd placed the other stones? But she didn't really believe that. And she was going to need his hands.

Damn her visions for never coming when she wanted them! What use were foresight and prophecy if she couldn't call them on command? And she couldn't trust her usual intuition because her feelings were so clouded by lust.

Damn, fuck, hells.

He still said nothing, so she put a hand around each cuff. A few murmured words and they sprang open. She walked them to a shelf built into the chamber wall.

"Now." She spun and clapped her hands together. "We'll need to find two reasonably-sized boulders and carve."

"Shouldn't they be made from the original keystone?" Ronan gestured at the big central stone.

"No. If we did that, the new spells would be weaker, because they would have to be grafted over the original."

"How are you going to coax the old group to merge with new stones?"

"Once we've carved the new stones, I'll cast a replication

spell. It will rebuild the new stones to match the old, but with the new carving merged into the overall matrix, so that it blends with the four already here. You'll not be able to tell it wasn't there from the beginning."

"Are you sure that will work?"

Under different circumstances, Sorcha might have spared the time to make a disparaging remark. At the moment, all she needed from him was that he follow her directions. "Just help me find two stones." She strode back upstairs and out into the cloudy afternoon. The air smelled like rain.

Ronan kept to her heels as she crossed the manicured grounds and advanced through the wilder portion of the property. In years past, this grass would be as short as the rest, chewed by sheep and cows. But ever since Lilias went to London at the turn of the nineteenth century, the Fay family had made a slow migration away from Skye.

The last nearly ten years, there'd been no duchess to manage the estates, and Sorcha had been forced to deal with an agent in London who saw no point in releasing funds to help maintain a "moldering pile" in the far north of Scotland, except in case of actual damage and repairs. She'd made do with what she could raise from the estate, and by offering her magic services to the islanders, but she lamented everything she'd lost.

It was her hope that Etta would restore Fay House to its proper glory someday, but if that was going to happen, Sorcha needed to protect what was left.

Walking the property, she felt for herself what Ronan had experienced. Knowledge of the other spell's presence allowed her to push through the surface layer—through the subtle hints that she should look away—to examine the counter-wards beneath. Whoever had designed this was also a master. The layer that resisted scrutiny was only the first of several interlocking wards, each of them specifically engineered to undermine an element of her system. They must have been in place for months, and were why she could never detect overt tampering.

She would need to counter all of these, and do it fast. Her wards needed renewing tonight, at the full moon, and if she was correct, that was when the true attack would take place.

She studied the spells and wished she knew where the keystones were, but there wasn't time to find them. A mage this sophisticated would have protected them well. She'd have to improvise and hope for the best.

They wandered through the unkempt former pastures, up the hills that would lead, if they walked farther northeast, to Sgurr Alasdair, the highest peak on Skye. But she found what she needed long before they left the property, much less before they reached the Black Cuillin.

Two boulders jutted from the softer earth at their feet, each rock proud and distinct, yet clearly once fragments of the same larger stone. Water and wind had worn them down and separated them, and now magic and her hands would make them one again.

"These two," she told Ronan, who hadn't spoken a word since they left the keystone chamber.

"How do you propose to transport them?"

"A spell, ye dafty." What else would he suggest? That she would lift two one-meter square boulders, each weighing maybe five tonnes, with her bare hands?

"Yes, a spell, but what kind? I've never cast anything that could handle that much heavy lifting. Literally." He patted the surface of the boulder.

"When this is over, you'll have to tell me exactly what sorts of spells you do cast."

Half of his lips quirked up. "Perhaps I will. And perhaps you'll enlighten me as to how I can help you here?"

"The spell is as old as human occupation on these isles.

What do you think made the henges and stone circles that mark our fair kingdom?"

"Yours." The word was curt, almost shouted.

"My what?"

"Your kingdom. Ireland belongs to itself."

"Ah, so you're a Fenian."

His lips straightened again. "Irish Republican, but aye."

"Well, no matter who claims to rule the land, all of it is dotted with standing stones. And I know the spell that lifted them from their quarries and placed them in distant soil."

"How? I thought all of the druid spells were lost."

"Druid is a name we coined well after the fact. This particular spell has been handed down in my family since before Hadrian's Wall was constructed. We've clung to this little rock in the sea for literally thousands of years, long before we had the name Fay."

"And you're the keeper of the clan's secrets, are ye no?"

"I am. Not the only one, but at present, the most immediate one. So." She raised her hands and sketched a wide circle. "Do as I do."

Ronan faltered. "I've not had any real training," he admitted. "I'm not as proficient at following spells as I could be." Most mages learned magic in tandem with the gestures and words of a teacher or mentor. Those copycat skills later allowed a trained mage to participate in much larger spell-castings. Sorcha had heard that in the Far East, they often had hundreds of mages working in tandem, using their entire bodies to cast spells. But Ronan was apparently self-taught. He'd probably studied drawings of spells or invented his own, which could be dangerous.

Sorcha held her hands steady in the air. "If all of this succeeds, I'll teach you. For now, do your best to mimic my gestures."

He swallowed a few times and shifted his weight back and

forth, but he finally settled into a casting stance and lifted his arms until they made the same, loose arc on either side of his head. She flexed her fingers, then slowly curled them down, twisting her wrists and lowering her arms at the same time so that she came to rest with her elbows at her sides, palms up and hands cupped, in a pose reminiscent of a supplicant.

Ronan's motions were not as smooth, but he managed to follow the general pace and shape. She kept her movements slow and steady. Her fingers danced, drawing magic from the air, from the earth, from the grass and diffuse sunlight, weaving it into a net that would cradle the boulders and shoulder their weight.

The two nets shimmered in the arrows of sunlight that pierced the grey cloud cover. Sorcha examined Ronan's. It wasn't bad, for a first attempt, and his first shadowcasting. It would not have served for one of the truly massive massifs that the ancients had lifted, but it would do for the boulder.

"There's a single voiced incantation that goes with the spell, but the torque will prevent you from saying it, so I'll do it for both nets. Be ready to toss yours over the stone."

He nodded, his concentration still on holding the spell together. Sorcha took a deep breath, and chanted. Both nets erupted with light, and—as though they'd practiced a thousand times—she and Ronan cast the nets around the boulders in one fluid motion.

Almost no sound accompanied the lifting of the stones, except the soft taps as clods of dirt fell from their bases to the ground. Ronan did grunt as the spell settled, probably because he hadn't braced for the minimal impact of the weight against his body. The spell carried nearly all of it, but in order to tow the stones along, they had to maintain a minor amount of contact.

"Let's head back then." She hid a grin when he cursed under his breath. Perhaps he imagined she had developed a spell that could instantly transport things from one place to another without using a portal. If she'd done that, she would have licensed the thing and wouldn't have to rely on the ducal coffers to improve Fay House.

They trudged back to the house. At the sight of the rambling stone building, Sorcha realized she was going to have to show him the cellar entrance. None of the upstairs doors were big enough to bring the stones inside. She watched him surreptitiously. He hadn't complained again, and her intuition kept shouting that she could trust him. If this were all an elaborate hoax, then he'd managed to outwit every instinct that she'd relied on since childhood.

From the brief bits of information he'd dropped over the last few days, he was an admitted thief, smuggler, con artist, and revolutionary. But her heart said he was telling her the truth.

She took the path to the cellars.

Because she kept her gaze on him, she caught the slight raising of his eyebrows and parting of his lips that indicated curiosity. He'd have to resign himself to disappointment. She would not allow him anywhere near the vault, or anything else except the main hallway and the keystone chamber. After tonight, she could renew the mirror spell and reveal exactly who he was.

Before that, she could only trust him so far.

6

S orcha moved quickly, and Ronan had trouble matching her pace. That fact proved to be the rule of the evening. He'd never had much respect for university-taught mages and witches, and he'd outwitted more than a few of them over the years. But Sorcha was in a class all her own.

It wasn't so much that she had a powerful talent, although hers was perfectly respectable. Rather, she utilized every iota of her talent with deftness and precision. She reminded him of the poor farmers in Ireland, who could wring every last drop of productivity from their land and their possessions.

Sorcha had learned to be creative and efficient with her gifts. He could admire that dedication, could admire *her*. He didn't want to hold her in any sort of esteem. If she could only be like the vapid, wasteful witches he'd known, and the hapless, destructive wizards.

But she glowed with steady purpose where they had flashed in an opulent blaze before going dark. He couldn't help his attraction to that constant light and warmth. Or to the woman who possessed them.

For hours, he did as she asked, and barely had time to

breathe. They carved the stones in tandem, her magic linked to his, his body an extension of hers. She didn't stop to eat or rest, and by the time the replication spell shimmered into existence, they were both exhausted.

Yet she somehow found reserves within herself to finish casting, to merge the new ward matrix, and to test that her efforts had not been in vain.

Thank the gods, the new wards worked. The tangled threads relaxed and straightened. The outer wards now repelled the other spell. He watched, exhausted but unable to stop, as she poked and prodded every conceivable point of failure, and then checked everything again.

"It's done, Sorcha." He took her hands, and she blinked at him, her vision slowly focusing on his face instead of her Sight. "You did well." His voice was hoarse, as though he'd been shouting all afternoon. Given that the torque restricted his ability to speak spells, that was an odd side effect, but perhaps it was disuse, rather than overuse, that caused the rasp in his throat.

"So did you." She, at least, had an excuse for her huskiness, but his body chose to interpret both the tone and her approval as invitations. His thumbs stroked hers. He used a light pressure against the base of her hand and she moaned with pleasure.

That was all he could take. He drew her close and bent to kiss her.

As she had both times before, she responded with eager abandon. Except those kisses had been meant to prove something, and this…wasn't. This kiss was yearning, and need, and pure, overwhelming passion.

She wrapped her arms around his neck and pressed her lush body against his far less yielding frame. He tangled one hand in her hair, pressing her lips closer to his devouring mouth. The other hand went straight for her round, perfect arse. Gods, it was made for his hands, the curve perfectly matched to his cupped fingers. She wiggled against his palm, and her belly grazed his cock.

He broke away from the kiss and gasped, "Gods, Sorcha."

Her eyes were glazed, her breath ragged, but she yanked him back. "I need you." The words were nearly a growl. "Take me," she demanded, and kissed him.

He needed no further encouragement. She still wore the loose red dress, and he took advantage of its big, square neckline to slip his fingers under the fabric and push the whole thing off her shoulders, his hands stroking her arms to her wrists.

He dragged the tips of his fingers back up to her collarbones, chuckling at the little hairs that rose in his wake. His lips moved to her jaw, and he nipped at the sensitive spot below her ear. She gasped and jumped, and he slid his tongue down the column of her throat to the tiny hollow at its base. She tasted of salt, and thyme, and Sorcha.

Her skin gleamed, luminous and lovely, in the glow of the fairy lights that danced in the corners of the keystone chamber. He couldn't stop caressing her, could not bear to take his flesh away from hers. He cupped her breasts in his hands and groaned as their heavy weight pressed her tight, hard nipples against his palms.

He abandoned her throat and pushed her backward, over the heartstone. She lay atop it, her lips swollen from his kisses, her body bared to the waist, the tips of her breasts dark and peaked and begging for him. He bent and took the nearest nipple into his mouth, teasing it with his tongue until she cried out.

Her hips lifted in an unconscious echo of his tongue as it flicked across her sensitive breast. With every flex and writhe, her cleft rubbed against his cock, stiff and insistent, trapped in his trousers.

She reached for his waist, tugging at his shirt until her hands found his skin. Her fingers were warm and raised fire along his belly and back where they stroked him. Then she pushed into the waistband of his trousers, reaching for his arse. But the damned things were too tight, and she couldn't go very far. He straightened and fumbled with the belt and buttons, and she sat up to help him wrench the offensive fabric down his legs.

His cock sprang free, and his lungs released a gusty sigh of relief. Then she wrapped those tiny, perfect hands, that cast spells like the finest tapestry, around his stiff flesh. He groaned. His body became like a spell then, blazing with magic and energy, longing for her touch, for her embrace, for her breath to bring him to sweet, desperate life.

She stroked him, teasing the sensitive skin with a firm, practiced caress. She made as if to jump from the stone and give herself better access, but if she took him in her mouth, he would spend as soon as those perfect lips closed around him.

Instead, he pressed her back to the warm surface of the heartstone, and pushed her skirts out of the way. Her legs parted for him, falling to either side in a wanton invitation. Her pale curls beckoned, the hair only a shade darker than the moonlight-strands on her head, and he wanted to stroke them, to part the glistening folds and find the hidden treasure at her core.

But he made them both wait, dancing his fingertips across her upper thighs, stroking the curve of her hip and back to her arse, and groaning at her little mewl of impatience.

How had he lived without this woman wanting him? How had he ever found another female form arousing or seductive? This was the only body he wanted, hers the only flesh he yearned to taste and lick.

He surrendered to the craving, and pressed a finger through her slit, gathering slick moisture and sliding it over her clitoris. The little pearl rose from the surrounding flesh and peeked out of its hood, and he couldn't have halted the motion that brought his mouth to suckle its sweet, red perfection.

Her hips bucked beneath him, and she cried his name. Gods, that was the best sound in the world. Sorcha Fay, begging him for more. And she did beg, gasping for him to lick her, to not stop, to go faster, harder, "Oh, goddess, don't stop!" she screamed, and then salty, musky moisture flooded his mouth as she came.

She shuddered uncontrollably as he drove her from peak to peak, her shoulders and hips lifting and falling as she writhed with pleasure. Her thighs closed around his head, and he finally had to stop to catch his breath.

He stood, chuckling, to find her lax against the keystone, her legs dangling off and one arm flung over her face. Her white-blond hair had settled around her head in a messy halo. His light. His Sorcha.

He waited until she came back to herself, until her gorgeous sky-blue eyes opened, and then he slid two fingers inside of her. Her inner muscles clutched him, the passage hot, and tight, and wet.

She lifted her legs and wrapped them around his hips. "Please," she murmured. "Now."

He guided his cock to the slick folds of her entrance and pushed inside.

Gods, her cunt was tight, like thrusting into heaven. She moaned, and opened for him, and he tried to take his time, to savor this first, exquisite joining, but once he was fully seated in her depths, his balls resting against her wet flesh, he couldn't stop the instinct to withdraw, and plunge back into her heat.

She urged him on, rising to meet his thrusts, and he leaned to lick her breasts, resting one arm on the heartstone, reveling in her gasps and moans. He wanted to wait for her to climax again, but his peak took him by surprise, pleasure surging up from his balls and bursting through his chest and into his brain.

Her name exploded from his lips, as though he called her to follow him over the edge.

Then she was panting and trembling again, and with the tiny portion of his brain left with any ability to reason, he discovered that their magic had somehow meshed when he cried out his release. His crisis had precipitated hers, each little quake and tremor in her body making her inner walls clutch around his cock.

Then he sagged onto her, spent.

Sorcha cradled Ronan's body against hers. She hadn't meant for this to happen, but no matter what the outcome, she would never regret that it had. Even if he left tomorrow, even if she never saw him again, she would have this one, perfect moment, this beautiful memory to cherish for the rest of her days.

She still wasn't sure of him, couldn't trust that she had not given her virginity to a man who would treat her like a conquest or a body without a real, human person inside. But she was at least now sure that he wasn't her interloper. Because, when their magic had joined, when there was no place for either of them to hide, she'd found only Ronan. Oh, there were secrets, still, and dark nooks and crannies in his soul that she doubted he cared to examine. But he hadn't come here to steal, and he didn't want to harm her.

That was not, she reminded herself, the same as saying he

wouldn't harm her. Intent and results often did not match. She tugged in a breath. Released it.

His cock was still buried within her and not yet softened. She clenched the muscles around him. He flinched as pleasure pain coursed through him and moaned, burying his face into the crook of her neck and shoulder. She wanted him again, although soreness had already settled into her muscles, and certain previously unused parts of her anatomy were swollen and raw.

Perhaps she could tempt him into a bath? She didn't have a water heater, but a few years ago there'd been a very good harvest, coupled with an unexpected dividend from one of her investments. She'd put the money into having plumbing installed to a handful of water closets, the kitchen and scullery, and two extra-large tubs. In place of the water heater, she used magic.

She nuzzled his head with her cheek. "Let's take this somewhere more comfortable."

He pulled away with a jerk, and their sweaty skin came unstuck with an audible pop. He hovered over her, braced on his forearms, and said, "Feck it, I'm sorry."

Not the response she'd been hoping for. "For what? For doing everything I asked, no, begged you to do?" Her stomach fluttered when he would no longer meet her eyes. "Is it because we're on a stone slab?" She shifted, and her back rubbed against the carvings. The magic shimmered and tingled along her skin. "It's no feather mattress, but it's warm, and we gave the wards an extra kick."

"No, it's not that. Shite." He levered himself off the stone, and his cock slid out of her. She wanted it back, wanted to hold on to that connection, but he was backing away and staring at his hands as though they'd sprouted thorns.

She sat up and started to lift the bodice of her dress. But his eyes tracked the movement, and she decided that covering her body was the wrong tack. Instead, she stood, and let the entire thing fall to the floor. She arched her back, stretching, and raised her arms as high as they would go. She left her eyes open in slits so she could watch him.

As she'd hoped, his gaze drank her in. Good. So he hadn't suddenly stopped wanting her. Was this a crisis of conscience? The fact that he had one—had any sort of morals or qualms after his disavowal of higher feeling or nobility—made a bright warmth fill her chest.

She picked up the dress and tossed it over her shoulder. "I'd like a bath. If you'll join me, you can do your self-flagellation in the warm water and then I'd very much like you to cum in my mouth."

His jaw dropped, and his gaze finally met hers.

"I wanted to taste you before." She bit her lower lip. "Not that I'm in any way criticizing what happened instead." She hoped the heat and desire glowing inside her was clear in her gaze. "But I still want to wrap my lips around your cock. If you'll allow it."

He made a guttural sound, neither yea nor nay, and she reached out her hand. "Come."

For a moment, she thought he wouldn't take it. Would allow shame to guide his actions. But then he grinned, and her own personal sun emerged. He laced his fingers through hers and said, "Lead the way."

7

After the bath, and another round of mutual pleasure—although no more intercourse—Sorcha remembered the mirror. Ronan helped her out of the tub so she could retrieve it.

"Thanks to you, I'm now brimming with energy, so I shouldn't have any trouble renewing the spell. We'll hope that the duchess is paying attention this time."

Ronan laughed and pulled her against him. They were still naked and flushed with heat from the bath, and his hunger for her turned ravenous. He kissed her, but she wriggled out of his arms.

"I have to hurry, or the moon will set, and then we'll have to wait a whole month to fill the mirror."

"Go on, then."

She wrapped a length of toweling over her body and went into the hall. He followed, and a door opened halfway down the corridor. The suite was of modest size, with an open door on either side, leading to a dressing room and a sitting room. He glanced into both of these as she strolled to the nightstand beside the bed.

He ought to have been sated, but he had to restrain the urge to tumble her back onto that bed and feast on her flesh once more. He would lick every inch of her, from her forehead to the tips of her toes, and then concentrate on the cleft between her legs. Once she'd reached her peak at least twice, he would lift her up on her knees and take her from behind, where he could wrap a hand around and fondle her clit while he gripped that lovely round arse with the other.

Yes, he would do all of those things. In a few minutes. She grabbed the mirror and plopped onto the mattress. The towel slipped off her shoulder, and her breasts jiggled. His cock had come to half-mast, and he had no intention of hiding his arousal.

After he'd taken her on the keystone and their passion was spent, he'd had a moment of…he wasn't even sure what. Perhaps it was shame. She'd been so wanton, so sure and willing and even demanding. He hadn't realized until that moment afterward—until they lay there with every defense down and their magic wide open—that she'd been a virgin.

The thought had flitted across her conscious mind while they were still linked, and he'd balked.

She'd seemed cold and cynical that afternoon in the pantry. Even after their other interactions had convinced him his initial instincts about her were correct, he'd still believed her experienced, if not jaded. She was indefatigable, and bright, and honest. But she'd also been putting on a façade of worldliness, and if he hadn't been so consumed by his own issues, it would have been obvious to him.

But it hadn't been, and when he'd understood that she'd been—not innocent, because she knew exactly what she wanted, but untouched—he'd panicked. His thoughts and emotions tangled. What sort of rake pounds into a woman on a stone fecking slab, not even holding back to make sure she peaks first?

She'd scoffed at his attempts to apologize and then had done perhaps the only thing that could have broken through the welter of his feelings. He'd been shocked that she used what most ladies would consider crass terms, but with emotion and craving behind them instead of shame and degradation. He hadn't known that he could be so aroused by a woman's genuine desire to have him cum in her mouth.

And he had. Gods, he had. And it was only slightly less earth-shattering than when he'd filled her sweet cunny with his seed.

The vision of him doing it again faltered and froze. He hadn't used a sheath. He'd never—since he was a raw lad losing his virginity to the older upstairs maid—taken a woman without a barrier. As soon as his mother's cousin found out about the maid, he'd told Ronan where to buy the sheaths, and how it would keep a babe from catching in a lass.

Ronan stared at Sorcha and imagined her swelling with his child.

The image should have scared him to death. And it did, but only because he wanted it.

He opened his Sight so he could watch as power danced around her. Her magic felt like a summer night, warm and soft, lit by the cool reflection of the moon. The smell reminded him of a night-blooming garden he'd once snuck through on his way to burgle a house, mixed with the earthier aromas of new-mown hay. It tasted like mulberries and thyme. He had to restrain his renewed urge to lick her and ascertain if her skin tasted differently when his Sight was open. He'd never had sex with a witch before her.

Sorcha wove her spell, pulling most of the magical energy from within herself, and part of it from the tidal energy of the moon that was a key element in the artifact's matrix. She worked with a little half-smile on her face, her posture relaxed and her movements fluid, unaware of the dark places his thoughts had gone.

Should he speak? Would mentioning the possibility of a child make her back away? Or would she embrace that future? He had no idea. He'd never considered a settled life, never imagined himself a father or in a relationship with a woman that lasted longer than a few brief, passionate encounters. He didn't know what a man was supposed to do next when he actually wanted a woman to stay. When *he* wanted to stay.

Gods, what the hells was he thinking? He couldn't stay here, on this little island in the middle of fecking nowhere. He had his Cause, and a purpose. He had a driving principle, and it wasn't homey and full of love. It was cold, and dark, and hard, and necessary.

He'd been soft, once. He'd imagined bright futures, as a lad. But then his father had divorced his mother, claiming that she'd been with another man and that Ronan wasn't his. She'd been his second wife, married because he wanted to take advantage of cheap property in Ireland. When that hadn't yielded a profit, he'd found a way to dispose of her and his unwanted Irish son. Before the ink on the divorce was dry, he'd remarried a much younger, very wealthy American heiress. Her fortune propped up the sinking viscountcy, and Ronan and his mother had lived on the McCarrick family's sufferance for the rest of his childhood.

Not that his mother had made it easy. She fought with her father, who blamed her for the divorce, and then with her brothers who briefly gave them shelter. They finally settled with a distant cousin, who'd paid for Ronan to go to school to remove him from the house.

It wasn't meant to be a kindness, but Radley had been the best possible choice. It was a new school, only forty years old, and didn't have the cachet of Eton or Harrow. It also didn't have the very long traditions of nepotism and intolerance for outsiders that those venerable institutions celebrated.

Unfortunately, the curriculum did not include magic, at least not officially, and so when Ronan's talents emerged, he hid them. He didn't want to be politely told that he needed to transfer somewhere that could teach him control. He doubted his cousin would pay the higher tuition at another school, and would likely pull him and put him in a free public school in Dublin, where an overworked mage would teach him enough not to kill himself and let him go.

When the cousin died before Ronan graduated, he and his mother moved into a tiny flat in Dublin. He went to a few classes and learned the basic tenets of magic, but they needed money, so he had to work.

Having left Radley without graduating, and with few connections in the city, he had difficulty finding a respectable position. He'd taken a job counting receipts for a gaming hell that had an attached fighting ring and brothel. It was there that his mother met a boxer and ran off with him to America. Within a year, she was dead.

But it was also there that he met Michael McCauley. He was a big man, brawny and charismatic. Where another man might have been called Mick, his temper and size earned him the nickname Donn, from *Donn Cúailnge*, the Brown Bull of Cooley in the Ulster Cycle.

Donn lit the fire of revolution in Ronan's heart. He was a member of a group of Irish Republicans, and through him, Ronan met with many of the leading members of their cause. Donn was the Alpha of a Circle, and he chose Ronan to act as his Beta. Together, they organized a group of thieves, con-artists, smugglers, and pickpockets to become spies and agents against England in the cause of Irish Independence.

Finally, Ronan had found something to which he could

give all of himself, and be accepted for all that he was. And the Cause gave back what it took, in the form of friendship, camaraderie, and eventually, love. Not romantic love, but the sibling relationship he'd never had with his much-older brothers. Evie became his sister in every way but blood.

It was for her sake that he'd quit the most dangerous missions and shifted the group's focus to smuggling and raising funds. It was so that she could learn proper magic that he'd eventually released her from their Circle. She'd run away to the Fay School, and once he'd tracked her down, she promised to return once she'd finished her training. But he'd eschewed her promise. If she wanted to stay in Scotland or, gods help her, England, he would not drag her back to Ireland.

No one else would have been given that trust, or that choice.

And now here was another woman, who had stolen something from him he'd never intended to give away. He, the consummate thief, had been unable to stop this honest, forthright woman from reaching in and plucking out his heart. She'd done it like the most brazen pickpocket, while he was distracted by other things. By his frustration at the cuffs and torque. By the danger of the attack on the wards. By the heady rush of casting spells in tandem.

By her bloody gorgeous body, and her pure, achingly beautiful soul.

Damn her. Because she was light and brilliance, and perfection, and he was a man who'd never made the right choice for the right reason. Sometimes the wrong choice for the right reason, but usually the wrong choice for the wrong reason.

She deserved better than him.

Sorcha jumped off the bed and raised the mirror. She hitched the towel back over her shoulder, and he wanted to rip the fabric off. She should always be bare for him, and him for her. "It's done. I wish I'd been able to set a meeting, but we'll try a few minutes at a time until I reach Etta again."

"That's the duchess?"

Sorcha's eyebrows drew down and her lips quirked in a frown. "Don't you know her name?"

Ronan crossed his arms over his chest. "I was hired through another party. My contact told me the duchess doesn't want to be linked to what I'm doing. Damned if I know why."

"Who's your contact, then?"

"Is that important?" Not that Sorcha would ever be a threat to Evie, but he'd spent too many years guarding his tongue. Keeping information close had become a habit.

"I suppose not. I just thought to ask Etta. If she hasn't met you, then how can I be sure you're the person she meant to send?"

"Ah. My contact is Evie Finn. She's a student at the Fay School for Magic. If we have enough time with the mirror, Evie will vouch for me."

Sorcha's expression relaxed. Proof that she was still worried that he'd lied to her. Maybe not about the wards, but about everything else. And yet, when they'd been together, she must have felt the connection as he did. His own truths must have been revealed to her, as hers had to him. She had to realize that he hadn't lied.

Maybe it wasn't lies, but the things he'd left unsaid that bothered her. He had secrets, more than most men, and a woman who could See would not appreciate his reasons for hiding.

"When we reach Etta, I'll keep the conversation brief and set another time to chat with Evie." She put the mirror back on her nightstand and placed her other hand on his chest. It was the hand that had been holding the towel.

The damp fabric slithered down her breasts and onto the floor.

She deserved better than him, but right now he wanted her, and she wanted him, and that was going to have to be enough.

8

Sorcha woke in the dim light of early dawn. Her room faced the west, so the house shielded her windows from the morning glare, assuming the sun was out today.

She wriggled and stretched, and her arm encountered a warm body on the other side of the bed. Ronan. He lay on his back, one arm over his chest and the other by his side, between them. They'd fallen asleep tangled together, but they had drifted apart overnight. The memories of their last coupling, probably only a few hours ago, made her body flush with heat.

He'd asked her about the possibility of pregnancy, and she'd told him about the spell her mother had taught her, to prevent a man's seed from entering her womb. The spell would last until her menses arrived, at which point it would dissolve and need to be renewed.

Not that she'd remembered to cast it, that first time on the keystone. But she'd done it the second time, and she wasn't fertile right now anyway. A tiny trickle of disappointment flowed through her. Because no matter what had changed between them physically overnight, Ronan would still leave once he got what he'd come for.

And wouldn't it be amazing if he left something of himself behind?

She propped herself on her elbows and drank in the view.

The sheet was bunched around his waist, and she'd stolen the heavier duvet. Only the bottom corner still warmed his legs. His breathing was slow, even, and she could watch the rise and fall of his ribcage for hours.

But she needed to contact Etta today, and a glance at the clock on her mantel told her she might already have missed Etta's morning ablutions. So she sat up and lifted the mirror. She'd almost engaged the spell when she remembered that she wasn't wearing anything.

Her movement must have woken Ronan, because he was suddenly taking advantage of that fact, his hand covering one breast and his mouth latching onto the tip of the other.

She squealed, in surprise and stunned pleasure, and let him lap at her nipple for a few lovely moments as liquid heat pooled in her core. Then she pushed him away. "I have to use this now. I may have already missed Etta at her mirror this morning."

He chuckled and came back in to nuzzle her neck. "You planning to talk to her like this?" His fingers stroked along her bare shoulder and collarbone. She slapped at his hand.

"Of course not. I'll put on a dressing gown. She'll understand." She hopped off the bed and ambled to her wardrobe. Ronan's gaze was like a brand on her, heating her skin even though she had her back to him. She took her time retrieving the dressing gown and then swiveled around so he could watch her as she wrapped it around her body.

"You're killing me, *a solas*," he said, and deliberately pushed the sheet off of his hips to reveal his thick, hard cock. He wrapped his fingers around the head and drew his fist slowly to the base, revealing the glistening glans that she wanted to tease, and stroke, and lick.

She bit her lip. It was either that, or drool. She needed him in her mouth again, and then in her cunny.

But that had to wait.

She tied the dressing gown and crossed to her vanity rather than back to the bed. If she peeked at him again, she'd go lick him from balls to tip and not stop until he begged her to mount him and ride them both to ecstasy. She'd done that once, with Duncan, though he'd had his trousers on at the time, and she wanted to try it again with Ronan's cock filling her.

Her regular mirror revealed that her hair was a mess, snarls of white-blond locks sticking out all over. She sighed. How could that possibly be arousing? Although it obviously was. She attacked the knots with her brush until she could manage a simple chignon. Then she swapped the brush for the mirror and activated the spell.

She'd found Etta's room by trial and error last time, but the mirror honed back in on its last location immediately. At first, the room appeared empty, except for a big four-poster bed and what she could see of the dressing table and its chair. But when she tapped on the mirror, a head entered her view.

"Ach!" From the brown wool maid's uniform the girl wore, embroidered with the Fay School crest, Sorcha surmised this was one of the school's servants.

"Hello."

"Sorry, miss. I was told to watch for ye, but it's been sae lang, I didna expect ye."

"Can you fetch the duchess for me, and a student by the name of Evie Finn? I don't want to waste the spell, so I'll make contact again in a half hour."

"I will, miss."

"Thank you." Sorcha eased back in her chair and made a widdershins circle with her left hand to disengage the spell.

Ronan stepped behind her, still gloriously naked, and bent to kiss the top of her head. "There's a lot we can do in a half hour."

FAST OR SLOW, PASSION WITH RONAN WAS SOMETHING SORCHA could easily become addicted to. They missed the half hour deadline by a good ten minutes, and when Etta and Evie appeared in the mirror, Etta was twisting her wedding ring and Evie fingered a silver chain that disappeared beneath her blouse. Both relaxed immediately.

"Sorry we're late." Sorcha's voice died in her throat. Evie was young and stunningly beautiful. Her hair was all coppers and golds and scarlets, a sunset transformed to individual strands. Her features were delicate and elfin, as though somewhere in her bloodline was a true faerie changeling. She had gigantic green eyes the exact color of early spring moss. Her body was slender and nearly ethereal, as though she were not completely tied to the mortal realm.

Sorcha had never considered herself a jealous person. Her world was comfortable and stable, and she loved her place in it. Her body's generous flesh and lavish curves did not match the feminine ideals of the age, but she'd not been forced to go to a fashionable city where she would have to compare herself with other lasses or be strapped into an impossible corset. She'd attracted plenty of lads and had no doubt of their delight in her endowments.

Evie Finn made her feel ponderous and heavy, thick as a seal out of water, and as ungainly. At Ronan's expression, her heart faltered and seized in her chest. His wide mouth had ticked up in a grin, and his eyes crinkled at the corners. In her Sight, he'd turned almost incandescent with joy. His magic had intensified, too, and his saltwater-scent suffused her nostrils. Sorcha tasted brine, but underneath it…something sweet. Apples?

And then she understood. He loved Evie.

A bitter taste filled Sorcha's mouth, and her jaw was tight with tension from her clenched teeth and pursed lips. Her hand holding the little mirror shook. If she didn't need to keep her Sight open for the spell, she'd have clamped every last magical sense and tried to ignore what she'd discovered. But she couldn't.

She forced her limbs to relax, and then her jaw. Ronan had promised her nothing. He'd not promised to even visit her again after his task was done, much less offer his heart. And that was the source of the sharp pain in her chest. Because he hadn't spoken of love with her, despite what they'd done and how close their magic had brought them. She'd thought the life he'd led had no opportunities for love, and maybe he didn't even understand what he felt.

But he clearly loved this girl.

And Evie obviously loved him back. Her already beautiful face transformed to radiance as she beamed at him. "Ro! Bart sent me a telegram saying you weren't on the beach last night as he expected, and your boat was still on the shore. They didn't land because there was some kind of ward."

"That's a long story." Ronan chuckled, and Sorcha had to force her gaze away from him and Evie. So she stared at Etta, her distant cousin. Etta was beautiful too, but in a different way. If Evie was elfin and waiflike, Etta was solid strength. She was only of average height, but she gave the impression of a tall warrior goddess.

"We don't have enough time for stories." Sorcha hated that her voice sounded so high-pitched and loud. Both Ronan and Evie startled. "There's not enough magic in this mirror." She tried to be softer and gentler that time, but the words still held an edge as she attacked the consonants and clipped her vowels.

"I'll be brief, then," Etta said, and Sorcha noted that her nasal American accent was almost gone. Instead, her speech was a mix of brogue, Appalachia, and London society. "Yes, I sent Ronan to acquire some items from the family collection. Didn't my note arrive?"

Heat suffused Sorcha's cheeks, and she clenched her hands to keep them from flying to her face and cover the tell-tale flush. "I've been having trouble with the wards. Someone has been tampering with them for several months, and I'd increased my security in response. Ronan stumbled into one of my extra wards, and I'm afraid your note was destroyed." She didn't mention that his clothes had been destroyed, too. No need to share that image with the other women.

"Ah," Etta said, but her dark eyes had narrowed, the nearly black brows drawing down. A streak of white—a family magical trait—that had barely been visible at her temple a year ago was now a wide slash above the left brow. "Why didn't you ask for help, Sorcha? It would have given me the perfect cover, and I could have come myself."

"I honestly thought it was a nuisance at first. The wards were a mess, but there was no evidence of direct tampering that I could trace. Someone had placed counterward keystones around the property and covered them with avoidance spells so I wouldn't notice. And it nearly worked. But Ronan helped me set new keystones into the House ward matrix, so we've stopped the intrusion for now."

"Someone?" Etta leaned forward. "Do you think it could be Amelia again?"

"No, definitely not. I rewrote the ward spell after last year to specifically exclude her. She did come poking around a month or so after you and Mal married, but she hasn't been back."

"That's good to hear. But I don't like that you're there alone guarding the house. I'm going to ask Muireall to send someone to stay with you. Maybe we can arrange a special training program for the students who are nearly ready to graduate. That would put more mages and witches into the house, and allow us to send more of the family to help you."

Sorcha bristled. "If you deem it necessary."

"It's not a punishment or a criticism of your abilities. We have an enemy, perhaps many enemies, and it's alarming that they've targeted Fay House. I want it guarded to the best of our abilities."

The chastisement stung, but Sorcha accepted the inevitable. Etta wasn't yet Le Fay, the official head of the clan, but she was the duchess, and she owned the property. Her word was law.

She also wasn't wrong. Sorcha did need help. Not that she liked admitting it.

"Very well. Once the new contingent arrives, I'll dismantle the counter keystones and study the spells. I might be able to trace them back to the mage who built them, though I'm sure he or she is long gone."

The mirror flashed. They had only a minute left. "Our time is nearly done. I'll retrieve the wand and the diadem and send Ronan on his way."

"Bart sailed 'round to Arisaig," Evie said. "I'll send him a telegram to come back for you."

"I'll be seeing you soon." Ronan grinned, and Evie's brilliant green eyes, anticipating their reunion, were the last thing reflected in the glass before the spell flashed again and the mirror cleared. Sorcha stared into her own eyes, dark blue as a stormy sea, and pushed the jealousy deep.

It was natural to form an attachment to a man with

whom she'd shared such exceptional passion. She shouldn't be so upset to discover that he was capable of deep love and affection. His ability to love in general did not obligate him to love *her*. He was not hers. She had no claim on him, and he none on her, beyond the agreement he'd made with Etta.

She would send him on his way, and never see him again.

"Well. Let's go to the vault then, shall we?" She made to rise, but he caught her hand.

"What's your hurry? Bart won't be here till nightfall, or perhaps the morning. We've plenty of time."

She pulled her fingers free and stood. "I need to ride to the village for everyone to come back." She bustled to her wardrobe and removed a coat and her heavy boots. "Chores haven't been done for days." She carried the boots back to the chair and sat to pull them on. "I've fed and watered the animals, but the barn's a mess and so's the kitchen."

"Sorcha." Ronan put his hands on her shoulders, and her fingers stilled on the laces of the boots. He pressed into the muscle, and she closed her eyes as he kneaded the tension away. "Why are you in such a hurry to toss me out?"

She closed her eyes, her head still bowed over her boots, and breathed. She could tell him the truth, but that would open her wide. She didn't sense he would be cruel and mock her feelings, but she was much more afraid he would be indifferent, or worse, pity her. She could picture his handsome face, dark eyebrows raised and grey eyes wide in disbelief at her confession. He would be chagrinned, and pat her hand, and explain that she was a good tumble, but he wasn't the loving kind. The lie would destroy her.

So she stitched a smile on her face and inclined it toward him. "I'm more in a hurry to resume my life. I've never had to deal with an attack on the house before, and the sooner we call everyone back and things return to normal, the better."

He pushed a strand of hair behind her ear, and his fingers

trailed her jaw in a soft caress. The contact tingled with warmth, though something in his grey gaze said he didn't entirely believe her. But he allowed her the omission. "I'm sorry your fortress was invaded. You've handled the threat, and all is well. I'll help you." With a slight exertion of pressure, he tilted her face a fraction closer toward his and captured her lips.

Heat and need swept from her core and met with a wave of desire cresting through him. This was not the same as when he saw Evie in the mirror, and she tried not to sob when she sensed the difference. What he felt now held no trace of that love. Yet she couldn't stop herself from wanting him, couldn't hold back the desperate force of her lips against his.

He must have sensed the shift in her emotions, because he pulled his mouth away and rubbed his thumb over her jaw and down her throat.

Before he could ask what was wrong, before he could say anything, she blurted, "Thank you. I know this isn't where you want to be."

His face was still close to hers, his breath still feathering her cheeks. "Right now, it is," he said, and kissed her again.

9

E vie had looked well, Ronan thought, hobnobbing with a duchess as though she belonged among the beau monde. And perhaps she did. Her lineage was a mystery, but her formidable magical talent implied that she had noble blood somewhere in her family tree. And she'd always carried herself with an innate grace.

Despite knowing for certain that his father was an English viscount and his mother the daughter of an Irish baron, Ronan had never had that quality that some nobles had, a mix of hauteur and the absolute comprehension that their blood was bluer and better than a peon like Ronan's. Evie might find a place in Society, but he would never be accepted by the *ton*.

He watched Sorcha as she finally got around to lacing her boots. This last lovemaking had been different from the others. She'd clutched him with an almost frantic desperation, had pushed him onto the bed and ridden him so hard he'd barely held back from climax long enough for her to peak. Perhaps her urgency was because their relationship now had a definite end point. He would leave, tonight or tomorrow.

That was for the best. He had to keep repeating it over and over until he believed it. Because a single night and day of passion with this woman made him want to stay with her forever.

Seeing Evie helped. She was a reminder of his Cause—of the course his life had followed for the last ten years. He couldn't let his yearning for Sorcha distract him from his purpose. Ireland must be free.

They trudged to the vault, which Ronan had expected to be in the basements with the keystones but was actually on the top level of the house. The most complex series of protections he'd ever seen in his life—including King's College and Windsor Castle, where the queen spent most of her time—surrounded the entire upper floor.

"Do these spells have their own keystones?"

"Some. Others use the leylines in the area for renewal. Most have pervaded the house for years, sometimes hundreds of years, but many of them were designed by the first duchess. This was her fortress."

Sorcha approached a door, and Ronan left his Sight open so he could watch her interact with the spell. Very little action was required. The spell wrapped tendrils around her hands and then, after the briefest of motions, retreated. The door swung open.

"I could tell that it was a sensing spell, but not much else. What was it doing?"

"Making sure I'm a Fay. In particular, one of the Fay who has access to this space. There aren't many of us."

"Ah." He followed her inside. Again, Fay House did not match his assumptions. Where he had expected thick walls and darkness, he found light. This was the glass-walled section he'd noticed from outside, and had assumed was an observatory or magical conservatory.

In some ways, it was a conservatory. Plants grew everywhere, each one feeding and being fed by the spells that interlaced everything. Warm, moist air settled over his skin, and little particles of magic danced in the thick humidity.

Ronan breathed in the complex sweet and earthy mix of good soil and green leaves and tasted something like mushrooms. Magic multiplied the assault on his senses and made him dizzy. He focused on vision, suppressing everything else.

The pots and plant boxes were set in what was probably a symbolic pattern, but which made crossing the room difficult. Sorcha took a particular path through the verdigris and stopped at a cabinet.

She hesitated, her hand partially outstretched.

Was she thinking what he was, that this was the moment their idyll would end? It might have started with animosity, but he'd come to crave her company and her touch.

He took a step forward, but she lifted her hand and engaged the locking spell on the cabinet door. Something inside clicked, and it swung open.

Inside sat a number of oddly-shaped objects, any or all of which he could fence for a not inconsiderable sum in any major city in the world. His fingers twitched. Instincts did not die easily.

She extracted a wand and waved the cabinet shut again. As had been described, three different kinds of wood were twisted in a complex pattern that could not have been possible without magic, even using modern steam-bending and machines. The wood had been fused on a level that no glue could replicate.

Ronan took the wand with reverence. It lay heavy in his palm, giving the sensation that it weighed much more than a simple wooden wand ought. Was that the magic, or was there a core of metal within the wood?

Sorcha moved on, and Ronan followed her rather than delving into the wand. She stopped at a chest this time, which required more spells to unlock. She withdrew a leather case. "This artifact you won't be able to handle directly. Only Le Fay can open the case."

The case was roughly circular and about three inches deep, as would be expected for a diadem. "How does the spell identify who holds the title of Le Fay?"

"When the new Le Fay is chosen, the family casts a spell to acclaim her. The title is invested within her magic, like a signature. There are many spells in this house set to respond to that signature."

"Amazing."

Sorcha passed over the case. "Perhaps, but not unusual. The military does the same thing with their mages, so that orders cannot be opened by the wrong hand."

"And if the mage dies and cannot open the message?"

Sorcha scrubbed a hand through her hair, dislodging a few strands from the hasty bun she'd constructed earlier. "They may have a failsafe. Ours is simply to acclaim a new Le Fay."

They were speaking of inconsequential things because neither of them wanted to address the consequential thing that stood between them, both massive and insubstantial.

"I'd like to—" Ronan began, but Sorcha's attention had been caught by something over his shoulder.

"*An Donas Dubh,*" she swore, and then she strode away through the foliage to a big wooden cabinet, much bigger than the one that had held the wand, and which stood with its doors wide open. "Great Goddess, no." She had picked up speed, and her foot collided with one of the pots. Ronan caught the tree as she stumbled onward. He set it upright, and she flung herself at the open cabinet.

She was swearing in rapid, low Gaelic, pawing through the shelves of the cabinet and yanking out drawers, until she'd handled every object, unlocked every secret compartment.

Then she started to do it all again.

Ronan wrapped his arms around her, forcing her trembling hands to her sides. "*A mhuirnín*, what's wrong?"

"They're gone."

"What are?"

"Only the most powerful artifacts that this vault holds. My most important task is to guard them, and I've failed."

Her whole body shook, tremors that reached into his magic and made him throb with her. Guilt, inadequacy, fear, shame. Waves upon waves of despair.

Ronan steeled himself against the onslaught, spun her in his arms and kissed her. For a shocked moment, she resisted, and then she threw herself into the embrace, clutching him like a rock in a stormy sea.

When her panic had subsided, he broke the kiss and said, "Let me help you."

She nodded, weakly, and he gave her another squeeze. There was a locked chest beside the cabinet, and he sat and drew her onto his lap. "Tell me exactly what is missing, and then we'll do a circuit of the room to see if anything else has been tampered with. After that, I'll cast a reconstruction spell to uncover what happened."

"It might not work in here. There are so many independent matrices, they'll interfere with anything you try to do."

Ronan chuckled. He'd spent his entire adult life learning how to do spellwork inside heavily warded areas without interfering with the existing matrix. But he didn't say that.

She didn't need to hear about more thievery right now. "I can handle it. Now, what's missing?"

"Two fully functioning Power Wells, and a smaller Well that was created during an earlier attempt to make them."

Ronan inadvertently squeezed her in surprise, and she grunted. He relaxed, and nuzzled her head in apology. "You weren't fecking joking. How much power are we talking?"

"Substantial. Lilias made them to fight Napoleon. The little one can wipe out a small city." She swallowed. "I know because it did. It destroyed a place called Badajoz in Spain."

"Black bollocks. Are you sure? In school, I read about a siege and that we lost five thousand men and a section of the city was destroyed, but nothing about a Well."

"I'm sure. They'd already lost so many men, and the city refused to surrender. It was supposed to be a contained explosion, but there was more power than Lilias thought. She leveled most of the city, not just a section. And the big ones are much more powerful."

"Bloody hells. That's not good."

"No, it's not. I need to get them back." She started to tremble again, and he put a hand behind her head to force her to meet his gaze.

"Come back to me, *a solas*. When was the last time you checked this room?"

"Right after you arrived, and again the night before last when I went to bed. Nothing had been disturbed."

"So it happened yesterday when we were distracted by the ward stones."

"That's the most reasonable assumption, yes. I'd have noticed if anyone entered the house after we recast the wards last night."

"That gives me a period for the reconstruction spell. But let's inspect the room and make sure nothing else was tampered with. The more localized the spell, the more likely it is to work. If I need to widen it to a broader area, it's best to know that in advance."

Sorcha wiggled as though to stand, and he held her still. "Relax a moment. You need to focus and stop flagellating yourself over something you couldn't have stopped. If we hadn't worked to fix the wards yesterday, the entire house would be vulnerable today. Yes, the situation is dire. But it could have been much worse."

He took her mouth again, to comfort her and to remind himself that she was here, and safe. How had she become so important to him in so short a time? The tension in her body ebbed and she leaned into him. He ended the kiss and nudged her forehead with his. She smiled. It was wan and pale, but still a smile.

"Now, let's have a look around and find out if anything else has been disturbed."

Two circuitous routes through the room proved that nothing else had, which Ronan found very odd. Or perhaps not. Most thieves were caught because they were greedy. They lost focus and tried to take more and more, made too many mistakes, or took too much time. This thief had been precise. A few protection spells had been brushed on the burglar's way to the Wells, but he'd avoided everything else.

"How could he have discovered the precise way through the room to the Wells?" Sorcha asked. "Why hasn't anything else been tampered with?"

"It could be a she. Some of the best housebreakers are women."

Sorcha's stiff stance told him she disliked that particular knowledge.

"But it was most likely a directional or compass spell. I'm sure they're the most powerful artifacts in the room. The spell would be cast to show the shortest feasible path, which would account for obstacles like your greenery."

"I've never heard of a spell that could do that."

"That's because you've never run with a street gang like mine. Each gang with a witch or mage has their own version. Some are better than others. Evie created one that could track across three whole city blocks. Best thing I ever saw." He grinned. Then he noticed that Sorcha's mildly curious expression had frozen, the muscles along her jaw and neck taut with tension. He'd told her of his past. Was this story so awful?

"But I'll know for sure what was done here when I cast the reconstruction." He lifted a hand a placed it on the torque at his throat. "It's time we dispensed with this."

"Oh. Yes." Sorcha flushed and came to him, lifting the metal necklet off his flesh. Magic surged in a welcome wave, and he captured her hand to lace his fingers with hers.

"That's better." He tried to initiate a link, but she resisted. Her energy was all tangled, pulsing in a thousand different directions. "Relax, lovely girl. I told you it will be fine. But you understand the energy of the room. It will help me if we're linked when I cast this."

She nodded and closed her eyes. Her magic contracted inward, settling along her skin and over her curves. He tasted mulberries again, and the air was redolent with the tang of a lightning storm.

Her fingers tightened in his, and her magic flowed down his arm. His met and meshed with hers, a casual joining that quickly deepened. She was afraid and felt inadequate, but she was also…jealous? He closed off his awareness of her. Her negative emotions would color the spell, and he'd already glimpsed more than he imagined she wanted.

What did she have to be jealous of? There'd never been another woman in his life like her.

Not now. Deal with it later. He kept the thoughts firmly behind his wall, where she couldn't overhear.

He pulled her back to the open cabinet and took a casting stance, feet shoulder-width apart, weight evenly distributed, legs relaxed, and knees bent but not locked. For very long spells, it was important to be still, and poor stance could make a mage lose balance and thus collapse the spell. Locked knees had caused more than one hapless mage to black out.

Sorcha mimicked him, her movements fluid and practiced. *Shall I shadowcast with you, or do you only need my understanding of the room?*

Her mental voice stroked like velvet against him, soft and decadent and desirable. Perhaps this would be harder with her linked to him, and not easier. *Just your familiarity, I think. But if I need you, be prepared to jump in and hold on to a few threads.*

She nodded rather than answer, and he began to weave.

The magic in the room resisted him, at first, until Sorcha gestured and it flowed with a rush through the first segments of his casting. If the thief had experienced the same difficulty...he quickly adjusted the spell to allow for that possibility. The new segment pulsed and grew, and he tied it back into the original plan with a mix of symbols. He nodded at Sorcha, and she raised her hands to keep the threads steady while he worked on a different section.

Sweat poured down his face and gathered under his jaw as he worked in the humid and too-warm room. The sun had emerged from behind a thick bank of clouds, and the temperature had risen by several degrees in the glass-covered space.

But at last the work was done, and the spell threads merged into a kind of living tapestry, mixing woven images with the motion of a zoetrope. A man walked through the weaving, holding a small vial in one hand and a nasty-looking black orb in the other. Sorcha gasped, but her emotions were walled away from him, and she didn't try to speak through the link.

Ronan didn't have any reservations about sending his thoughts to her. *Shite. That's a null orb.*

It took her a moment to answer, her gaze flicking around the reconstructed image and settling on what was held in the man's hand. *Really? I didn't know those actually existed.*

Very few of them do, and the fecking British Army has most of them.

He's with the army? That makes sense.

It does? Has your clan angered anyone in the government recently?

Sorcha flushed from the roots of her pale hair all the way to the neckline of her dress. But she answered. *Remember how the duchess mentioned a woman named Amelia earlier?* He nodded. *That would be Amelia Upton, Dowager Countess of Falcestershire and Queen's Sorceress.*

Fecking hells, woman. You've riled Queen Vick herself.

They watched as the thief, a man with ash-blond hair, indeterminately colored eyes, and a big frame, opened the cabinet and seized two large, roughly urn-shaped artifacts and one smaller object, more like a cup. He deposited them in a duffel and retraced his steps across the room.

Ronan adjusted the shape of two sections of the weaving, and the image moved backward. It also shrank so that, instead of nearly life-size, the man was now the size of a toy soldier and the weaving showed a cutaway-style projection of the house. The images raced faster, back through time, and then Ronan shifted something, and it started to flow forward again, showing the thief as he laid his plans. He'd come every month during the single hour when the wards were vulnerable and scouted the house until he found the vault.

There had been a gap of two months, presumably while

he obtained the necessary items to actually breach the vault spells. Then the night when he must have accidentally encountered a servant, who Sorcha said was named Ross MacRae, in the dark, and had knocked the man unconscious rather than be discovered. Ronan's spell couldn't reach beyond the house, but Sorcha estimated that the earliest incursion was seven months prior, when she'd first woken from a nightmare and felt something wrong with the wards. He had probably been there for at least a month before that, though, because he would have needed time to craft his counterward stones.

The weaving went dark, and Ronan loosened the tied ends so that the power would dissipate back into the room. He let go of Sorcha's hand and released the link. "He's been planning this for a long time."

"Ever since Amelia came and tested the boundaries nine months ago. Damn." Sorcha pulled away and went back to the chest. She sat hard and put her head in her hands. Her voice emitted from behind a curtain of pale blond locks. "Even with a Null Orb, he couldn't have gotten past the outer vault spell without something from one of the few people keyed to the vault. Right now, the only ones with access are myself, Le Fay, the Duchess, and the Marchioness of Hazelby."

"What would he have needed? Hair? Fingernails?"

Sorcha shook her head. Her hair parted, revealing her beautiful heart-shaped face. He wanted to kiss her again, wanted to stroke her and make her forget everything bad that had happened in the last hour.

"He would have needed blood. And fresh, if possible." She crossed her arms over her chest and sank into herself. "How would he have gotten that?"

"There are ways. I've employed some of them myself. I assume we will find that one of the other women has recently had a mishap where a bribed servant 'accidentally' drew blood with a dressmaker's needle or a hatpin. Manufacturing a shaving nick for a male mage is another favorite method."

Sorcha forgot to hide behind her hair and openly stared at him. "That's—diabolical."

He chuckled. "I believe you mean practical. And, since pragmatism appears to be my role here at present, I'll suggest that we now cast a tracking spell and go after your Wells."

She stumbled up from the chest. "You can do that?"

"I can."

"Without a piece of the items to follow? How?"

"Sorcha, *a solas*, those Wells have been sitting in this vault for years. They're chock-full of the energy of this house, and of the leylines that run beneath the foundation. I assume that's why the house was built here, and why the old duchess wanted her bits stored here. So it's a simple thing to find power that isn't where it ought to be."

"Simple to you, perhaps. Did you make this spell?"

Ronan coughed and rubbed at the back of his neck. He still hadn't replaced his hair tie, and his fingers tangled in the curling strands. "It was a group effort years back. I can't take all the credit."

"You told me you had no training."

"Enough to not kill myself. Which I then promptly ignored. Needs must."

"Indeed. I'll cast it with you this time unless it is very complicated. It will be better if we're both tracking. That way one of us can rest."

"Let's link more deeply like we did with the keystones, so there's a single spell from both of us rather than two spells. Then we can pass it between us without any loss of power or integrity."

Sorcha hesitated. "Are you sure? A deep link put us in this mess. If we hadn't been so wrapped up in each other…"

"He was long gone by the time you assaulted my person on the keystone." He took her hands and their magic flowed together, almost without his urging. "Trust me. It's better this way."

Sorcha stared at him, her eyes so blue he had a moment of disorientation, as though he were falling through the sky. Then she swayed against him. "I trust you."

S orcha helped cast the tracking spell, but she kept her thoughts rigidly separate from Ronan's. What would he say if he heard she'd been having visions of this man for months? Ever since he'd arrived, apparently. Was it only because he'd been violating her borders? Had the visions been trying to warn her? To show her who was causing the problems with the wards?

How irritating not to grasp the truth, even now.

The tracking spell led them, as they might have expected, to the village of Kinlochfay. Although their thief had probably lived in the wild, unclaimed land beyond Fay House's property line, in the foothills below Sgurr Alasdair, he would have needed to resupply occasionally from local sources. But he hadn't been staying in the village proper, or Sorcha would have been told about him long before now.

Had she seen him? Had he seen her? He'd stayed away from her wing of the house, had always come when the staff was gone, or asleep, except for that one night with Ross. Every question she'd ever had about him and the visions came back with brutal force.

Who are you?

"Och aye, he come through mebbe once a fortnight, or a mite longer. Said he was up here researching seabirds," Angus MacLeod, the owner of the public house and general town busybody, reported to Sorcha. If her intuition hadn't told her where to go for information, her knowledge that he was the town's biggest gossip would have led her here in any case. "It were right strange that he stopped in last evening, after only the twa days."

"Yes, well, he got what he wanted, didn't he?"

"If I'd'a known that, lass, he'd nay have left me pub."

"Thanks for saying that, Angus, but it's better that you didn't try to stop him. We believe he's with the British Army."

Angus spat onto the floorboards by her chair, which was all anyone in the Highlands had to say about the British Army, Highland regiments excepted.

"So ye'll be off after him, then?"

"Aye. I've locked the house and sent a telegram off to Herself. Wee Fingal is going to see to my livestock until someone can come from the school and take over for me."

"Safe travels to ye, then, lass, and yer man, too, for all he's an Irish lad."

"He's not mine," Sorcha protested, and she hated that her cheeks heated. "He's just helping." At that moment, Ronan sauntered into the pub and pulled her into his arms, dropping a kiss on the top of her head. Angus winked. Damn, this was going to take years to live down.

"Telegram is sent. I tried trick I know that wards the lines, but it doesn't always work when the cables go underwater. With luck, no one will be able to tell what you sent."

"At this point, it's more important that Etta understands things have gone terribly wrong. Do you think my code was not obscure enough?"

"It was fine. Maybe obvious to your enemies, who already

know what to listen for. But not so obvious as to reveal your secrets. What do you guess the duchess will do?"

"Send people to secure the house, though I would have expected to see someone tomorrow or the next day in any case. Possibly try to rendezvous with us somewhere, once we locate where our thief has gone."

"Yes, I meant to tell you. I followed the trail to the inland road."

"The inland road? I was certain he would have gone to the harbor and taken a ship from Loch Fay."

"Maybe he still intends to do that, but when he left town, he was headed inland."

"That's so odd. But I assume he had a reason. We'll need to borrow horses and buy provisions. Oh! What about your captain? He's coming here."

"Already added that to the telegram going to the duchess. Evie is instructed to tell Bart to wait until he hears from me directly. He should still be in Arisaig since he would have needed to wait for the afternoon tide. The trials of using ancient methods to power one's ship."

"There's not much in the way of modern communication methods inland. How will you tell him where we're headed?"

"We'll find a way."

She wished she shared his confidence.

THEY RODE OUT OF KINLOCHFAY AND INTO THE CUILLINS. Ronan had suggested they stay in the village for the night, but the summer sun would not set until nearly ten and Sorcha refused to waste time. She couldn't be sure whether it was magical intuition or anxiety pushing her onward, but she wouldn't be happy to stop until dark. And perhaps not even then. In the Isles in summer, the sky never became truly dark, and they would need only a handful of fairy lights to guide the horses.

The thief kept to the main road, either because he wasn't well acquainted with the land, or because he realized that the road was his quickest option. "I still can't comprehend why he didn't have a ship come for him," Sorcha said as their horses walked along the packed-dirt and cropped grass from the verge.

"Your wards are impressive, *a chuisle*. He may have expected you to have a spell over Loch Fay to tell you when ships approach, and perhaps to sink or repel unwanted visitors."

Her cheeks heated at the compliment. "I don't, but you can be sure I'll try that in the future. Although I may need Muireall to cast it. She's better at spells over water."

"That's the woman you call Le Fay?"

"Aye. She has a water affinity, like you."

"Does Clan Fay have mostly water gifts?"

"There are a few, but they're not the majority." She considered the magically-talented people in the family for a moment, and their various elemental leanings. She couldn't find any sort of pattern there. "We Fays are interested in practical magic and have typically followed our hearts into marriage instead of social rules. Because of that, we've brought in a good mix of affinities. The duchess is aligned with earth, and her husband is a mix of water and fire. The rest of the family runs the gamut, including one weather mage who is mostly air."

"And you're light."

"Well, in the Classical sense, I'm fire, and in a practical sense, I often feel affinities to air. But yes, my magic is attuned to light." She glanced at the setting sun behind her.

"But perhaps more moonlight than sunlight, if I have the choice."

"I've never known another mage or witch with a light affinity."

Sorcha chuckled. "Nor have I. But it's not as rare as some affinities."

"Is it hereditary? Did it come from one of your parents?"

Her gaze fell from the distant peaks to her horse's saddle. She pressed a hand against a tingling behind her breastbone. But she wanted him to know the truth. She tried to make her voice bright, her tone casual, but it came out forced and shaky. "Not from my mother. I have no idea who my father is, so that's no help."

Ronan twisted in his saddle and his horse spooked from the sudden movement. It took a moment to calm the animal back to a gentle walk, and then he said, "I assume there's a story there. If you want to tell it."

Sorcha's shoulders hunched inward. "It's not much of a story. My mother had no interest in marriage, but plenty of interest in taking lovers. Here in the Isles, we haven't been too polluted by English ways, and so she wasn't shamed for it as she might have been in the Lowlands."

"Or in Ireland, I'm sad to say." His acceptance and lack of condemnation made warmth return to her chest. "We've wandered far from our Druid roots."

She grasped at the change of subject. "Not so far as to embrace the English."

He convulsed with laughter. "Never so far. Never." After a few more chuckles, he regained control and glanced back toward the southwest, in the vague direction of his home. "Though there are many who are overfond of the Magisterium, and many of those are shouting the loudest for independence. I fear for what may happen when we free ourselves from the English yoke. Those who choose the Academies or the old ways may no longer have a choice."

"That would be a sad thing, indeed. Particularly the old ways. We've lost so many traditions here in Scotland, too. And so many people."

"All gone to America," Ronan said. "And who can blame them?"

"But Etta came back to us, so perhaps not all is lost."

"How does the rest of your clan feel about having an American lass as the duchess?"

"There have been stumbles and obstacles. It took a while for us to understand her and trust that she would take her place and protect the clan. But she has, and she will."

They lapsed back into companionable silence. The road took them past the fairy pools and the stone dances that once had been the home of actual fay. When she was a child, Sorcha and her mother and an elderly Lilias had come one midsummer to pay homage to their fairy kin, and a few had crossed the veil between worlds to speak to the old duchess. The place still teemed with magic, and Sorcha and Ronan both dismounted to use it to supplement their internal resources while they ate their supper. Ronan claimed their enemy had not stopped to renew his magic, although the spell clearly showed him passing by the pools.

"I wonder why he didn't use the fay energy?" Sorcha asked. "There's so much of it, and they aren't here to care anymore."

"Maybe he believes in the legend that such power still carries with it certain obligations to the wee folk. Or he is too rigid in his magical training to use wild power."

"Or both."

"Or neither. It's difficult to glean a sense of him. He's pretty far ahead of us."

"Show me."

Ronan took her hand and drew her into the spell-net. She allowed the spell to mesh with her internal map of Skye and frowned. "I'm pretty sure he's in Portree. It's one of the bigger towns on the island, and he may have had a more permanent base there. Or an accomplice. If he's working for Amelia—the queen's sorceress—she may be staying there, which would explain why he went overland instead of taking a ship immediately south."

"But that's a port town, right? He could board a ship today and be gone before we arrive."

"Will your spell follow him over water?"

"Maybe. I've only tried that once before, and it was only partially successful."

"We'll hope that their ship departs in the morning and ride all night."

Sorcha unwrapped the meal Angus had prepared for her and dispelled the stasis spell she'd placed on it earlier. The fish steamed as she snatched one paper-wrapped portion and handed it to Ronan. They ate quickly and mounted again.

Right before sunset, they rode into a small village at the crossroads of the two main paths. The town had an inn with a telegraph office. It relayed through Portree, so any message might alert their enemy, but Ronan took the risk and sent a message that would eventually make its way to Bart and his ship.

"They ought to be there by this time tomorrow, or earlier if my weather mage can coax a favorable wind. I swear I'm going to discover how to send messages to a ship without the magic currents interfering."

Sorcha pushed her horse harder than she ought on the last leg of their journey, and boosted both mounts with magic when they might otherwise have flagged. They reached Portree a few minutes after dawn, to the news that a large private yacht had sailed only a few hours before. Worse, the ferry had suffered a very coincidentally-timed boiler explosion and the local fishermen who might be willing to take them for the price of a day's catch had sailed at the same time as their quarry.

"Damn," Sorcha said as they breakfasted a few hours later in an inn near the water. She'd resorted to using the Duchess's name for credit to have the horses boarded for a week until someone from Kinlochfay could retrieve them, and afterward had changed from the rumpled bloomers and shirtwaist she'd worn for riding into a more respectable morning dress. Ronan still wore his ill-fitting castoffs from Fay House.

"The harbormaster is a friend of a friend," Ronan said. "He was surrounded by official-looking folk earlier, but I'll chat him up when he's alone and see what he can tell us about their destination."

"What about Amelia? Do you think she left with him?"

"Probably. My guess is they'll make for the nearest port on the mainland with a railway station. I don't know where that is, but I'll ask the harbormaster. We may even be able to take the ferry if they fix the boiler quickly."

"I'll find a quiet place and scry out where Amelia stayed. I've only spoken to her twice before, but the connection I have after warding the house against her should be sufficient."

"Excellent. Once we're in that room, I can cast another reconstruction and find out if they spoke about their next steps."

Sorcha shoveled eggs and kippers into her mouth, then went to find their host and request a private place and a glass of wine.

"I can get you seawater," Ronan offered.

"Not from the harbor. It's too polluted. And I don't wish to go all the way back to the river. Wine will do."

A serving girl returned with a goblet of wine and took Sorcha into one of the private dining rooms. Ronan stayed in the common room to assure she had as much silence as possible. He finished off another helping from the sideboard and then couldn't help opening his Sight to check on her progress.

Instead, he found a different spell. It had a particular scent to it, like burning wood. Not entirely unpleasant, but odd and unexpected. It was possible that another mage had that same scent-marker, but not likely. The problem was, the spell was far too complex and powerful for the mage whom he'd identified.

Donn.

What would he have been doing in this little backwater? And how had he cast this fine, intricate net? There wasn't anyone in their cell who could do work like this, not even Evie. Or perhaps she could now, after training with the Fays, but none of the others had this much finesse. Ronan stood and followed the net onto the street. The threads were like gossamer, or a spider's silk, barely visible. If he hadn't been trying to see the much fainter evidence of scrying from Sorcha, and hadn't recognized the caster's magical aroma, he'd never have noticed it. It resembled a natural channel of power.

"Ronan?"

Sorcha's voice drew his attention back toward the inn, and he realized he'd gone all the way across the street to the edge of the quay. A few more steps and he'd have been in the harbor. He went to her and said, "Open your Sight and look at this spell."

She tilted her head away from him in confusion, but she did as he asked. Then she leaned forward to focus on the spell-threads. "That's interesting. A very deft hand was used. I'm not sure what it's doing. It's somewhat like a spell Lilias described in the clan's Book of Shadows and Light. She used it for information-gathering against Napoleon. But who would want information in Portree, other than us?"

"Who else is aware of…what we're looking for?"

Sorcha's eyes widened when he avoided using the word 'Wells.' But she caught on quickly, and her expression of surprise converted to one of concern. "Before yesterday, I would have sworn that only three people alive knew about them. Now?" She lifted her hands in a defeated gesture. "It wouldn't surprise me if everyone on the island knew."

"I don't think the news is so well-spread. But I do think your…enemy either has a loose tongue, or there's someone on her staff who does."

"The latter is more likely. She's a thorn in our side, but she's loyal and devoted to her mistress. She has as much invested in secrecy as we do. Maybe even more. She believes the only safe place for the…objects is in her mistress's hands."

"Hmm. Well, it's possible that the person who cast this was only aware that our quarry had been staying here and was curious."

"Then we'll hope the net didn't catch any inconvenient fish."

"Yes. Did you determine where she'd been staying?"

"Across the harbor, and into the town. One of the bigger hotels." She gestured away from the water and up the hill. "I'm sure it's the most expensive one in the town."

"Likely so." He offered his arm, and she took it, as though they were any fashionable couple promenading on the quay. But no fashionable gentleman would broach the subject of money, and he had to. "How much are you carrying if we need to pay for the room?"

"Enough. And now that everyone knows the duchess is covering my bills, I'll have credit anywhere on the Isle. I dislike using her name, and I couldn't before, but Etta will pay the expenses now."

"Before?"

"There hasn't been a Duchess of Fay in almost ten years. Well, I suppose there *was*. Etta's mother ought to have been named to the title, but she wasn't. Trustees held all the accounts until the Committee for Privileges officially approved Etta as the Duchess less than a year ago. The trustees' man of business gave me enough money to make structural repairs to the house when needed, but would not allow me anything extra for improvements or expansion."

"It sounds like the old duchess made poor decisions in her estate planning."

"Or good ones. While most of the aristocracy is seeking cash from American entrepreneurs to refill their empty coffers, the Fay holdings have multiplied."

"Perhaps, but that house contains so many of your clan's treasures. She ought to have made provision for its welfare. And yours, as its caretaker."

Sorcha shrugged, jostling his arm in the process. "The house itself wasn't in danger. The trustees would release money for repairs, but nothing to help run the estate in lean years or provide for the tenants. Lilias wouldn't have considered that. She was not a…caring woman." She paused, and when he glanced over at her she had a contemplative frown on her face. "That isn't the right word. She cared very deeply about many things. But she wasn't a nurturer. It was unfortunate that she considered it her duty to have children, because she was a very poor mother. She loved them and was an excellent teacher to them, but her goals and her ambitions always came first."

"And that's why the youngest one ran away to America?"

Sorcha snickered. "With an Irish rogue no less."

Ronan pulled her against his side, far closer than a respectable gentleman would. He thickened his accent and murmured into her ear, "So the Fay colleens have a weakness for a bit of the Irish, do they?" A tremble ran through her body, and he swept his tongue along the outer shell of her lobe. She shuddered again, and her hand on his arm squeezed involuntarily. If she hadn't changed into a fashionable dress complete with corset and bodice, he'd have been able to see her nipples pebbling against her shirtwaist. He missed the flowing red chemise dress that she'd worn the first time they made love. This one would require far too long to remove.

"Perhaps we do," she admitted. "Will you steal me away to America, then?"

He nipped at the earlobe and then retreated to an appropriate distance. "Alas, I've no plans to cross the Atlantic. I can only steal you as far as Dublin."

She tripped and would have fallen without his arm to steady her. But even as he said the words, he knew full well she would never permanently abandon Skye. And he would not take her from the place that she loved. It was an empty offer, no matter how much he wanted her to follow him there.

"I would like to see Ireland. Perhaps you'll show me when this is all over."

That wasn't what he wanted, but more than he deserved. "I would love to show my country to you, *a chuisle*. I grew up in lots of places, but my favorite is in Kerry, on the western shore. The land there will take your breath."

As she was taking his by smiling at him and imagining a future where he could be anything but temporary to her. And by all the gods, he wanted that to be true. But she wasn't for him, not for forever. He would only pull her with him into the dark.

They reached the inn, and she strolled inside. He had to compose himself on the threshold because everything inside of him ached. He wanted to hold her and never let go. He wanted to run as far as he could and never sully her bright light with his tarnished soul again. And damn it, he wanted a room where he could strip her bare and make her scream his name. Where she would come for him, over and over, until they joined and he could let himself go—let himself fully experience lovemaking and desire and bliss—in a way he'd never been able to before.

But the room she sought was a specific one, and they would have a specific task to accomplish inside it. Not heights of pleasure to which he'd never dared aspire to reach, but the far more serious effort to recover dangerous magic and put it back where it could do no harm.

Remember that, old man. You are here to help her keep others safe. It's your job to keep her safe. And he would. He swore that by whatever gods might be listening. *I will protect her. Sorcha, le solas mo chroí.*

He slowly approached the clerk at the lobby counter, staying beyond the point where the man might ignore Sorcha in favor of a male customer. He could already tell that the man did not much care about former guests. He only wanted to rent rooms. Eventually, Sorcha realized that and started to tailor her requests accordingly. Once she'd agreed to take a room for the night and paid her deposit, the clerk became friendlier and more helpful. He provided her with a key and informed her the room was a suite on the second floor, with a private bathing and dressing chamber. The best room on the premises.

The clerk did not lead them upstairs. He left that duty to a bellhop who stood stiffly, his uniform too big and his hat too small, looking miserable with his lot in life. The boy brought them to the room and then escaped, saddened that they had no luggage and no reason for a larger tip than the few pence Sorcha pressed into his palm.

"This room probably cost you a pretty penny." Ronan settled into the plush armchair beside the fireplace.

"It cost the duchess a pretty penny," Sorcha corrected. "Though I don't expect we'll be in it long."

She crossed to the center of the room and held out her hands. Ronan came to her, and instead of matching her pose, he closed his hands around hers and pulled her against his chest. "Perhaps we have a little time?"

Her gaze met his, and there was still too much wariness in it. Something had changed, and he couldn't grasp what caused the shift. The woman who had flung herself into passion with an abandon that delighted him had disappeared, her brilliant light shuttered by hesitation. It wasn't shame. She hadn't been ashamed of anything they'd done, and with his Sight wide open, he couldn't sense that now. Only... caution. Perhaps distrust.

He softly probed her magic with his, and after the barest of hesitations, she opened to him, letting their gifts coalesce and merge. *Will you tell me what's wrong?*

There's nothing wrong.

You've closed an element of yourself that was open before. If that isn't something wrong, what is it?

Unexpectedly, tears welled in her eyes. "*A solas,* don't cry." What pulsed through their link was a deep discontent, almost a weariness. She wasn't sad or upset so much as resigned, and exhausted from her attempt to build a façade. He could have told her it wouldn't work.

As their magic sunk deeper into each other, he an image flashed in her mind. Evie.

What does Evie have to do with anything?

A sob broke free of her mouth, and she almost pulled away, but then steeled herself and met his gaze again. *You love her.*

Now she'd startled him. What did loving Evie have to do with Sorcha?

I do, he agreed. *She's my sister in every way but blood.*

Sorcha nodded, as though he'd confirmed something, or perhaps answered a question she'd not voiced. Had she thought he and Evie were lovers? He wasn't old enough to be her father, but only by a handful of years. And he'd met her when she was a thirteen year old girl who routinely passed as an eight year old boy. There'd never been a moment of attraction between them, not even on Evie's part. He'd been something between brother and father and mentor to her.

You love her, Sorcha repeated, *and that proves that you* can.

So can you. Why does that make you distrust me?

Sorcha pulled his magic deeper, then, and showed him a memory. It was a smiling woman, taller than Sorcha but no less shapely, with honey-blond hair and a magnetic grin. In the memory, she was wrapped around a big red-headed man. The memory-image was replaced by another, of a different man, and then a woman, and then another man, and another, and another, partner after partner until Ronan had to squeeze her hands to make them stop.

She was happy, Sorcha said, and that was what mattered to her. They were all good men and women, nice to me, and very pleasant company. But no one stayed. She loved all of them, and she accepted when they left our lives almost as willingly as when they entered it. I don't want that for myself. I want someone who will stay.

Ronan froze. What she wanted was the one thing he could not give. Even though he wanted to. And damn it, but he wanted to. *Sorcha, I...*

She pulled back then, disentangling her magic from his, but not so fast that he didn't feel the hurt lancing through her, a bright flare of despair and loss, mixed with resignation and disappointment.

"Let's cast this spell and keep moving." She started pulling threads of power together, mimicking the reconstruction spell he'd done in the Fay House vault.

He watched her work and tried to contain the tangled mess of emotions poking and shredding him inside. She was better at putting the pain aside than he, but he managed it, at least enough to show her where to tweak and change the spell to allow for local magic conditions. He added a layer over hers that revealed not only images but sounds.

They watched as a maid cleaned the room, her motions odd and jerky as the spell moved back through time. His sound layer played the clinking of the coal scuttle and the maid's tuneless humming. Then silence and stillness, and finally, in the early hours of the morning, light bloomed in the room, revealing Amelia Upton, Dowager Countess of Falcestershire and Sorceress to the queen, standing beside the blond man. Ronan gestured for the spell to move more quickly, back to when the man had entered the room. Then he changed the direction of time's passage, and they viewed the thief giving the countess a brief bow.

The man handed Amelia the bag he'd been carrying.

"I've got them heavily warded," he said, "so their power doesn't make everyone with a hint of talent in the area come running."

"Well done, Mr. Blake." Amelia accepted the big leather bag and peeked inside. She swore softly. "Lilias, you old liar." Her cupid's-bow mouth widened into a stunned smile, and she gasped. "I've suspected she had these for so long, but I didn't really believe it until now."

"The vault was full of powerful artifacts, but only these three resonated with the spell you gave me."

"I'm not worried about potential power use in their other artifacts. They are still tied to the available magic in an area. Thesc…these are far too dangerous for a private citizen to hold."

Mr. Blake agreed. "Where will you put them? With the others in the Tower?"

Amelia's head jerked up from examining the contents of the bag. "That will depend on the queen's wishes."

Mr. Blake started to say something, but he stifled the words when Amelia snapped the bag shut. "Get some rest. My yacht is awaiting us on the quay, and we'll sail with the tide."

The mage bowed to her again, and raised his hands with splayed fingers, a traditional mage-salute that was meant to indicate the willingness of the saluter to perform a spell at the salutee's command. He left the room, and Amelia sat with the Wells for almost an hour, holding them in her lap like a mother might hold a babe. Then a knock sounded on the door, and she rose and left the room.

Ronan loosened the knots holding the spell together and let it dissipate back into the energy of the room.

"They didn't say where they were headed with her yacht." Sorcha's voice held disappointment.

"No, but if they're headed to London, I stand by my guess

that they'll be going to the nearest port with a railway stop."

"I suppose you'd better speak to the harbormaster."

"I will. But…did you notice, before she dismissed him, the mage started to say something?"

"Yes." Sorcha frowned at where the spell had been, as though she could still perceive the images there. "He looked like he wanted to contradict her or tell her something that she might not like. That's why she stopped him."

"I imagine he was going to remind her the queen is a private citizen. She no longer holds the power to make laws or even officially call Parliament. She still does it ceremoniously, but after mad King George, they changed the rules so Parliament can convene itself."

"So perhaps all is not well in their little partnership."

"I don't believe it is. He wasn't wearing a uniform, but everything else about him screams military, from his possession of a null orb to his close-cropped hair and well-groomed mustache and sideburns."

Sorcha's face flushed with color, and she continued to stare at the empty space where the spell had been. Why was that?

"I agree. And that means he doesn't answer to the queen."

"He may have been loaned to the Sorceress for this purpose, but no, he would report to someone in the Army's hierarchy. They will do many things for the queen, but they ultimately answer to Parliament, not Old Vick."

"You know an awful lot about English politics for an Irishman." She stopped examining the empty room, and her odd actions were overshadowed by her accusation.

No point dissembling. She'd seen deep inside him, had discovered the sort of man he was. Time to put words to those impressions, to disillusion her from any dreams that they might have a happy, idyllic future. "I am a true Irishman. I have worked for years to free Ireland from English rule. I've learned much about the inner workings of the government and its enforcers. It's amazing what one can discover by means both fair and foul. Not to mention the amount of material one can gather to later *influence* certain parties to act on one's behest."

Her blue eyes went even colder than they had before, when he couldn't tell her that he would stay. "So you spy on people and then blackmail them to do what you want."

His Sorcha, speaking the truth outright. No dissembling or shadowy language for the lady of light. Gods. He wanted to pull her back against him, to kiss her until she forgot that he was a bad man, who'd done much worse than espionage and extortion. Instead, he said, "And when they don't do what we want, there are consequences."

She stared at him, and he nodded. She could infer what he meant. But she asked anyway. "Permanent consequences?"

"Sometimes. If it can't be avoided."

"Murder can always be avoided."

He didn't defend himself. He could have. He could have argued that every man whom he'd killed—and there had been far fewer than he'd implied—had been a terrible person anyway. Their ranks included an owner and frequent customer of a brothel that specialized in children as young as five; an army traitor who had sold secrets and supplies in the Crimea, causing the deaths of many soldiers and pocketing the profits; and a baronet who had compromised, married, and then murdered four wives for their dowries.

But he would not speak of that. Let her assume the worst, and pull away. Let the promise of a future die here, before either of them fell too much farther toward a word he would not use, even in his thoughts.

She did jerk away, leaving him alone in the dim chamber. She took the light with her in far more ways than one.

The harbormaster proved to be a chatty fellow who had handily recognized Ronan's casual mention of a fictitious "friend" in their previous conversation as code. Smugglers throughout the islands would ask a new acquaintance if they knew so-and-so. For Ronan, that fictional person was "Jack Cleary." That name told the harbormaster Ronan ran a smuggling operation out of Dublin. If he'd said "Jimmy Callahan," he'd have been signaling he was from Cork.

There were other names for other major ports all over Ireland, England, Scotland, and Wales. The names changed every so often as un-bribed excise men caught on, and as Ronan spoke with the harbormaster he updated him on a few changes by saying so-and-so had died, but had he ever met so-and-so?

By the end of their cheerful conversation, Ronan had discovered that the yacht's destination had been logged as a town called Stromeferry, where, as predicted, there was a train terminal. The line made a direct connection with Inverness, and from there he assumed their quarry would go south to Edinburgh and then take the sleeper to London.

He went back to Sorcha with a copy of the train tables, and the news that the ferry should be fixed by the next day. But fortune finally smiled on them when Bart sailed into the harbor late that afternoon. With a weather mage in the crew, Ronan's ship could sail against the tide when absolutely necessary, so they departed as soon as he and Sorcha boarded. The ship moved more slowly than she would have had the tide been going out instead of coming in, but they made good time once they were in open water.

In the captain's cabin, Ronan apprised Bart of the events of the past several days. Bart, never one to yield a chance to say "I told you so" to his employer, was uncharacteristically silent.

"Out with it, man," Ronan said when Bart frowned at the charts in front of them instead of remarking on the tale. "I've never known your tongue to sit so still betwixt your teeth."

"It's only that you have what you came for. Why are we running this colleen all over creation and not taking your items back to the woman who's paying us?"

"Evie said we could write our own check on this job. The longer it lasts, the more we're paid. Don't worry on that score. I'm keeping a good accounting up here." He tapped at his forehead.

"There's jobs you take for good pay that you might not otherwise accept." Bart scratched at one bushy eyebrow. "And then there's jobs as are not worth any price, no matter how high."

"And you think this is one of those?"

"The queen and the army are involved, Ro. It's time to write that check and run. We'll drop the girl off at the train and be done."

Ronan couldn't meet his captain's gaze. He ought to do what Bart suggested. Every instinct honed over years of running cons, heists, and intelligence-gathering operations shouted at him that it was time to cut anchor and go with the tide—in the opposite direction.

But he'd long since stopped doing this job for money, no matter what he claimed to Bart, or anyone else. He was doing this for Sorcha, and it was because of her that he would not run. He would see this through. He'd already sworn to protect and assist her until she retrieved the Power Wells and was safely ensconced back in Fay House.

Only then would he retreat back to the endless monotony of smuggling runs, shipping schedules, and filling the Cause's coffers. To the empty bed in a barren flat in a bad neighborhood in Dublin, where he couldn't imagine ever bringing Sorcha. The darkness there would smother her light until it extinguished.

No, he would leave her on Skye, and she would always be there, like a lighthouse in his memory.

For now, he had a job to do, and that job meant silencing his instincts and ignoring his captain's advice. "Not this time, Bart old man. I'll be on that train with her, as far as it goes."

"All the way to London?" Bart said the word London as another man might say dung heap.

"If need be."

"Donn's not going to like you coming on his turf without having an assignment." He leaned back in his chair and tapped at one of the hinged arms, swinging it out and then back into position. "Though word was he's been drilling in Killarney, so maybe you'll not even see him."

"If he does discover me, he'll have nothing to say. We don't have anything pressing." But Ronan very much doubted that Donn was still in Killarney. Not that he'd mention that to Bart.

"There's that shipment from Boston of rifles and Gatlings we're to collect in Liverpool in a sennight."

"If I'm not done by then, we'll send part of the crew to do

the run. It's the usual route, and Ahearn needs the practice running the ship on his own."

"They're not going to give the guns to Ahearn."

"Why ever not?" He'd never had a problem sending proxies before.

Bart shifted forward again, his paunch grazing the edge of the desk. "Because the last telegram said they wanted it to be you. Apparently, there's…conflict over the use of violence in the Supreme Council."

"Danu preserve us. I'll bet I can guess which side Donn's going to be on." Ronan's fingers curled. He forced the fingers to relax against his thighs.

"He's not named after *Donn Cúailnge* for nothing."

"I wish I'd never been made an alpha. I never used to have to do these things as a beta."

"Better you than me. But you need to be in Liverpool in ten days, or the guns go to their intended destination in bloody Africa."

Ronan swore, this time in Irish. "I'll be there. But I must finish this first. Or take her as far as I can, anyway."

Bart met his gaze, and they stared at each other for a long stretch. Finally, Bart nodded. "Very well, but the bloody duchess better come through with the money."

"She will. I've been informed that their holdings are lucrative. No impoverished titles for the Fay clan."

Bart closed his eyes and swiped a hand over his forehead. "I suppose that will give us an excuse when Donn roasts us later."

"What's that saying about asking for permission or forgiveness?"

"Yes, yes." His fingers dropped to his beard. He smoothed it a few times before giving it up as a bad job and growling, "Well, go on with ya. I saw the way you looked at the girl.

You've time enough between here and Stromeferry for a good tupping."

Ronan wheeled and snarled. "Don't."

Bart wasn't intimidated, and instead leaned back in his chair, the picture of a man at leisure. "Ah. Like that, is it? I suspected so. Well, when Donn asks what by Badb's hood were we thinking, you can be the one to tell him why."

"I will, and you'll speak no more about Sorcha. If I hear so much as a crude suggestion while she's with us, I'll dock everyone's pay for a month."

Bart's chortles chased him out of the cabin.

SORCHA STOOD ON THE DECK, WATCHING AT THE RAIL AS THE mainland came into view on the other side of Rona, one of the smaller islands to the east of Skye. She'd never come this way before. Usually, she rode to Armadale and took the ferry there to the mainland, or sometimes all the way 'round to Kyleakin. They'd taken a circuitous route because the ship's captain wasn't certain of the waters between the isles of Raasay, Scalpay, and Skye. But he promised they would arrive in time for the evening train in Stromeferry.

That still put them several hours behind Amelia and Mr. Blake, who would have been able to make the earlier train unless something had gone very wrong on their sail southeast.

Sorcha chafed at the delay. At this rate, there would be no way to catch up before the Wells reached London. And if their destination was the Tower? Even Ronan had never attempted a theft of such magnitude.

A patch of cloud scudded away from the sun, and its light fell on her with welcome warmth. She closed her eyes and drew the warmth into her core. She was so cold, and so afraid. She'd not yet had a chance to stop and process the full extent of what had happened. She'd had Ronan beside her, to distract her with his conversation and his crooked grin and the way her body lit up beside him.

Without him, she was forced to admit that she'd failed. She'd sworn an oath to the clan, to the duchess and Le Fay, when she assumed the post held by her mother before her, and her mother before that. Where the females in Lilias's line held the title of Duchess, the females in Sorcha's line were the protectors of Fay House.

She'd failed to uphold that oath of protection. She'd lost the two most powerful items the house had hidden, and lost herself to a man who would not care for the heart she'd dropped into his hands.

Even the sunlight could not warm the knot of ice that had formed in her belly.

She sensed him long before he approached her, and believed she'd prepared for whatever he might say or do. But when his arm settled around her shoulders, her traitorous body woke and blazed for him.

How could she still want him, now knowing for certain what she'd always suspected?

Love was beyond her control. Hadn't her mother taught her that? Gavenia had loved so many men and women, each excellent in their own ways, and had always told Sorcha that her heart had an infinite capacity.

Sorcha's heart might be capable of the same, but it had never chosen to exercise that capacity until now. Until Ronan. And she had the Seer's knowledge that, for her, its infinite love would always and first be for him.

Her mother had derided the concept of soulmates, saying that everyone could potentially be a mate, and there was no such thing as 'one true love.' But while that may have been the case for Gavenia Fay, it was not her daughter's Truth.

Great Goddess, I am going to love him until I die.

She swung around, and looked into the seal-grey eyes of the man she loved. She would take whatever he could give her, for as long as he was willing to give it. She had a very long lifetime ahead of her without him, and she wanted every last memory she could horde against the loneliness to come.

"It will be a few hours yet," he said. "You should rest."

"I wouldn't be able to shut my eyes."

"Lie down at least."

She made her decision. "Show me where."

At the cabin door, he stopped, as though he wouldn't enter. She clasped his hand and tugged. She closed the door and pushed him against it, rubbing her body over his chest, belly, and hips.

He made an inarticulate noise. She hummed in appreciation of the swelling that quickly rose against her belly. She splayed her fingers on his chest and bit through the fabric at the place where his nipple ought to be. He groaned and finally wrapped his arms around her, but only so he could grasp her head and tilt it back. He captured her in his gaze.

"Are you sure you still want me?"

"I wouldn't touch you if I didn't want you, Ronan McCarrick. I understand my own mind."

"Even after…"

"Yes, damn you. Even now. You want me to believe you're a monster and cold, that you'll not be stirred by softness or pity or compassion. But I have seen inside you, and I recognize the kind of man you are. I want you."

If she'd been wearing the red dress, she would have dropped it to the ground. In a damned corset and blouse, all she could do was grasp his head and bring it down to kiss him. He didn't balk, but kissed her back, his tongue darting in to tangle with hers. Her pulse raced, and heat pooled between her legs.

"Damn it, I want you, too," he said against her lips. And then his hands went to work on the buttons down the front of her blouse, and she leaned back to give him greater access.

It was an agonizing few minutes while he unbuttoned her blouse and then popped open the busk on her corset. Her skirts fell away more easily, and then she stood in a thin lawn chemise that outlined her breasts and belly and hips.

"Fecking hells, you're gorgeous." Ronan molded his hands over her, cupping and stroking until her skin fairly sang with pleasure and her nipples protruded, hard and taut against the fabric. She made short work of his waistcoat, shirt, and trousers, and in moments he had her on the bunk and was stripping away his undergarments and shoes. She still wore her laced boots and stockings, but he didn't seem to care as he pushed her legs apart and lowered himself between them.

He crooned something in Irish that she didn't catch, and then he was pushing up her chemise and taking a nipple between his lips. He suckled and she writhed, shocks of pleasure sparking along her body. "More, Ronan. Please."

He stripped the chemise over her head and shifted his attention to the other nipple, teasing it with quick strokes of his tongue until her moans were interspersed with pants and her hips lifted instinctively off the mattress, seeking his caress.

His clever fingers found her, teasing the sensitive outer folds and skimming across the slippery inner ones. She pressed against his hand, wanting the gentle pressure to be harder, wanting him to fill her. "I need you inside me." The words were half-moan, half-spoken, and Ronan kissed her rather than answer them.

Sorcha pulled him until his chest pressed against hers and she rubbed her nipples on the lightly-furred muscles. Her fingers danced down his back and to his arse. Her hands closed over the tight, round globes, and they both groaned. Pulses of pleasure surged through her body, and she broke the kiss to gasp, "Please, Ronan. Fill me. I'm so empty."

This time, he did as she asked. He levered himself until he knelt between her legs. She lifted her hips, and he guided the tip of his cock to her outer folds. He teased her only a moment more, rubbing the crown against her wet clit, and then he thrust deep within her.

Sorcha shouted his name as sensations burst in her chest and belly and brain, heat and light rising with every stroke of his flesh into hers. This would not be a slow, gentle climb to a soft, pleasant peak. This was an assault of pleasure, his cock surging through her sensitive cunny, his hipbone grinding against her clit with every thrust.

Sparks burst behind her eyes, and every plunge sent the wave of passion higher and higher until it swamped her in a burst of light and love.

RONAN HELD SORCHA AS SHE DOZED, THEIR BODIES NOW COOL but still joined. He couldn't bear to go even so far away from her as to slip his cock out of her cunny. He had pulled them both to their sides and draped her leg over his hips after he came hard inside of her, but that was all.

They hadn't used magic this time—hadn't merged their minds and their gifts—and although the passion was intense and fantastic, he mourned the loss of connection.

But even this much was more than he'd expected to be given. He'd assumed she would withdraw completely, excluding him from her bed and her heart. She'd kept the walls tightly around the latter item, but he was more than happy to share the former.

She was exhausted, and he ought to pull away and let her settle more comfortably into sleep, but he still couldn't take his flesh away from hers. He almost wanted her again, his cock twitching and indicating that it could achieve the necessary hardness in a few more minutes if required.

But he wouldn't press her. Wouldn't wake her. He couldn't leave her, either.

So he nestled her head against his shoulder and closed his own eyes. Someone would wake them before they reached Stromeferry.

13

In Inverness, the vagaries of train schedules and the vanity of Amelia Upton worked in their favor. The ticket attendant in the station was more than happy to recount how the lady had fumed at him when he explained she had missed the last train of the day and would have to wait until morning. Her companion had been much calmer and had suggested they find an inn.

"But her ladyship was having none of that. She ordered the poor man to take her to Castle Inshesmuir, which is more than twa miles away, on account of her knowing the baron."

"There's no accounting for the whims of the aristocracy," Sorcha agreed. She and Ronan were dressed well, with Ronan finally back in his own clothes from the ship, but not in the first stare of fashion. More like well-to-do Cits than true upper class. "Thanks for telling us." They purchased tickets for the next train to Edinburgh, due to leave in four hours. Sorcha was certain Amelia would be on that train, but they had a good chance now to find her and obtain the Wells.

Outside the station, Ronan checked the tracking spell.

"Our man has the right of it. She's somewhere to the southeast. Or at least the Wells are."

"She won't go anywhere without them, I'm sure."

"Then our best option is to find a quiet place on the road they'll need to travel and then accost their coach, highwayman-style."

Sorcha started to nod, but then a vision punched into her mind like a right cross to the temple.

An open expanse of moorland filled her view, dotted with gorse and marshy patches, and heather all in bloom. Several stands of trees clustered together near a stream. A dirt road passed through the purple and green, a slice of brown until it reached the stream and disappeared into a ford. A carriage drove briskly over the road, raising a great cloud of dust in its wake. As it approached the ford, it slowed.

Two riders burst from a copse of trees near the road, and Sorcha recognized Ronan and herself despite the masks they wore. The coachman whipped the horses to go faster, but Ronan tossed a cutting spell that snapped their harnesses and disconnected them from the carriage. Freed, they continued to run, obeying the last order they'd received, and they splashed through the ford and up the road on the other side. Sorcha incapacitated the driver and the footman with a sleeping spell she typically used when someone in the house was ill or injured. The coach slowed, and Sorcha braked it with a net of air, but it was warded, and neither she nor Ronan could pass through.

Ronan shouted for the passengers to show themselves and give back what they'd stolen.

When the coach door opened, it was not a terrified passenger but an infuriated sorceress who exited. And in her hand, she held the smaller Well.

The vision blinked and transformed to pure white. When the haze cleared, it revealed total devastation. Smoke filled the air, and the grass of the moorland had burned to ash. Of the carriage, there remained only tiny bits of rubble. Of the horses and people, no trace beyond a few smears of blood.

"We can't!" Sorcha shouted, and the words were muffled against Ronan's shoulder. He'd pulled her into his arms while the vision coursed through her, and she breathed in the scent of him: warm wool, soap scented with rosemary, the musky animal scent that was his alone, and with her magic senses still reeling from the vision, his magical essence of salt and apple. The rough nap of the wool against her cheek grounded her back in her own skin.

"Can't?" He stroked the nape of her neck and down her spine, his voice soft and soothing.

"I've Seen what will happen if we do, and it isn't good. Amelia will try to use the little Well, and she'll kill herself and us." She pulled away. His shoulders were stooped with resignation, but then a wry smile tugged at his lips and he straightened, setting his jaw.

"I suppose I can forego my desire to add 'highwayman' to my list of exploits. What do we do instead?"

She groped in the dregs of the vision for inspiration, but as always she could not bring it back to show anything useful. Instead, she wracked her brain for any ideas and trusted her intuition to help her choose the right course.

"Watch for them, I suppose, and make sure we take the same trains. Shadow them to London, and discover where they're going to store the Wells." As she spoke, the plan resonated with her magical senses. She added, "It will be better to retrieve them from wherever they put them—even if it's the Tower—than to risk Amelia killing everyone on the train."

"A fair point." He let her go, and offered his arm. Sorcha took it and leaned into his warmth as they ambled away from the station. He'd pulled her into a shadowy alcove while she had her vision, and the other pedestrians gave them only a brief glance as they emerged into the morning light, diffused by a quantity of grey clouds.

"Let's not go too far from the station."

"We won't. And I'll check the tracking spell often, so we are ready when they move back toward the city." They passed streets lined with shops and small eateries and stopped to purchase meat pies from a street vendor. After they had eaten, Ronan broke the companionable silence.

"What is it like, having a vision?"

Sorcha missed a step, and he steadied her.

"You don't have to answer if it's upsetting."

"Not upsetting. I don't think anyone has ever asked me that. Most members of my family have had at least one vision, usually during puberty when their magic is potent but hasn't been trained into an outlet."

He stared intently at her as she spoke, and she blushed at the attention. "Did that not happen to you?"

He shook his head. "No, and if it's that common, it should have. I wasn't trained to use magic, at all, until I was seventeen. And that was just enough not to kill myself."

"Hmm. Maybe it's only common in Clan Fay. We almost always have a few members with the Sight. I never thought to ask how often it happens to others, and I don't go to the school much." She cocked her head to the side. "But I haven't answered your question, have I?"

Every answer she considered sounded trite or contrived. She could explain how it felt physically, or what she sensed was happening magically, but none of that truly encapsulated the experience of a vision.

"I'm not sure how to put it that won't be completely underwhelming. Sometimes they slip into my head, little snippets of things to come, often of people I will never meet and times I will never see with my physical eyes. This time, it was like being punched. They usually come with more force when they are relevant to my own life, or are something that I can affect or change."

"And you said you can't control them?"

She sighed. "No. And that's unusual. Not that they come on their own—that happens to everyone. But most Seers can summon visions, too. They enter a trance-like state and meditate on what they wish to See. It's like scrying, but for the future instead of distant places or things. And I can't do it."

"So that's why you don't want to be called the Seeress of Skye?"

She couldn't help the flush of heat to her cheeks, even though he was being sympathetic, not mocking or derisive. "Yes. I'm not a proper Seer. I simply have a lot of uncontrollable visions."

"I'm sorry. That sounds awful."

It was the first time anyone had ever said that, and his words unlocked a chain around her heart that she hadn't understood was there. Yes, it was awful. The visions could be a tool, and a warning, but that didn't make them a gift. They hurt, and often she had no idea what she'd seen or what to do about it.

There was something else that she hadn't told him. Once she had a vision, they sometimes came back to her at odd moments, or in her dreams. Usually, those were the worst ones, of violence and death, as though they clamored for her to do something to change them. But she couldn't.

Ronan must have sensed her desire to change the subject, because he asked, "Will Amelia recognize you? It's going to be harder to shadow them if she can identify you by sight."

"Unfortunately, yes. She's been to Fay House twice, and the second time I'd warded the house against her. She found me in the village and demanded to be allowed onto the property, but even the queen's sorceress doesn't have that authority without warrants and cause. And her suspicions were not cause enough for a Scottish judge to swear out a warrant." Sorcha smirked. "Which really made her angry. I suppose that's why she took this tack when intimidation and legal means didn't work. But yes, she does know who I am."

"Can you maintain a glamour for long?"

"Not long enough. And it's harder to maintain spells on a train because the ambient magical energy is constantly changing."

"Then we'll need to disguise you. How do you feel about dyeing your hair and dressing up?"

She boarded the train a few hours later as a brunette in a velvet and satin gown that had been hastily altered for her, with only a tiny glamour over her face to obscure the shape of her eyes and mouth. That small of a spell could be maintained indefinitely using only her personal magical energy.

Ronan had shown her a type of link that he'd often used with Evie during their thieving days, a way to keep a very light magical contact and be able to speak mind-to-mind without actually merging or accessing the other person's magic. She hadn't yet grown accustomed to the idea of thinking to him rather than speaking, or suddenly hearing his voice inside her head.

Amelia and Blake were visible through the windows of an open first-class car, not sequestered in a private salon. Ronan chatted with the conductor and learned that their few private cars were carrying an earl and his party back from sporting in the Highlands. Though she was a dowager countess and the queen's sorceress, Amelia and a single gentleman could not have ousted a dozen titled men.

"That must have made her peevish," Sorcha murmured as they came to the door of the first class parlor. Ronan tapped his forehead, and she pursed her lips in chagrin. The conductor ushered them in and they took seats as far from Amelia and Blake as they could.

Sorcha settled back into the plush cushions with a delighted sigh.

Better than second class, eh?

Much. I haven't been on many trains, but this is much nicer than anything I've ridden in before.

They'd given their names as Robbie and Sarah Grant, which ought to be innocuous enough. Ronan's Scottish accent was nearly flawless, pitched to match Sorcha's musical island tones. He'd brushed powder through his dark hair to streak it with grey, and had procured a false mustache and sideburns from a barber who sold them to men who could not achieve appropriately bushy specimens with their natural facial hair.

You're very good at this. I suppose you've run many confidence games in the past where you had to adopt new roles. Have you ever performed on stage?

Only at school. And it's not at all the same thing, standing there declaiming memorized lines. This takes a very quick mind, and an ability to commit your entire being to the role. People want to believe you, but they aren't stupid. They sense when you make mistakes.

I'll keep that in mind if I ever need to do this again.

You're doing well, a solas, but I'd not recommend you adopt this as a career. You're too honest, and everything you feel shows on your face. It's fine to have an expressive countenance, but if you want to run a con, you must control it. It cannot be a mirror to your soul.

He grasped her hand. Even through her unfamiliar glove and his, the contact burned like a brand. Did he know everything about her? Yes, he probably did. And whatever he couldn't see for himself she'd told him, freely.

Except the fact that she'd been having visions of Blake for months. She hadn't disclosed that yet. Why not?

The train whistle sounded again, and the car lurched forward. At the other end of the parlor, Amelia held herself rigidly against her seat until the train settled into motion. She said something to Blake, who scowled at her openly. Whatever had transpired overnight, it had not enamored the queen's sorceress to her military companion.

Sorcha tried to reconcile this first in-the-flesh viewing with her many visions and two instances of magical voyeurism. As a child, his hair had been nearly as white-blond as hers, but it was now sandy and nearly brown.

He wore it short and had close-cropped side whiskers and a well-trimmed mustache. How had he kept himself so tidy, living wild outside her grounds at Fay House? He'd probably had a valet tend to him this morning, but in the two reconstruction spells Ronan had cast, he'd been perfectly groomed then, too. Most of the island men grew a full beard rather than deal with a razor and scissors.

His posture was rigid and correct, too. By contrast, Ronan sprawled beside her in a pose that matched the fashionable traveling suit he'd found while a hairdresser had changed her from a blonde to a brunette.

She had often asked herself who the man in her visions was, and now she knew, at least a little. He was a member of the mage corps, and his last name was Blake. What was his given name? Where had he grown up? The places she'd seen could have been almost anywhere in Britain, except for when he was older and was clearly in more tropical or desert locales. From things she'd seen, she guessed he was from a well-to-do family, but was he in line for the peerage or landed gentry? Or, perhaps, from a family that had gotten rich through industry?

It was rare for Sorcha to encounter people whose entire

lives and backgrounds were unknown to her, and her curiosity had been more than piqued by the little she'd seen of his life. She glanced at Ronan, and then back at Blake.

Ronan intrigued her, too, but for very different reasons. He was willing to talk about the many outrageous and less-than-legal things he'd done in his life, but shared very little about his family or childhood. She'd seen him interact with the crew of his ship, and they all seemed friendly enough, but he didn't care about them the same way he cared about Evie Finn.

In many ways, she understood Blake better than the man who'd been sharing her bed, and that troubled her.

Ronan nudged her, and she watched as Amelia cast an anti-eavesdropping spell. Damn. They wouldn't be able to hear what was said. But their body language was still visible, as were the shapes of their lips as they spoke.

He's really not happy, Ronan thought to her. *I bet he's trying to get her to agree to give him back custody of the Wells.*

I agree. That last word looked like 'Parliament.' I wonder if he'll succeed? Sorcha tried to watch them without being obvious that she was watching, but all she managed was a crick in her neck.

He might. You know the lady better than I do.

Not really. But the duchess does. They've been in skirmishing at society functions for the better portion of a year, ever since Amelia tried to bring Etta around to the queen's way of thinking and Etta refused. Amelia tried to have her imprisoned, and her power stripped away, but Etta escaped. Now they spar verbally over bad lemonade while Etta draws more and more politicians to her side.

Ronan had no difficulties at all with the deception. He sat, perfectly relaxed, one hand resting open in his lap, the other up behind his tipped-back head, like he had no cares in the world.

Sorcha gave it up and pulled a book out of her reticule. Maybe she could glance surreptitiously over the spine.

Why didn't the duchess make what happened public? It would have ruined the sorceress.

It serves her purposes more to keep the threat of exposure hanging over Amelia's head. If the truth is revealed, the queen will remove Amelia from power, and the next sorceress or mage might be worse. Etta likes understanding who the players are, and how they'll move.

Wise of her. But that doesn't help us much at the moment. He grinned at her book, and she glared at him behind the open pages.

No. But from what Etta has told me of her, she won't surrender the Wells until she's presented them to the queen. At that point, Mr. Blake may have a chance to convince Her Majesty that they need to be in a safer place than Windsor Castle.

I wouldn't much like having to steal them out of there. The wards might not be the same as in the Tower, but the queen has better guards, and there's more risk that we'd all hang if we were discovered. She still fears assassination attempts.

Sorcha peeked over her book at Amelia and Blake. Amelia's pursed lips and Blake's tense jaw shouted their disagreement despite the soundproof ward.

Then we'd better hope Blake is able to convince Amelia the safest place is with the national arsenal.

14

They shadowed their quarry all the way to London. Amelia managed to claim a private sleeper car for the overnight journey from Edinburgh, but Ronan and Blake slept nearby in one of the men's open cars, and Sorcha had a bunk in the women's car. Ronan's casual adoption of a very tony English schoolboy accent had even garnered him more information. Mr. Blake was a mage-captain, and his given name was Lucien. He'd gone to Rugby, and they had a mutual acquaintance whose brother had been at Radley with Ronan, although Ronan had not given his real name.

In the morning, Blake went off with Amelia to her private car and Ronan returned to Sorcha in the first class lounge. When they arrived at the station, Sorcha and Ronan had to decide whether to disembark with Blake at King's Cross or continue on with Amelia to Windsor Castle.

"She's taking the Wells with her," Ronan said. "The tracking spell shows them still on the train. Do we follow her, or Mr. Blake?"

"I don't know." She rubbed the bridge of her nose and hoped

her insight would give her an answer. "I don't think it's wise to go to Windsor." That felt right, like a wise decision. Following the same impulse, she added, "We need to bring Etta here."

So they disembarked and sent a telegram off to Glasgow. Then they plopped wearily into chairs at a café not too far from the station. It had been a long night, and neither had slept well in the open sleeper cars.

Ronan took a long pull of very strong tea and sighed with pleasure. "I have a few contacts of my own I can check with while we wait for the duchess. People who can tell me more about Mage-Captain Blake, and whether he's susceptible to suggestion."

Sorcha stopped him with a penetrating stare. "Are these willing contacts?"

He decided not to try and lie to her. "Some, yes. Some, not. Does it matter, as long as we uncover what we need?"

"It matters to me."

Ronan groaned. They were seated at a corner table where he could keep an eye on the door and the other patrons. No one was close enough to overhear them without magic, and they'd already checked the place for active spells. So he leaned closer and said softly, "Does it ease your conscience to know that the woman who is my contact for the army is a compulsive liar, adulteress, and embezzler? She used her position in society to join the financial committees of several large charities and seduced the bankers to funnel away a large amount of money before one of my associates caught her at it. Her husband is at the Home Office and now she passes on information to us."

"So because she's a bad person, it's fine to take advantage of her weakness?"

"If she hadn't done anything wrong, there would be nothing to blackmail her with."

"She should be punished by the proper authorities, not forced to do even more reprehensible things."

"Helping the cause of Irish Independence is not reprehensible."

"Not in the abstract. But you're making her betray *her* country."

"You must live in a comfortably idealistic world up there on Skye. I am fighting for my country's freedom. Sometimes that means making difficult choices, and sometimes those choices take me to dark places. But if it means Ireland is freed from the English yoke, every single thing I have done is worthwhile."

Sorcha sighed. "You're right. I do live in isolation, with only a few people around me whom I trust and love. Perhaps that gives me the luxury to believe that everyone should be treated with compassion, and that wrong action should be punished justly."

"I happen to believe that it is absolutely justice that she's being made to pay for her actions this way. The courts would transport her to Australia."

"They haven't sent prisoners to Australia in thirty years. She'd earn a long prison sentence, but nothing more."

"My point exactly. That's not justice. At least this way she's contributing to something important."

Sorcha took a deep swallow of coffee. She'd dumped sugar and cream in it until it was almost as pale as her skin. Ronan gazed at his unaltered cup. Bitter and potent it might be, but he preferred the way it woke every corner and crevice of his mouth with flavor.

She put the cup back onto its saucer with a decisive *click*. "Do what you must. I told Etta to send her reply by way of the Seward's house. That's where she usually stays when she's in London, so we'll sleep there tonight, and decide on a plan of action for tomorrow."

"The Sewards?" It couldn't be the same Sewards.

"Yes, the Marquess of Hazelby is Roland Seward. The duchess is married to his second son."

"Ah." Ronan's breath hitched in his throat, and his muscles involuntarily clenched. It was the same family. He'd been at Radley with the sons of their neighbors in Scotland, the MacAlasdair boys. The older son, Lachlan, had died several years ago. The younger had inherited the barony and married one of the Seward girls. And the marquess was on some of the same committees in parliament as Ronan's father.

Not that anyone *knew* Viscount Ashtondell was his father. McCarrick was his mother's family name. His father and half-siblings bore the much more respectably English surname Dunning.

But he'd located his father when he reached manhood and had studied him from a distance. The resemblance between them was stark. He didn't want the marquess to notice.

"You stay there. I'll find my own lodging."

"It's better if we stay together," Sorcha insisted. "If you don't want to be in Mayfair, I'll go with you, but I'd like to go somewhere that has a bathing chamber and hot running water, at least for tonight."

Images of what had happened the last time they'd been in the same room with a tub full of hot water cascaded through his head.

When she put it that way, so did he. Perhaps the marquess would not recognize him.

RONAN HAD CONSIDERED TRYING TO ARGUE SORCHA OUT OF accompanying him on his fact-gathering mission, but he wasn't interested in fighting with her again, and when she met his acquaintances, she might finally appreciate the sort of man she consorted with.

First, he took her to a secondhand clothing shop and bought worn but clean outfits for them both. Neither were well-fitting, but the shoddy cloth would blend in where even Sorcha's casual woolens would stand out.

In Spitalfields, they passed through a square surrounded by shops, many of them crowded next to and on top of each other in buildings that had seen better years. Many people jostled through the shops, all of them too-thin and dirty. The roads leading off of the square were narrow, lined with the doors and windows of overflowing boarding houses, punctuated by the occasional bawdy house and pub. These narrow passages, Ronan had explained in the cab, were rookeries. Here, the clothing changed from even the dregs of respectability in the square. Women wore very little, men did not bother with coats, and the urchins darting about or sitting desultorily in doorways had bare legs and feet covered in muck. Ronan hustled her down one lane, through an even tinier alley, and up a set of sagging steps into the third floor of a building with heavily chipped plaster and more than a few broken windowpanes covered by fabric or paper.

Sorcha dared not open her Sight here. Even with it closed, the magic in this area felt strange and choppy, as though someone had placed hurdles under the leylines so the energy would pool like water behind a dam and then burst over like a spillway.

She didn't like it at all.

Ronan pulled her through a cramped hallway. The boards under their feet creaked and groaned, and their steps raised clouds of dust that further obscured the dingy, peeling wallpaper and the few boards that remained of what was once wooden paneling. Probably long burned to keep someone warm in the winter. At the moment, Sorcha would have given much for the air to be chilled. Cold kept the worst aromas at bay.

She tried to take shallow breaths through her mouth, but without even the hint of a breeze provided outdoors, the stench of unwashed bodies sweating in the summer heat, mixed with refuse, chamber pots, and the reek of beer and gin, almost overwhelmed her.

Ronan knocked at one of the doors along the corridor and it opened to reveal a small, wiry man with a pile of flame-red hair on his head and an equally-brilliant beard, and a nose that must have been broken a half-dozen times or more. When he spoke, his Irish accent was so thick Sorcha almost couldn't discern his words, even having grown up with a rather thickly-accented family and community.

The man's speech patterns posed no difficulties for Ronan, who answered in what she assumed was the same dialect. After a few exchanges, the little man backed away to let them into the room.

They stepped over the threshold and through a low-level ward. It wasn't sturdy enough to keep a determined inter-loper out, but would likely give warning to the occupants of any forced entry and possibly place a kind of magical tracer on the intruders for ease of locating later. Ronan had explained how such things worked on their journey south, and she would insist that they check each other for the tracking spells as soon as they left the premises.

The tenement was crammed with boxes, tools, and old furniture, but almost empty of people. When the door closed, Sorcha realized it was nearly empty of the foul odors as well. She risked opening her Sight long enough to distinguish that the ward was also a barrier against sound, scent, and sight. Anyone peering in the windows or the door would see only an empty room, the wallpaper stained and peeling. She'd been too busy watching their "host" to notice the change in the background before they passed through.

A dark-haired and dark-eyed woman with an olive complexion sat in the far corner in front of a door, practicing making shapes and patterns with twine. Most schools of magic used that method for instructing apprentices, so Sorcha assessed the woman's power without probing her, judging by the way her magic affected the room. A good talent, but obviously still learning. Although it was unfortunate that she wasn't being taught the Fay method. Lilias had believed the twine or yarn exercise made for shoddy spell-work. Physical substances could never mimic the texture of magic threads, and the muscle-memory of the mage or witch would tend to reign at times when they should be adapting to variations in the local magic currents.

The door behind the woman opened, and a giant of a man with light brown hair and pale blue eyes walked through. The woman leapt to her feet and stuffed the twine into her pocket. She wore a modified bicyclist's costume, almost more trousers than skirt. The man was dressed in a suit that would not appear incongruous on a clerk or shopkeeper. Yet he carried himself as though he wore perfectly tailored evening dress made of silk and fine wool, and belonged in any club among the powerful men of London.

"Donn," Ronan said, and his tone only slightly missed being an exclamation. He hid his surprise quickly, and his lips formed a smile, but behind the geniality and strong handshakes they exchanged, Sorcha sensed his disquiet. Something wasn't right.

"Didn't expect to see me here, did ya boyo?" Donn had a lighter accent than the first man, but she suspected he had tempered it because of her presence. He'd only glanced her way, but that glance had assessed and judged her in moments, then dismissed her. Sorcha forced herself to relax and ignore the slight. He wasn't nearly as powerful as she, and she was only a middling talent. She could have him wrapped in a binding before he could even open his Sight.

But she stilled the impulse. He may have dismissed her as not important to him, but he was canny enough to realize that Ronan wouldn't have brought her if she weren't important to Ronan.

"I never try to expect anything where you're concerned," Ronan said. "But no. I heard you were running the circle out of the West End, and that you had taken recruits for drilling at home."

Donn chuckled. "I go where I'm needed. Now, what brings you to London town?"

"My client had several items stolen from her home. The man that did the stealing was with the army, and the woman he did it for is the queen's sorceress."

Donn whistled, and leaned back on a stack of boxes, crossing his arms over his chest. "Must have been something very…attractive."

Sorcha stiffened. That word wasn't chosen by accident. Power Wells attracted ambient magical energy, quickly storing a massive charge that could later be released at a mage's discretion.

Most attempts at making Wells produced only minor results—the sort of thing that could power household spells or perhaps one moderate-level working. But Lilias had devised a way to create Wells with a very high capacity for energy storage, and she'd left them to fuel for the last fifty years. They were a component of her plan to provide magical power when the drain became too much to support English magic. They ought to provide enough energy for a few more years even when the deep magic was gone.

Or they could provide enough energy for a very large, very destructive single spell. That was what Amelia and Mr.

Blake likely feared. And what someone like this Donn would be most interested in creating.

Ronan didn't fall for the trap. "The nature of the items is private. But I'd hoped the Circle would help us locate them, and perhaps provide assistance getting them back. We aren't sure where they are now, but they may end up in the Tower."

Donn's gaze lighted first on the little man, and then the woman. Some message or signal passed between them, and they both shuffled into the hallway. "Come back in the morning. They'll check with the usual people."

Ronan watched Donn for another moment, as though trying to scrutinize the bigger man's skull. "Including Lady Wiltbury?"

"You can take that meeting if you like. As I recall, she offered an abundance of *extra* information when you were her contact."

Since Ronan had called the woman an adulteress, it wasn't a giant leap to imagine exactly what she'd offered. And that he'd accepted. Sorcha had managed not to react to anything so far, had kept her stance loose, her posture relaxed, but at this, her hands curled into fists. She didn't want to believe it was true, but Ronan didn't deny it.

"She and I understand one another. But if you'd rather have your usual person handle the exchange—"

"Not at all. She'll be happy to see you again." Donn glanced again at Sorcha, and his hard mouth turned up by a tiny fraction at the corner. "When I last saw her, she was looking very well indeed."

Ronan acted as though he hadn't noticed Donn's malicious enjoyment of her discomfort. He hadn't reacted at all, treating this exchange as though they were ordering tea at a café. "Does she still check the same location for instructions?"

"She does."

"Then I'll return tomorrow evening, not morning. She'll need time to gather what I need."

Donn's expression barely changed, but Sorcha caught the slight tightening of his jaw muscle and the minute shift in his posture. He didn't like Ronan telling him what would happen. "In the evening, I'll be at Covent Garden. The Royal Opera House is putting on a production of Mancinelli's *Ero e Leandro*."

"We'll be there," Sorcha said. Both men were startled away from their contemplation of each other, and their probing gazes now swung to her. She was startled, too. She hadn't meant to speak, had been prepared to let Ronan handle this meeting. The words had emerged from her mouth without any conscious intent. She followed her intuition and added, "But for now, we have another appointment."

She held out her hand. For a moment, Ronan hesitated to take it. But he did, placing it on his forearm. He gazed at her for a heartbeat longer, then back at Donn.

"We'll see you tomorrow at the opera."

Sorcha followed his gentle lead into the hallway, and then they walked briskly back to the square and the market. She started to speak, and he silenced her with a gesture. He hired a hansom and told the driver to take them across the river to Guy's Hospital. Sorcha didn't ask why, and Ronan again bade her be silent while they drove.

At the hospital, he took her to a side entrance and then through a maze of corridors to an office. He spoke to a secretary and left a written message for whomever the office belonged to, and then took her back onto the street. There, he said, "Open your Sight."

She followed his instructions and found the tracking spell tangled in his magic. She extracted it and unraveled the weaving. He did the same for her.

"Now we can speak. I don't know for sure that the spell

relays what we talk about, but it might, and I didn't want to take any chances." He put her hand back over his arm and walked away from the hospital.

"Don't you trust them?" She asked the question already suspecting the answer, but she was interested in the why of it more than a yes or no.

Ronan snorted. "Do you?"

"No, but I'm not one of their number. I thought you were a member of the same cause."

"We are, and I trust them all to do what's best for Ireland. In this case, they're more likely to view that as confiscating your property and using it for a very different purpose."

"Like what?"

He gestured off into a nebulous distance. "Maybe something as simple as augmenting Irish magic. That would do the trick and give all of us a boost for years. That's what I would do, anyway." He handed her up to a waiting cab at the stand on the corner and gave the driver the Seward's address in Mayfair. He ought to have taken the seat opposite her, but Ronan had little interest in propriety. She allowed him to haul her against him and snuggled her head against his chest.

"You don't believe your colleagues would take such a benign action." Again, it wasn't a question, because she already knew the answer. But she did not like any of the three people they'd met, and she wanted to grasp why Ronan called them, if not friends, then at least compatriots.

"I would argue for it. We all receive a say, and if I can convince enough of my fellows that it's the best thing to do, it might happen."

"That's unlikely. No one wants to take the slow, steady path when a big spectacle is offered."

"Or the peaceful option when there could be violence?"

She couldn't see him well, but that didn't stop her from lifting her head as though she could. "I don't know about the general run of people, but I would assume that revolution-aries are naturally the types that don't shy away from violent action. And your friend clearly recognizes what we seek, so we should assume at this point that Amelia keeping it in Windsor Castle is not the worst case scenario anymore."

"Yes, I'm afraid so." His arms tightened, and his discomfort made her own belly queasy. "The net we found in Portree smelled like his magic. I'd hoped because no one spoke the words during that scene we witnessed, and we didn't say anything outright, that perhaps he didn't know. The Queen's Sorceress must have mentioned it on another occasion."

"So how do we stop him from stealing it first?"

"We make sure he keeps helping us and don't let him lead. But that shouldn't be a problem. It's easier for him if we do most of the planning and work. Then all he has to do is keep his agenda separate, and attempt to double-cross us."

Her fingers tapped his shoulder in an unsteady drumbeat. "That's the part where you lose me. We know he's going to try something, but not what. We'll have to wait until he acts."

"It's one of the reasons I wanted to be the one contacting Lady Wiltbury. I want to control whatever information she provides. That will give us the advantage."

Sorcha stiffened in his arms. He stroked a hand over her side, but the touch didn't help. "Would you trust her to only give the information to you, and not share it with him, too?"

"Not really. I actually assume that he's going to make contact with her, too. That's why I waited to remove the tracking spell. I wanted him to be aware that I'd already left a message at the drop point."

"So how will you keep her from spilling to him?" His features made only a rough outline in the dark. She needed to ask, even if she couldn't observe his face when he answered. "Will you sleep with her?"

A tremor ran through his hands, and that was all the reply she needed. "I don't intend to. But you should know that I did, before. It was how we acquired the information to blackmail her."

"And she isn't angry about it?"

He shifted, making a negative gesture. "She took it in stride. In the world we live in, you can only ever consider yourself. When we slept together, she wanted something, and I wanted something. We both got it, but it wasn't the same thing."

"What did she want?"

"Prestige." He stroked down her spine, then up again, dancing his fingers along the tiny bit of her skin exposed at the back of her neck between the high ruffled collar of her dress and her hair. "Her circle of ladies all had their eye on me that season. They were in Dublin with their husbands and bored, and it was a coup for her to take me as a lover first."

Sorcha pushed away, unable to remain quiescent in his arms. "That's awful. You didn't mind?"

"Not at the time. And not now, really. I realize it hurts you to talk about it, and *that* I mind. But I would do it again. It was necessary, and she's given us a great deal of information since then."

Fabric bunched between her fingers as she squeezed handfuls of her cheap skirt in her fists. "I don't want to live in your world, Ronan. I don't want to exist in a place where such things are necessary and people only care about their own lusts."

He took her hands and squeezed so tight it hurt. "I don't want you to live there, either."

15

Sorcha moaned as her tired and stiff body sank into the welcoming warmth of the tub in one of the upstairs bathing chambers in Seward House. Though the house was nearly empty of Sewards at the moment. Cecily, the marchioness, was in Glasgow helping to train Etta. Malcolm, the second son, was there, too, since he and Etta were married. Giles, the heir, lived nearby in Mayfair with his wife and daughters. Viola, the eldest daughter, was in Scotland with her husband and baby twins. Olivia, the youngest daughter, was on the continent traveling as a companion to the dowager marchioness. Percy, the youngest son, was at Oxford, preparing for a career in the army. Term was finished, but he'd stayed for summer drill with his volunteer battalion.

The marquess had told her all of this over dinner, while Ronan fidgeted and ate very little. It was only Sorcha's second trip to London, and although she'd explained to Lord Hazelby the circumstances of the visit, she had only mentioned that things had been stolen from Fay House, not what those objects were.

After the meal, a messenger arrived with a return telegram from Etta. It read:

Fay House secure will arrive in London on overnight train

And that was all.

A very cheerful maid had shown Sorcha her room and the guest bathing chamber, and promised to have her clothing ironed and hung, a necessary procedure after being first stuffed into saddlebags and then tossed into a newly-purchased valise in Portree. But what Sorcha had most anticipated was taking off the goddess-blasted corset. Each busk hook that came undone became a leap toward freedom. Then she'd stripped and found the almost-too-hot bath.

First, she plunged her head beneath the water and scrubbed at her hair to remove the dye. Not all of it washed clean, leaving her with a more traditional golden-blond rather than her own nearly-silver shade. But the streak of Fay silver cleared almost immediately. It hadn't taken the dye well in the first place.

Once she'd restored her hair to rights, she sank back against the side of the tub where a spot had been molded for a bather to recline against a provided pillow. She breathed the humid air, redolent of the oils that had been added to the bathwater. Lavender, tangerine, and walnut were the primary scents, and underneath something almost smoky, like sandalwood.

The door to the bathing chamber opened, letting in the cooler air from the hallway. Sorcha shivered as the latch clicked shut again. She closed her eyes and pretended she hadn't noticed.

There were many things left unsaid between them, places that neither of them seemed willing to go. But she hadn't stopped wanting Ronan, hadn't changed her mind about stealing every last moment she could before he inevitably ran.

After a moment, warm hands clasped her bare shoulders, kneading the muscles and leaving her body lax and languid in the hot water. Then the hands drifted past her collarbones to her breasts, and a warm mouth found her nape.

It seemed that Ronan had come to a similar decision.

"I recall a very lovely hour spent with you in the bath not too long ago," Ronan murmured. His breath made the little hairs on her neck stand to attention. His fingers stroking her nipples under the water made her whimper.

"Would you—" she broke off into a moan when he nipped at her throat, then gasped, "care to join me?"

By way of answer, he stood. She tilted her head to watch him. He was gloriously bare, his cock stiff and erect and at the perfect height for her to take it into her mouth. He came around the tub and she leaned to grasp his rigid flesh in her warm, wet hands, stroking and teasing until he panted and begged for her.

Then she licked her lips and slid them over him. He groaned as she slowly took him into her mouth, licking and suckling his smooth skin, loving the hard, solid flesh beneath. She'd enjoyed it when he'd lost himself and spent in her mouth, had loved the way he'd moaned again when she swallowed the essence of him and licked him clean.

But this time, she wanted a different kind of connection, wanted the assurance that—for now—he was hers. Tomorrow he might choose to take another woman, but tonight, she would take him into her body and tease and torment him until he completely lost control.

She slipped his cock out of her mouth and stood. The water sluiced over her skin, and Ronan tracked its progress with his gaze. He groaned as she fondled her breasts, her belly, and her thighs.

"Come here." She lifted one hand, and he took it, stepping over the side of the tub to join her in the steaming water. She pushed at him, and he sat with his back against one edge. There was enough room for her to straddle him, so she knelt with her knees on either side of his hips and let her wet body glide over his chest.

Then she tentatively brushed him with her magic. If he chose to go to Lady Wiltbury's bed tomorrow, she didn't think she could bear to touch him again. So if this was their last lovemaking, she wanted it to be real, and true, and deep. Even if that meant that her heart broke wide open later.

Who was she kidding? Her heart was going to be torn to pieces, no matter what.

His magic met hers with an almost desperate surge, all of his desire and need rising to meet her as she grasped his cock and lowered her hips. She sank onto him with a moan, and he grabbed her arse as she gripped the side of the tub and began to move.

Everything smelled of apples, of Ronan's true magical scent, of the secret self he tried to hide with years of bitterness and salt. But she could see it—could taste and hear and feel it. The man who had this sweet, crisp, sensual center was entirely worth fighting for.

If only he would allow her to.

She kissed him, letting her tongue and her lips say against his what she could not form into speech. Except, with magic, her thoughts washed over him like the water that splashed against the tub, and all her words flowed into him. *You are more than your fears, more than your past.*

Heat and pulsing pleasure built and crested, again and again as she rocked against him. His passion twined and twisted with hers, and his pain and his doubt. *I have nothing left to give you. It's all been taken away. I'm not enough.*

Love doesn't ask for anything, Ronan. I don't need anything from you. She broke the kiss and moved her hands to his chest. His heart pounded against her palm, but she focused on his storm-grey eyes. *I love you, and I'm not going to stop. Take my love. It's yours.*

She ground her hips down, hard, and rode him until he gasped and groaned and her own release gushed in a flood of his water magic, illuminated by a million sparkling points of her light.

RONAN STOOD IN A QUIET NOOK IN HYDE PARK AND WAITED for Isabella Landen, Viscountess Wiltbury, to arrive. She'd sent a message to meet here this morning, and he'd managed to talk Sorcha into going to meet the overnight train from Glasgow instead. Bella would not appreciate another woman at their meeting, and even if Sorcha remained hidden, Ronan would be too distracted by his lover's presence to keep his focus where it belonged—on the treacherous viscountess.

Even reflecting on Sorcha, remembering the way she'd taken him, made him experience her love through every last cell in his body, was too much of a distraction. So he deliberately closed off the lingering connection between them and aimed his attention at a different tangle.

Donn.

No matter how much of an asset the Wells would be for the Cause, they belonged to Sorcha and Clan Fay. Ronan had promised her he would help recapture them, and he always kept his promises. Which was why he rarely made them, and why he shouldn't have made this one now.

There was no outcome in which Donn would not try to take the Wells, had never been one from the moment the Wells left the vault at Fay House. The only option was to stick close and foil whatever attempt he made. Once Sorcha had them back in her possession, Ronan's oath would be fulfilled and this would stop being his problem.

He sighed at that outright lie, but wouldn't take it back. He was going to have to walk away soon, or risk tangling himself with Sorcha forever. Already he could imagine a future where she waited for him on Skye, taking him into her arms and into her body whenever he could steal the time to come to her. He could see their children, growing up partially on Skye and partially in Dublin, learning magic with them, and fighting by his side for Ireland's freedom.

And damn it, she'd clouded his mind again.

Isabella glided to him out of the morning fog. She wore a very fashionable walking dress of raw silk with enormous puffed sleeves and rows of bunched fabric running vertically down the bodice. Her waist was impossibly small beneath a wide ribbon. She looked like an overstuffed mattress tick, but he kept that thought to himself.

"What are you doing in London, you gorgeous thing?" Isabella prowled over and leaned against him, her hazel eyes sparkling with something between mischief and malice.

"I'm on a job, as my note should have made clear." He thickened his accent, though not so far that she couldn't interpret his words. She'd been wild to slum with a low-born Irishman when they met, and he'd played the stereotypes until he'd caught her well and good.

"Ah, yes." She lifted a hand and stroked a gloved finger on his jaw. "I was so surprised to receive it yesterday. I quite exhausted my lover last night in anticipation of seeing you again."

So she did expect him to come to her bed.

He tried to imagine that, tried to rouse himself with the memory of her flesh, with the feeling of her pushed against him now, but all he could picture was Sorcha, gliding over him, his cock buried so deep inside her he imagined they'd actually become one flesh. And her voice in his head, saying, *Take my love. It's yours.*

"I'm afraid there's no time for pleasure on this trip, birdie."

Her mouth quirked down in a little moue. "Not even a smidgen?" She deliberately curled her tongue out and licked her top lip in what she must deem a seductive fashion. But the only mouth he wanted near him was Sorcha's.

He shook his head, forcing a wry smile so she'd believe he was actually sorry for rejecting her. "More's the pity. Perhaps next time." He pressed his thumb to her lower lip in a pretended promise. "What do you have for me?"

She wrapped one leg around him and ground herself against his thigh. "It's too, too bad of you to rouse me so completely and not release this tension."

Ronan kept the growl of frustration tamped deep inside. She wasn't going to let this go. He pulled her back into the greenery, away from any watching eyes. She giggled, and he pushed her against a tree trunk. It wasn't big enough to support her, and there wasn't room in this little nest for them to lie down, so he had plenty of excuses not to take the act to its conclusion. He said nothing, though, as she writhed against his thigh and tried to kiss him.

He avoided her lips by pulling away and reaching for her skirts. She let him hike them to her hips, revealing a pair of lacy bloomers and the bottom of her corset. He delved between her legs and she threw her head back, moaning as he found the slit in the bloomers and fondled her moist flesh.

"Oh, yes, Rory! Harder!" Her cries pushed his thoughts to the past, to the time he'd played Rory Donnelly. He was a very different man now. He continued to stroke her with practiced precision, drawing out her pleasure, and wondered when he had started to change.

He'd not taken any spying missions for several years now.

He'd even gotten away from the street-level work of house-breaking and running cons. The smuggling had been far more lucrative and had taken all of his time. But it had also given him a certain distance from the rest of his cell, and until he'd sensed Donn's net in Portree, he hadn't realized how large that distance had grown.

Bella had her eyes closed, writhing back against the tree trunk, her hips thrusting against his fingers. Once, he would have been more than happy to take the rest of what she offered, because they both understood the boundaries of sex and both got exactly what they wanted from it. But what he wanted from sex had changed the moment he kissed Sorcha Fay on the beach. Or perhaps even when he'd helplessly emptied his bag against a cave wall because the pull between them had already been so great.

Bella held no attraction for him, only a mild distaste. So he drove her faster and harder until she climaxed, and then withdrew his hand.

She mewled in disapproval as he moved farther away, but shimmied her hips until her skirts fell back to her fashionably-booted ankles.

"Still tense?" he asked, affecting a leer and a grin.

"If only we had more time," she purred. "I would raise some tension in *you*."

"Alas, birdie, we haven't. Now, what have you got for me?"

She pouted again, and said, "Your man is Mage-Captain Lucien Blake. He's recently returned from Africa, where he worked to suppress some uprising. He was loaned to the queen's personal guard at her sorceress's request."

"Anything I can use on him?"

Bella frowned. "Not a thing, actually. The word is, he's squeaky clean and annoyingly so. A loyal, honorable servant of the British Empire."

Ronan scoffed, but she shrugged and made a 'what can you do' gesture. "It's difficult for people like you and me to accept, but it seems he's a true believer."

"What about the people around him?"

"At the moment, he's acting autonomously, and I can't find anything on his commanding officer. He did report in yesterday, and they sent him back to the queen."

So the army wanted to keep an eye on the Wells and didn't trust Her Majesty to protect them. "Anything about his mission?"

"Only that he was to report back today to the Tower for new orders. Whatever those orders are is hush-hush."

The Tower of London. Damn. "When is he to report?"

"They didn't specify. I imagine once he's finished whatever he's doing in Windsor Castle."

Yes, Ronan imagined that, too. And that it might take the good Captain a while to convince the queen and her sorceress to surrender their new prizes. But with the weight of the ministries behind him, old Vick would have to relinquish the Wells to his custody.

"If that's all, I'll be off." He parted the leaves beside him. She stopped him with a hand on his arm.

"Are you sure you can't find time when your mission is completed to visit me properly? I'll even pay for the hotel suite."

"This is a side job. After it's done, I'm back to what I was doing before. Perhaps the next time I'm in London."

One corner of her mouth lifted in a sly smirk. "You remember how to reach me."

He nodded as though in promise and pushed out of the shadowy space. The fog still lay heavily on the park, and in a few steps, it swallowed him.

He had no intention of keeping that appointment, and

frankly had very little desire to ever return to London at all. He'd have Bart tie him to the mast of the ship and stay on the water for the rest of his life. Then he wouldn't have to remember this ugly encounter, and wouldn't have to face Sorcha with the knowledge of what he'd done.

16

The train's brakes made a squealing hiss as it finally came to a full stop on the platform. Sorcha waited on the platform, wondering which carriage held the duchess. She could scry for it, but instead she started walking. Her intuition almost never failed her, and it didn't now.

A porter handed the duchess down from the train, and then Etta's husband Malcolm Seward descended to the platform. Behind him came Evie Finn.

Sorcha made herself stand still and relaxed her muscles. She wouldn't embarrass herself in front of the woman Ronan loved. Evie might be more sister to him than anything else, but he had acknowledged that he loved her, and that made her the most important person in the world to him. Sorcha tried not to envy the girl, or at least to keep her envy well hidden.

Etta saw her and tramped across the platform to take Sorcha into a hard embrace. Then she pulled back and tapped at a strand of Sorcha's hair. "What's this?"

"We used a disguise for a while. Not all of the dye washed out."

"Ah." This time, Etta traced a finger over her cheekbone, beneath the dark circles Sorcha had noticed in the glass that morning. "You've had a difficult time of it, haven't you?"

Sorcha pulled away. Her American cousin was forthright as well as prone to tactile contact. "I'm sorry I failed the clan."

Etta prodded her arm. "I'll have no talk of failure from you, Sorcha Fay. What's done is done, and you did what you could to prevent it. Now we need to focus on getting our property back."

"Ronan and I are working on that. He's spoken to people he knows and is meeting with a contact right now."

"Who've you spoken to?" Evie stood behind Etta, and Sorcha had to shift to the side to see her. Etta was only average height, but Evie was tiny. Perhaps even an inch shorter than Sorcha. Her vivid red hair was contained in a braided bun and stuffed under a far-from-fashionable hat. Her clothes were too fashionable for her, as her shape did not match the fad for hourglass waists and waspish silhouettes. The old Regency style would suit her best, or perhaps a medieval cote and girdle like one of the women in Waterhouse's paintings.

Sorcha answered the question, though she wished Ronan was here to answer it for her, not meeting with a woman who had once been his lover. And might become so again. "A man named Donn and two of his group yesterday. Ronan's speaking to a Lady Wiltbury now." Goddess, she hoped he was only speaking to her.

Evie frowned at Donn's name, then curled her lip at the mention of Lady Wiltbury. "Damn, not that harpy. She's a sleeveen, that floosie is."

Most of those words meant nothing to Sorcha, but she translated their intent well enough. Ronan's description hadn't been flattering, either. And yet he'd slept with the woman. And might be fucking her right now.

She made her voice even, but couldn't keep her hands from clenching. "Yes. He told me a little about her. But she has contacts who have information we need, so he felt it was necessary to speak with her."

"Make sure and watch yourselves. Ronan got lucky when he blackmailed her, 'cause she sees passing information to the Cause as more of a lark than a punishment. But she'd sell him or any one of us to the Brits, no mistake."

"I'm sure he'll be careful. He understands what's at stake." But she wasn't sure of anything. Hadn't been since she woke one night seven months ago to find her wards out of sync. Nothing had been certain or simple since.

"He knows what's at stake, and yet he brought Donn into it?" Evie's skepticism vindicated Sorcha's opinion about Donn.

"That was a surprise. Ronan didn't expect to see him here."

"Nor would I. Last I heard, Himself was in Kerry, training with the new rifles that Ro's money bought."

"Ronan's money?" Sorcha asked.

"Aye, from the smuggling. Though Ro says most of it is legit shipping these days. He's making a bundle, not that you can tell by where he lives or how he dresses."

Etta looked askance at Evie, but she made no comment. Sorcha stifled a snort, and reminded herself there were important things to discuss. "In any case, Donn's here now. And he knows what we lost."

"Damn," Etta said. "That's unfortunate."

Evie nodded emphatically. "It is, truly. Shite flies high when it's hit with a stick, and that aul git has been angling to make decisions for the Cause for years. I don't like him being here at all."

Mal spoke from Etta's other side. "I think it's time we took this conversation behind wards."

~

MAL'S FATHER RELUCTANTLY AGREED TO CONTINUE TO HOST A group of mages and witches in his home, though Sorcha's intuition told her he was secretly pleased to have his son back in the house. Mal had been living with Etta in Glasgow for the last year, although they'd come to London more frequently since the Season—and this session of Parliament—began. Before that, he'd hidden himself away on an estate on the northern coast of Scotland, near Durness, for nearly two years.

The marquess left them with a late breakfast in the family dining room, and Etta asked Evie to ward the room. "She's just learned a new type of ward," Etta murmured to Sorcha, "and needs to practice."

As the spell shimmered into place, the door opened. Ronan stood on the other side with one of the footmen, but when he stepped forward, he slammed against the ward. He stood there staring in at them, rubbing his nose, until Evie adjusted something in the spell's weaving so he could pass through.

"Ler's ballix, Evie. That hurt."

"You should always open your Sight to check for active spells in a house with magic users," Evie recited, as though from one of her lessons at the Fay school.

"Aye, as you say." Ronan's heated look brought back the memory of the last time he'd forgotten to check for active spells. He'd been gloriously bare in the dim summer night, his muscles bunched with fury as he swore in several languages. Her response now was no different than it had been at the time. Her mouth watered, her pulse skipped and tripped along faster, and heat built between her legs.

He sat beside her, and she wished that everything in their lives could be different, so she could haul him to her room and prove to him again that she loved him and was never going to stop.

No matter what he'd done today, no matter what now changed between them, she was going to love him for the rest of her life.

"It's nice to see you in person, Mr. McCarrick," Etta was saying, and Sorcha dragged her attention back to the group around the table. "This is my husband, Malcolm Seward."

Etta's introductions were not drenched in formality as one might expect from a duchess. She didn't mention her husband's title, or insist on the use of her own. But considering that she'd spent the first twenty-odd years of her life on a mountainside in America, Sorcha supposed that her manners were fine indeed.

"Call me Ronan."

He nodded across the way to Mal, who said, "and I'm Mal. Etta would smack you if you called her 'Your Grace,' so I'll warn you in advance."

Ronan grinned and nodded his agreement. "What have you all been on about in my absence?"

"Not much," Etta said. "Sorcha informed us of your progress so far, and of your meeting with Mr. Donn yesterday. I'd like to be apprised of the results of your encounter with Lady Wiltbury this morning. I've not met her before, but Evie seems to believe we can't trust her."

"We can't. But Bella can be counted on to give fair value for what she's given and to act in her own best interest."

"And it would not be in her interest to reveal our activities, as that would reveal her connection to your cause, correct?"

"Just so." Ronan relayed the information he'd gotten from Lady Wiltbury. Etta tapped her fingers on the table as she considered the news. A tingle of magic nagged at Sorcha, as though Ronan had skipped a chunk of the story, but she decided to pursue it when they were alone.

"We could set a watch on the train stations, but we'd need to watch every platform in the city. He's smart enough not to go directly from Windsor to the Tower. He might not even take the train, although that's the fastest option and the hardest for thieves to disrupt. We're not exactly in the wild west." She addressed Sorcha. "Have you tried scrying for him?"

"Yes. He's warded. We were able to follow the Wells because that kind of power isn't easily masked, even by spells intended to dampen them. They also retained the essence of Fay House, and Ronan was able to track that."

"Then that should still be our best option."

Ronan shook his head. "It should be, but it isn't. I don't understand what happened, but when I tried to cast the tracking spell after I met with Lady Wiltbury, I couldn't find them at all. Last night when we went to bed, they were still west of the city, in what I assumed was Windsor Castle. Now they're nowhere."

"Queen Victoria most likely has a null-warded vault," Malcolm said. "Bertie had a little one that one of his continental cronies made for him. He used to keep…" his voice trailed off, and he coughed. "Well, he used to keep private spells in there."

Etta gave her husband an incredulous glance at the emphasis on *private,* but otherwise she ignored the more salacious comment. "If that's the case, we'll check again at intervals for the rest of today until we can sense them moving."

"And if we sense nothing?" Evie asked.

"I'm already planning to appeal to the Home Office on a different matter. I'll see what I can do about this."

"The queen isn't going to let them go without argument,"

Sorcha said. "She and Amelia went to a lot of trouble to plan this. And you're going to have a difficult time convincing the Home Office that we need to keep the Wells under our control. It's better to whisk them away and pretend we know nothing."

"They have no legal reason to take them from us," Etta said. "Muireall and Cecily checked for me, and there isn't a single law or statute that requires such an artifact be surrendered to the crown or any other government body. And I would fight against any law proposed in Lords."

"Perhaps not," Mal said, "but once they have control of them, it will be a legal battle for you to procure them. You'd have to prove that they belong to our clan, and the judge is going to be sympathetic to the government's case."

"Damn," Etta murmured. "Then I suppose you must proceed with gaining your…other associate's assistance." She directed the words at both Ronan and Evie.

Ronan glared at his adopted sister. "I don't want you back in this, *a chara*. You took your chance to flee his madness, and it has served you well."

"I should have told you where I was going," Evie said. "I can't regret where it brought me, but I owe you this." There was a story there, and Sorcha wondered at it, though now was not the time to ask.

"You owe me nothing, *deirfiúr bheag*." That sounded enough like the Scots Gaelic *piuthar bheag* for Sorcha to interpret the endearment as 'little sister.'

"I'm still going with you. You need someone to watch your back who knows his tricks."

Ronan opened his mouth to argue again, but Sorcha said, "We're going to need everyone if this is going to work." She put her hand on Ronan's where he'd pressed it against the table in frustration. "Let's talk about what happens if we can't intercept the Wells on their way to the Tower."

They debated plans for the next two hours, sending Ronan outside the ward every fifteen minutes to check for evidence that the Wells were moving. He finally located them, but it was too late.

He burst back into the dining room. "They're already here in London. I can't figure out how, unless the null vault was portable. They're already here, and judging from the direction," he gestured almost due east, "they're already in the Tower."

THE THEATER BUILDING THAT HAD LONG STOOD IN COVENT Garden had only recently taken on the new name of the Royal Opera House, but very little else had changed since it was rebuilt in 1858.

Sorcha fidgeted in her gown. It didn't match the standards of the women visible from the Duchess of Fay's box, but she'd been unable to find anything ready-made during their hunt for clothing this afternoon. Evie's gown had been hastily altered down from a shop sample, and the seamstress hadn't tried to force her into a fashionable silhouette, but worked with her slender shape. Sorcha's was her own best gown, meant for special family occasions and town meetings, but several years out of date and lacking the flourishes of puffed sleeves and a full bustle.

She must look the dowd beside her striking cousin, the ethereal Evie, and the two resplendent gentlemen who might have been born to wear tail coats and starched collars.

"Do you see him?" Evie whispered to Ronan, reminding Sorcha that they weren't here to be seen, or even to watch the production of *Ero et Leandro*—Hero and Leander—that would be performed tonight.

"Not yet," Ronan murmured back. By the stage, the musicians had begun their tuning. Soon the lights would be dimmed in the house—although not so low the audience members couldn't see each other—and the production would begin. Someone was doing magic behind the stage, probably an illusionist hired to enhance the performance.

The house went dim all at once, and the rumbling sound of the patron's conversations died away. In times past, those conversations would have rarely stopped completely, and they might have witnessed crowd members bantering with the actors or singing along. But times had changed, and audiences had, too.

Light flared on the stage and music filled the air with sound. Actors and actresses moved about the stage in precise steps to the music. Magic flared somewhere nearby. Everyone in the Fay box shifted in the direction of the surge, but it was only an illusion, part of the play.

Underneath the illusion spells Sorcha sensed something else. Another layer. Everyone else was paying attention to the house and stage, and she wasn't sure that she was correct, so she slipped out of the box and made her way down the hall. She opened her Sight, let her gaze go unfocused, and walked wherever her feet took her. When something tugged at her, she stopped and placed her hand on the door to that box.

Someone had cast a ward on the door, or perhaps around the whole box, but it was not a tough spell or difficult to manipulate. She let her magic twist through the strands of the weaving and then the sounds from the interior came through the ward and into her head.

"Are you sure?" The voice was deep and rumbling, like distant thunder or a waterfall. She didn't recognize it.

"As much as I can be." That was Donn. "I've not seen anything with these two eyes, but everything I've discovered points that way."

"Then I suppose it's time to begin the next stage."

A hand came down on Sorcha's shoulder, and she startled back from the door. Ronan pulled her against his chest. He smelled of soap and brine, his physical aroma meshing with the magical. She mourned the loss of the apples, but ever since his return from the meeting in the park, he'd buried that sweetness with salt.

"He's in there," she whispered. "With another man, and I think someone else, although no one else spoke."

"You should go back to the duchess. I'll talk to him."

"I was with you before. He'll recognize me."

"Yes, but right now you're just the owner of the property we're tracking. The more Donn sees you with me, the more he'll guess…" Ronan trailed off.

Sorcha watched him, wondering how he would finish that sentence. His arms tightened around her, and he kissed her forehead.

Finally, he said, "He would use you as leverage against me."

"Someday you'll have to explain to me why you went so willingly to this man's cause."

"Not his cause. The Cause. He happens to be there."

Sorcha reached out with her magic. "Link with me, then. I won't be in the box, but I'll be able to listen and help if things go wrong."

Ronan accepted the tentative graze of her power and wrapped his around it. As long as both of them maintained the connection, the merge would hold unless they went more than a few miles away from each other.

"Now go back. Relay whatever you see to the others."

RONAN WAITED UNTIL SORCHA DISAPPEARED AROUND THE curve of the corridor and duchess's box door clicked shut.

Then he rapped quietly on Donn's box.

It took a minute before anyone responded, while he waited and squashed every nervous gesture his body attempted to make. But then a crack opened, and two dark eyes peered out. The woman from Spitalfields. He didn't recognize her, which was worrisome. Kevin O'Malley, the diminutive boxer, had been with the Cause for years, he and had been Donn's right-hand-man for the last four or five of those years, since Ronan became the alpha of his own circle. But this woman was different. Ronan didn't even think she was Irish. Although he supposed skin color and ethnic origins had little to do with nationality or love of country. She might be as keenly devoted to independence as he was.

But it still worried him that he had no sense of her as a person—or as a witch. She kept her magic dampened so that it wasn't easy to sense, although from what he could tell, she wasn't very powerful. And her perpetually blank expression gave away no hint of emotion, thoughts, or even humanity. She could be a golem, performing Donn's orders, except for that spark of magic. Golems were animated by magic, but could not do spells of their own.

"Good evening," Ronan said. "Donn's expecting me."

She opened the door wider, and Ronan stepped into the box. There was no sound from the stage or the crowd. The ward he'd passed through kept all of that out and assured that the conversation within was private.

"Ah, there ya are, Rory." Donn grinned. "I feared ya might not be coming." Why was Donn using his old cover?

"I'm here," Ronan agreed, shifting into the Mayo accent that had been an element of the Rory persona. He would play whatever role he needed.

"Good, good." Donn gestured at the witch. "I don't believe you were introduced to Miss Fina Toro at your last meeting."

"No, I wasn't." He inclined his head to her. "I'm very

pleased to make your acquaintance, Miss Toro." Though Ronan doubted that was her real name. It was too much of a coincidence that her surname would come from the Latin word for bull. But he wasn't about to mention it when there was another stranger seated a few feet away.

Donn gestured at the chair by his side. It was the same type that had been in the duchess's box, comfortable enough but not particularly lush. Yet Ronan hesitated to sit. He would be putting his back to the woman, and he did not want to do that.

I'll watch her. Sorcha's voice was only a tiny sound in his head, but it comforted him. She would warn him if he needed to act. He sat.

"Now, let me introduce you to my friend." Donn gestured at the other man in the front of the box. He was big, but in a portly sense. Donn was enormous, well over six feet and packed with muscle, and this man was average height but probably weighed the same. "Lord Kildunnen, this is Rory Donnelly. Rory, this is Patrick Moran, Baron Kildunnen"

"Pleased to meet you, Lord Kildunnen," Ronan said. Was Kildunnen someone who'd been acquainted with him, or known of him, back in the days when he'd been playing Rory? Ronan didn't recall the man, but that was years ago, and many men had hung around the edges of that scheme.

"And you, Mr. Donnelly. I've heard much of your contributions to our Cause." Kildunnen's voice was deeper than Ronan had expected, a soft bass with the lilt of Kilarney and the southwestern shores. He kept the frown of confusion entirely on the inside. He'd believed he knew all of the titled members of the Circles. Was Donn recruiting?

"I do what I can." He kept his tone light, nonchalant.

"And now I hear there's a prize to be had for a spot of burglary."

"Yes, I'm on a job that's paying well. It should fund a large quantity of munitions or bribes or whatever is needed."

Kildunnen's dismissive nod and fatuous smirk proclaimed that he recognized Ronan's deliberate side-steps, but no one in the box acknowledged the evasions.

"I believe I can help. Donn mentioned that your…items may find their way to the Tower of London. My maternal uncle is one of the Royal Fusiliers still stationed at the Tower. He's ridiculously loyal, but a bigger numpty you've never seen. I'm meeting him later, and I'll see what shakes loose when he's drunk and garrulous."

"I thank you for the help."

"Oh, it's no problem at all. Anything to help the Cause."

When he said it, the word made Ronan's stomach twist, and acid burned into his throat. There had to be another way.

"And how did your meeting go this morning?" Donn asked, drawing his attention away from Kildunnen.

Ronan had prepared this answer in advance. "Well enough. She had a name, but she's got nothing on him."

"A dead end, then?"

"Aye. But it's a question answered, anyway, and that's what matters. I've some of my crew with me, so once we know what Lord Kildunnen's uncle has to say, I'll take it from there."

Donn wasn't going to argue the point now, although Ronan had no doubts that he would attempt to commandeer whatever Ronan planned.

"I need to return to my client," Ronan said. "When do we meet again?"

"Day after tomorrow at noon. We'll go to the Tower and take a tour."

The day after tomorrow, Ronan needed to be on a train to Liverpool to receive a shipment of guns. But Donn wasn't supposed to hear about that. He sided with the segment of the Council that wanted to put the weapons to immediate use, rather than waiting until they had enough to incite real change.

In the end, the choice was between keeping Donn from the Wells, or taking that shipment. It was not a difficult decision.

At the Marquess of Hazelby's residence that evening, Ronan attempted to avoid everyone, including Sorcha. He didn't want to be recognized by Lord Hazelby, and he didn't want to have to lie to the woman who held all of his truths.

The duchess's husband found him wandering the back garden. He sidled up to Ronan and stared with him into the cloudy sky. After a long pause, he spoke. "My father spent the evening at his club, arranging a meeting for Etta with members of Parliament tomorrow. She's been courting this particular committee for the last six months, seeking support in her fight against the drain on English magic."

"Will they help her retrieve the Wells?"

"Maybe. Probably not. Parliament will be content to have them in custody. We're hoping to force the ministers to acknowledge the illegal nature of the seizure, and not to watch too closely should they...disappear back into our hands, lest we reveal damning information to the newspapers."

Ronan's jaw tightened and his mouth twisted with bitter humor. "Don't tell Sorcha. She dislikes blackmail."

"I wouldn't call this blackmail, but near enough."

"Do you need my help, or is this idle chatter?"

"I'm telling you because the committee member my father spoke to was Viscount Ashtondell."

Ronan's whole body went rigid, every muscle tensing, from his toes to his forehead. But he forced his voice to remain calm, nonchalant. "And?"

"Let's not pretend. You're the spitting image of him."

"Shite."

"Are you his bastard?"

Ronan nearly swung at Malcolm. He checked his fist and noted with reluctant admiration that the other man hadn't flinched.

"No." Ronan spat the word. "He was wed to my mother when I was born. Had been wed to her for eleven months. Stayed wed to her for nearly another ten years, three miscarriages, and two stillborn girls." He made his finger straighten, though tension still stiffened the joints. "Then she started fighting him on tenant's rights on the Irish properties he'd gotten in the marriage settlement. The depression hit, he started losing money, and we were a liability rather than an asset. He claimed she'd cuckolded him and I wasn't his son. He divorced her, sold off the properties, and married a young American heiress who sailed back to New York five years later with their daughter. Though as far as I know they're still legally married." He'd never seen the woman or his sister. Hadn't even learned their names. Told himself he didn't care to know.

"Father mentioned there'd been a scandal, but he didn't give me the particulars."

"What do you intend to do, now that you know?" Evie

trusted the duchess, and Ronan trusted Sorcha, but Malcolm and his father were unproven quantities.

"No matter what he said during the divorce proceedings, if your parents were married when you were born, you're still legally his son."

Ronan's pulse beat erratically in his ears, and his chest and shoulders tightened with tension. "I don't want to be anything to him. And that doesn't answer my question."

"My father thinks you should talk to him." The other man's open stance and relaxed posture were as cool and unruffled as a frozen lake. Ronan's insides were a choppy sea. "I assume you realize your older brothers are both dissolute gamesters?"

"I know." He bared his teeth in a false smile. "I once fleeced my oldest brother at cards for almost five hundred pounds. He had no idea who I was, even though I resemble our sire more than he does. But I spoke with a thick Irish accent, so he saw what he wanted to see."

"Are they not aware of you?"

"They knew me when we were boys." When he'd worshiped the ground they walked on. "But Edmund is ten years older than me, George twelve. I was not of much interest to them as an infant, and they were both young men pursuing their own lives during the divorce. They cared very little for their cuckoo little brother. Probably even less for our sister, poor girl." Ronan stopped that line of thought before it could go farther. The girl was with her mother, and he had a sister of the heart to worry about.

"In any case, the viscountcy is destitute again. He's cut off both boys, but it's too late. Sorcha introduced you as something of a shipping magnate, and Father believes, if you approached the viscount with an offer, he would have to take it, and then he'd be beholden to you."

Ronan released a long, heavy breath as his muscles relaxed. To have that power over his father...it would be heady, and possibly dangerous. And gods, how he wanted it. But why would Lord Hazelby suggest this course of action? "Aren't they friends?"

Mal barked a laugh. "Not in the slightest. My father has very little respect for peers who can't hold on to their property or navigate the waters of the new century that's nearly upon us. He made shrewd investments and is raking in profits. To him, your father is a relic at best, and an imbecile at worst."

This time, Ronan shared in the laughter. "More likely both. But my shipping company is only about seventy-five percent legitimate. I run several completely above-board vessels, but my flagship is manned by a totally republican crew, and we like to thumb our noses at the excisemen. A good portion of my profits are funneled back to the Cause, as my connections there are the reason the venture succeeded. If I offered to shore up the sinking viscountcy, my sire might discover my republican leanings. He'd repudiate me in an instant. I'd be jailed, and he'd obtain my profits as a reward."

"Ah," Mal said. "I see. So then I should tell Father to forget it?"

Ronan paused. He allowed the sensation of lightness to suffuse him at the idea of finally besting his sire. Then he thrust it away and rubbed at his temples. "I wish I could say otherwise—it would give me no greater pleasure than to make the old man squirm as he was forced to accept my help —but I can't risk it."

"Fair enough. I won't mention the smuggling or Irish independence to my father, though. He's a liberally-minded man in the sense that he claims happy people spend more money and make him richer, but he would feel obligated to report treason."

Ronan dropped the hand from his forehead and deliberately stared into Malcolm's eyes. "I don't consider it treason."

The blue gaze met his, unwavering. "Neither do I, which is why I won't be reporting you."

Ronan shifted, widening his stance as though he would need to throw a punch to defend his views. "You truly believe Ireland should be free?"

"I do, and Scotland, too." Mal's posture never changed, though he quirked a grin at Ronan's suspicion. "But I can't guess whether it will happen for any of us. Perhaps you'll find it first. You at least have the luxury of water between you and the English. We have to share an island with them." Malcolm's accent broadened as he spoke into something much closer to Sorcha's. So far, he'd only used inflections that were pure Harrow.

"I didn't realize you were Scottish."

His shoulders shifted, not quite in a shrug, but more in evidence of discomfort. "I'm not, really. My father's line is all English as far back as you can trace. My mother's line is, too, with the one exception of my great-grandmother Horatia, who was a Fay MacLeod before her marriage, and all Scots. But from what I recall of her, she tried to be even more English than the English." He waved that off. "In any case, my mother's dowry included a Highland estate, and I spent a large portion of my childhood there."

"That explains the accent. But do you consider yourself Scottish, or English?"

Malcolm pondered that for a moment. Ronan appreciated the time. He'd often wondered who he would have become if his father hadn't thrown him and his mother away. Would he be like Mal, a man drawn back to his mother's people and his mother's land, who saw himself as one of them, or would he have become another copy of George and Edmund?

"Scottish." Mal leaned against an arch covered with green leaves. "It's Lilias's fault."

"The first duchess?"

"Aye. She lived until I was fourteen, so she was a not insignificant figure in my life until that point. My sister and I were the only ones of our siblings to develop magic, and she took an interest in us. She trained us herself, rather than through the school, and she was as Scots as it is possible to be. She spoke like Sorcha, in that musical accent from the Hebrides, and she had little time for social niceties or strictures. She was a pragmatist—and a hellion. I loved her. But she was also stubborn, and unyielding. She had very high expectations of everyone in the family, especially the girls. I assume she knew I would one day marry Etta, because I was the only male in the family singled out for her attention."

This Lilias sounded like a right bitch, though one that had managed to capture the loyalty of her descendants. "Sorcha said she made an oath to her, and then again to the other duchesses, to protect the Fay property on Skye. She takes that very seriously."

"I know, and it's unfortunate. This is only the second time Sorcha has ever left Scotland. We can convince her to travel to clan events in the Highlands—births and weddings and such—but she's only come to London once."

He hadn't known those precise details, but he could have guessed. She was so alone on her island. He hated for her to go back there and return to that solitary existence of duty and family pressures. But the only life he could offer her was even worse.

Sorcha fidgeted in the forward-facing seat beside Etta

on the way to an afternoon concert hosted by the Countess of Wrothem. The Earl of Wrothem was the head of a parliamentary committee that oversaw the Ministry of Defence, and Etta had been courting him all Season. He'd agreed to grant her a brief interview today, along with Viscount Clastery, the head of the committee that handled home affairs, including oversight of the Home Office. If all went well, they, Etta, and Lord Hazelby would then approach the Home Secretary, the Defence Secretary, and the Prime Minister on the issue of the magic drain and the use of the Wells to buttress their rapidly-eroding magic stores.

"Don't worry," Lord Hazelby said. Sorcha flushed, embarrassed that he'd noticed her nervousness. "Afternoon events are more relaxed than evening affairs. You'll do well."

Mal grinned at her. "I won't leave your side, I promise."

"He stuck with me when I first started attending these things," Etta said. "Try not to howl at his jokes."

Right. If Etta could do this after growing up on a mountainside in America, so could Sorcha. She flattened her hands on her thighs and tried to relax.

As soon as she stopped worrying about the coming social maze, she remembered that Ronan hadn't come to her last night. And he'd been gone again this morning, leaving only a note that said he had business to see to. She'd understood. After all, he'd not contacted the rest of his ships since he first stumbled onto Skye. He'd need to contact his Dublin office and his captains.

But he hadn't spoken of his meeting with Lady Wiltbury in the park, and he hadn't made love to her last night. What had he done in order to acquire the information about Mage-Captain Blake?

The carriage halted, and Lord Hazelby helped Sorcha down. They moved as a group into the house, and then after introductions were made, broke off in pairs: Lord Hazelby and Etta going one way, Mal and Sorcha another.

Mal drew her along to a group by a refreshment table. He was greeted by one of the men, and Mal introduced Sorcha to everyone. Not that she would remember any names. And then her gaze caught on a familiar profile across the room. She startled, and whirled.

But no, it wasn't Ronan. Although the man with very similar features. He was much older, probably in his sixties, with steel-grey hair that had begun to go white at his temples. He was clean-shaven, though, which made the resemblance to Ronan even more striking. So many of the men here had mustaches, muttonchops, or full beards.

She nudged Malcolm. "Who is that, talking to Etta?"

Mal followed her gaze. "That's Viscount Ashtondell." His focused gaze filled with curiosity, as though she ought to have identified that already.

Viscount? "Is he on one of the committees she's courting?"

"He is. The home affairs committee."

"He looks…familiar."

Mal sighed. "I shouldn't tell you this, but I think you deserve to know."

"Deserve to know what?"

"That's Ronan's sire."

"His…sire?" Why use that word, and not father?

"He tossed Ronan and his mother out when he was a boy, and called him another man's bastard. But it's pretty clear that was a lie."

Sorcha sucked in a ragged breath. This was a portion of the past Ronan wouldn't talk about, part of the life he kept from her and was ashamed to have her see. But Mal was right. She deserved this knowledge. Tonight, she was going to make him talk about it.

ETTA SUCCEEDED IN GETTING HER INTERVIEW, BUT WHILE THE most powerful men in the Empire agreed that her conclusions were sound, and they wanted her help deciding what to do next, they claimed ignorance on the location of the Wells.

"Probably because Her Majesty is mixed up in this," Etta speculated to Mal and Sorcha that evening after they finally returned home. The three of them sat in the small family parlor upstairs. The housekeeper said Evie had gone to bed and Ronan hadn't been seen since he came in a few hours before.

Etta settled onto a loveseat and propped her feet on the small table. Definitely not the actions of a woman trained from birth to be a duchess. "The queen can't actually tell them what to do, but she can make their lives difficult in a thousand ways if they cross her. So they won't give the Wells back to me, but if I return with them in my possession, they will gladly discuss terms for their use." She rubbed at her temples. "I hate politics."

Mal sat beside her and shifted her so he could rub her back. "But you're so good at them, love."

"Ugh," she muttered. "I should have stayed on my mountain. My cabin was perfect. I had to walk for a half hour before I would encounter another human being."

"I rather prefer having you within arm's reach." Mal squeezed her shoulders. Sorcha made an excuse and left them alone. The affection didn't embarrass her or make her uncomfortable. It was only that their obvious devotion made her heart sore.

She would never have that with Ronan if he wouldn't trust her with the truth about himself.

He wasn't in her room, so she located his.

He sat in a nightshirt in a chair by the fireplace. It wasn't lit, but a paraffin lamp had been placed on the mantle. There were gaslamps in the room, but he hadn't lit them.

"I saw your father today," she said without preamble.

He startled and leapt from his seat. "You what?"

She walked calmly toward him and sat in the other chair. "He was at the concert, speaking to Etta. I thought he was you at first glance, until I realized he was too old."

Ronan's body trembled, and he sat back, hard. "How did you know?"

"Mal confirmed it." No need to tell Ronan that she hadn't known the truth until Mal told her. She'd been intrigued by the resemblance, but would not have made that leap on her own.

"I would like you to confide in me about your past, Ronan. You keep saying I don't belong in your world, in your life. But I want to decide that for myself. That means you have to tell me."

He stood abruptly and went to a cabinet. Inside was a decanter full of golden liquid and two glasses. He dashed several finger's-worth of liquor into each glass and handed her one, then sat. She'd expected brandy but tasted very fine Scotch whisky.

Ronan took a healthy swallow, then spoke. He told her of his earliest memory: his parents fighting. Of moving permanently to Ireland when they separated and then divorced. Of being shuffled between houses until a distant cousin took them in. How he'd been sent to school more out of annoyance than kindness. And then ripped away from school when the cousin died. Of his mother running off and dying in America, and his work in a gaming hell in Dublin. Then meeting Donn and finding his Cause, and finally finding Evie.

"My father threw me away when I was barely ten years old," he said. "My mother tried, but she had a temper, and we never got on as we ought. Then she found a man who promised her riches in the new world, and she ran off with him. So I didn't recognize what family was until I was twenty-five years old and a thirteen-year-old waif tried to pick my pocket."

He ran a hand through his hair, which pulled a few of the strands free from their tie. They fell into his face. She wanted to sit on his lap and stroke them, to trace the line of his forehead and his brow, now furrowed with tension.

So she went to him, plopped on his thighs, and put her fingertips on his face.

"I already told you that my mother loved too much and not enough, all at once. I never had a father. The duchess treated me as something more than a servant but less than family. So if you're trying to frighten me away by saying you have no idea how to be in a relationship, it isn't going to work. Because neither do I."

Her lips were only a breath away from his, and it took no effort at all to close that final distance. He resisted, at first, and a tendril of magic tickled the back of her mind, a reminder that he'd gone to Lady Wiltbury and come back with information. If he'd done what she assumed he must have to obtain it—

But he was fragile now, and he needed her acceptance, not her suspicions. So she shoved the worry deep and slid her tongue along the seam of his mouth. Finally, he opened, with a groan that told her he didn't want to give in but couldn't help himself. She wouldn't allow him to doubt, not now. She wouldn't allow anyone else in this kiss or in their bed. Tomorrow he might confess what he'd done, and rip another piece of her heart away. But tonight, he'd given her a piece of his. That would have to be enough.

And even if he had done what she suspected, while it

would hurt, it wouldn't change anything. Because damn him, and damn her, she loved him.

She broke away to murmur, *"Tha gaol agam ort.* Forever." He didn't respond, except to stand, and lead her to the bed. And when they mingled their bodies and their magic, she understood he was trying to tell her in the only way he could that he loved her, too.

Evie insisted on going to the Tower with Ronan. Sorcha, Etta, and Mal went as well, but separately, so as not to spook Donn with their presence.

Ronan tried not to think of Sorcha out there on the grounds, or about the possibility that Donn had brought his team, and she was in danger. No, not possibility. High probability.

Ronan very much feared that this afternoon would end with an attempt to steal back the Wells, whether he wanted to do it now or not.

Donn engaged the Yeoman Warder who led their group of tourists in conversation, asking questions and receiving colorful answers about the history of the place and the many prisoners and deaths the Tower had seen.

Evie watched everything, using skills long-honed by their days on the streets of Dublin and even, twice, London. They'd merged a dash of magic before they arrived so they could speak mind-to-mind, and she kept him apprised of what she noticed, like the number of guards posted, the size of other tourist groups, and various methods of ingress and egress from each location they toured.

Lord Kildunnen's uncle was not a warder, only an infantryman quartered here at the Tower. He'd been more than happy to chat about his current home, and had given Kildunnen information about a few places they could use to hide or as shortcuts between towers.

His information had not helped them discover the precise location of the Wells. This tour was meant to provide Ronan with the chance to scout using the tracking spell. He was nearly certain the Wells were in the White Tower, in the munitions storage with the army's other weaponry, but he would have preferred to draw closer to be sure. Unfortunately, that was one area not on the tour. The crown jewels could be seen by anyone who wanted, kept safe behind iron and magic, but the Ministry of Defence did not want to reveal their armament capabilities.

That makes sense, Evie thought to him. *And meshes with what our source said about the guard rotations.* The guards were positioned all around the Tower, but the bulk of them—and the on-site garrison—were stationed at the White Tower.

Something's not right, he thought back. *Not with the Wells, I mean. With Donn. He shouldn't be so visible. That Yeoman Warder is going to remember him. And possibly us, by association.*

Yes, but he's going to remember a good tourist who asked funny questions. If anyone asks, he's not going to consider him suspicious.

I still don't trust him. I don't know where Kev is, or that new witch he's taken on. They could have a lot more information from Kildunnen's uncle than what he passed on.

He probably does. So we stick with him and leave the rest to the duchess. She's capable. As is your Seeress.

She's not mine, *Evelyn.*

Oh, yes, she is. It's plain for anyone with eyes to see. Now, whether you decide to be hers is another story yet to be told.

Let's stay focused on the task at hand.

Evie sent him a playful mental nudge and ceased teasing him. He loved her to distraction, but there were times when he wished he hadn't acquired a little sister.

Sorcha followed Etta and Mal past the tower where the crown jewels were held and glanced back at the White Tower. Every instinct she had told her the Wells were there, but running off from her group to investigate would rouse suspicion. Instead, she listened to Mal, who had gone to school with the son of a Warder and knew stories about the history of the Tower. Unfortunately, much of that boy's knowledge of was useless, as the Tower had undergone "improvements" to the buildings and layout of the fortress.

One entire tower had been rebuilt to better match some architect's ideas of medieval life. Sorcha tried to wrap her brain around the fact that an actual medieval structure had been demolished in order to better match what someone believed or imagined about the period, but couldn't.

She took advantage of the demolition that had cleared a visitor's view of the White Tower, and stopped scanning the grounds when she recognized the witch from Spitalfields. Fina Toro wore a female Fusilier's uniform with a witch-badge, a sign that she was the magic-user assigned to a particular infantry brigade. With most of the regiment housed in Hounslow, she might actually be able to fool the soldiers here.

Sorcha tapped Etta's shoulder. Once she had the duchess's attention, she gestured with her chin toward the masquerading witch.

"Damn," Etta said, her voice barely above a breath. "Ronan was right. They're plotting something. They're going to try now, while the place is full of people and the guards are distracted."

"What do we do?" Sorcha asked.

Etta pivoted to her husband. "You're the one who's had battle training. What do you think?"

"First, we all link. Then one of us shadows her. The others hang back, watching for accomplices. We stay close enough together to help with casting, and Sorcha contacts Ronan to tell him what's happening."

Sorcha immediately put that component of the plan into effect. It was easy to find him, perhaps because they'd merged so many times lately, or because their magic was so well-suited to each other. *Donn's witch is here. We don't see Mr. O'Malley yet, but I'm sure he's here, and probably others we haven't met. Fina is wearing a Fusilier uniform. They must have gotten it from Lord Kildunnen's uncle.*

Ronan's thoughts came back to her from the far side of the Tower grounds. *Damn. I knew he was going to try something. Keep an eye out, and be ready for anything. The tracking spell shows the Wells in the White Tower, probably in the lower levels with the munitions storage as we guessed. We'd better go for them now, before he has a chance. If you can make your way there by the route we discussed earlier, I'll try to meet you.*

No! Don't make Donn suspicious. I can do it alone. I'm very good at glamours and wards, as you know. She made those last three words a reminder of the night he'd stood naked on her beach, and she'd wrapped herself in moon and starlight to hide from his angry eyes. The night her heart had taken a short tumble out of her chest and landed at his feet.

Dark God take you, a chuisle, a chroí. Don't put yourself in danger.

We're all in danger, a ghràidh. I can do this. No one will see me. Tha gaol agam ort.

She broke the contact, but not before she felt the swelling

of fear and panic in his heart. He would have to trust her, and do what was best for all of them.

"I'm going to go," she said aloud, but softly. "Ronan says they're most likely in the munitions depot below the White Tower. You watch for mischief."

"I'll stay to watch," Etta said, "but Mal goes with you. If you're discovered, he's better than you at fighting his way out of trouble."

Sorcha wished she could refute that, but it was true enough. Active battle spells were not her forte. "Let's link, then," she said instead. Etta and Mal each took one of her hands, and Etta initiated the merge. With Etta in control, Mal and Sorcha could focus on casting other spells while Etta held the link together.

Their group started to move off, circling around the central fortress, and Etta pulled all of them into a shadowy space made where two buildings butted together at an odd angle. Sorcha guessed this was a section of the later renovations, as no medieval architect would be so stupid as to create such an obvious point of shelter for an enemy who managed to breech the curtain wall.

Once in shadow, Sorcha opened her Sight and attuned herself to the local magic currents. There was water from the nearby river, plant energy from trees on Tower Hill, human energy from the crowds who had flocked to the Tower on this mild summer day. But the most abundant source was the one she found easiest to use. Sunlight.

She scattered sun dapples around their nook to hide her weaving, then crafted a glamour. It would both confuse the eye and deflect attention. If the guards were alerted to their presence, it would not keep a determined searcher from seeing them, but it should work on the complacent tourists and the ceremonial guard who stood staring into the middle distance at nothing in particular.

Good luck, Etta thought to them once the glamour was in place. They advanced from the alcove and down Tower Hill to the White Tower.

I'll watch for wards and inversions, Mal thought. *You make sure to adjust the glamour as necessary.*

They made it to the side entrance they'd been directed to use, a secret door spelled to look and feel like an unbroken stretch of white stone wall. Sorcha reached for the hidden latch, and then her intuition screamed. She gagged and nearly threw up onto the gravel path.

Mal, we shouldn't go this way.

He pulled her close while she shuddered from the after-effects of nausea. *Is it a set-up?*

Yes. I feel like I'm going to vomit when I contemplate gripping that door latch.

Then we go another way. You lead, and I'll follow.

Sorcha took a step backward, then another, and the nausea subsided. Another step and it was gone. She took a deep, cleansing breath, using more of the sunlight to enhance the glamour and open her mind to the possibilities of the universe.

No outcome was ever completely assured, but over the years she'd learned to tell when she should and should not heed her magic's warnings. This was one of the times when disaster would have followed them through the door. She let her gaze go fuzzy and trusted her instincts to tell her the best way to go.

To the east. She tugged Mal in that direction, and they moved slowly around the White Tower. They reached the corner and her heart seized in her chest. She pivoted. Ronan had come, even though she'd begged him not to.

He stood at the door, checking for anyone nearby. She flung her magic toward him, but he'd already grabbed the latch and pushed. It opened easily, and someone's hand grabbed his coat and yanked him inside.

She would have screamed for him and to the hells with secrecy if Mal hadn't grabbed her around the waist with one hand and clamped the other over her mouth.

You mustn't, Sorcha. We'll never get him back if we give ourselves away now.

Where the hells is Evie? That was Etta, who must be watching through Mal's eyes.

I'm here. Evie appeared coming from the other direction, wrapped in an illusion of a male Fusilier. She must have caught the attempt that Sorcha had made to link with Ronan, because she walked right to them despite the glamour. She took Sorcha's hand and entered their merge. *Donn disappeared, literally, and Ronan rushed off here to meet you. I took a different path.*

Are you still linked with him? Sorcha's mental voice was so loud Evie winced. The male face she wore flinched as though he'd been bitten by a hornet, proof that she'd overdone the glamour.

Yes, but he's not responding. I felt something, probably a sleep spell.

We have to find him. Sorcha tried to force down the frantic worry, but it refused to go.

We will, Etta soothed. *Fina is still here, just standing. Whatever plot they have in motion, her role hasn't started yet. Evie, please check for any ambient spells and relay them to me.*

Evie scanned the grounds and listed all of the usual wards, some practical spells in the lodging areas, and a few trapwards in places where visitors were not supposed to go. *Ah, there it is. Something like a sleep or suppression field, and a lookaway suggestion. They're moving into the White Tower. If they go deeper, I won't be able to track them. I'm not good underground.*

I am. My element is earth. Evie, you swap with me and keep an eye on the witch. I'll go with Sorcha and Mal.

The two women moved quickly, and rather than maintain the illusory Fusilier, Etta asked Sorcha to bring her under the glamour. It would stretch Sorcha's abilities to keep three people hidden, and she hoped they would make it far enough into the building before she tired too much to hold the threads together.

The aversion to the door was gone, so Sorcha led them the same way Ronan had been taken. But Fina appeared first. She stood guard in front of the door, waiting for her compatriots to return. *I'll draw her off,* Evie sent, and dropped her glamour. She ran at the Italian witch, tossing spells that burst with angry pops around the woman's head. Then she switched to a slash that would have done real damage if Fina hadn't twisted away and darted for the shelter of the wooden staircase that led to the main entrance. The woman flung a hastily-constructed burst behind her. Evie dodged it, but it whistled far too close to Sorcha, exploding against the stones by her head. A fragment of rock flew away from the impact and scored a line across her cheek. The glamour wavered.

Evie chased after Fina, and Etta opened the secret door, pushing Sorcha inside. Etta was on her heels, and then Mal pulled the door shut.

A spike of pain from Evie struck them all at once.

Are you hit? Mal sent to her.

I'm fine. She clipped me with another nasty spell, but I can take it. She's sticking tight to her hiding place.

We're inside, so clear out, Etta ordered.

No. She's staying under cover. I think she needs to be here for whatever Donn has planned. I'm going to try and force her into the open.

We need you keeping watch, Etta insisted. *If you two fight much more, you'll bring the whole guard station down on us. Cut and run, Evie.*

Gods damn it. Fine. But I am keeping her in my sights.

Understood.

Sorcha rubbed the cut on her face. It stung, and her fingers came away wet with blood. But it was only a scratch. She started to move into the building, and Etta stayed her with a tap on her elbow.

Dressed stone blocks surrounded them, chinked with ancient plaster and worn smooth on the floor by hundreds of years of footwear passing through the corridors. Etta pointed to the right. *That way.*

Sorcha stretched the glamour further to muffle their steps. It was nearly to the breaking point. A single curious guard could have pierced it even now.

We have to do this fast. The glamour won't hold for long and I don't have enough magical sources in here except myself. You two need to hold your strength for other things.

Already her internal magic strained with the effort of the spell, translating that strain into a physical experience like carrying a stone slab over her shoulder. She whispered a prayer to the goddess that she would have enough strength to make it to Ronan.

Etta took the lead, tracking the sleeping spell used on Ronan. Now that Evie had used her talent to identify the unique signature of the weave to Etta, the duchess could follow it even through layers of rock, earth, and wood.

They passed through a larger hall, where someone had displayed everyday items from the sixteenth century. They didn't stop to contemplate Henry VIII's bowls or Elizabeth's cutlery, however. At a side entrance, Mal stopped them with a hand on both of their upper arms. *There's a ward here. Sorcha, can you—?*

She had already stepped forward and eased the few

threads of her magic that she could spare into the ward. It was a fairly standard working, and it was easy to convince the spell that her glamour was another fragment of itself. It accepted them and no alarm was raised as they passed through. But the stone slab she carried had transformed into a ship's anchor, and her feet had begun to drag with every step.

If I have to do another, I'm going to lose the glamour, Sorcha warned. *I can't keep this up with all three of us.*

The next hallway wasn't warded at all. The first barrier was meant to keep visitors out of the guard quarters and recreational areas. At one intersection, they all froze as two guardsmen strode down the cross passage. Mal took two hasty steps back out of their way, but the men didn't notice. They argued good-naturedly about a gaming loss and the merits of a particular whore who was supposed to bring good luck if she sat on a man's lap when he tossed the dice.

Sorcha trembled. One of the men glanced up at the intersection, but his thoughts were too full of his conversation and his gaze slid over the glamour and past them.

The men cleared the corridor, and Sorcha huffed out her long-held breath when the sound of their footfalls receded past earshot.

Etta waved Sorcha and Mal on. They passed a mess with long lines of trestle tables and came to a stairwell spiraling down.

There's another ward here, Mal warned.

I'm going to have to release the glamour once we're through. It's nearly finished anyway. And letting it go would keep her from having to crawl.

This ward took a good deal more convincing than the last. If it had been anchored to a keystone, she'd not have been able to change it, but though it was more complicated and powerful than the first one, it was still the sort that had to be renewed each day, likely by a mage or witch assigned to the Fusiliers or the Yeoman Wardens.

Finally, she coaxed it to accept her glamour, and they started down the twisting stone steps. Sorcha had to clutch the wall at the sudden lightness in her body once the glamour lifted.

One floor below, the last shreds of the glamour dissipated into the rapidly cooling air, and she drew in a cleansing breath. Though the heavy weight was gone, so were most of her magical resources. She wouldn't be able to offer much assistance in whatever they faced next.

Something's big and powerful ahead, Mal thought, *and it's drawing in heat like an inverse bonfire.*

That would be the munitions ward, Sorcha thought. *I won't be able to trick it, so we're going to have to cross it and face the consequences. This is the part where I hoped speed and stealth would win the day.*

We'll have to hope that Donn's come up with something. Etta's mental voice was wry and not amused.

Donn plans to trip the wards and leave Ronan as a scapegoat. The idea had come to her the farther they traveled, and the truth of it rang in her mind, making her words confident.

They were nearly at the bottom now, and her intuition was talking again. This time, it warned her that something irrevocable was about to happen. But it did not give her any helpful suggestions about how to assure that the outcome was in their favor and not Donn's.

The three of them exited the stair into a cave-like room stuffed with rifles, cannon, swords, bayonets, and artillery shells. On the far side of the room was a massive steel door, standing open. Voices issued from the other side, and Mal lifted a finger to his lips and then his ear to indicate that they should be quiet and listen.

"This man here is a known smuggler, thief, and Fenian.

He's worth a lot if you were the one to bring him in. And I'm willing to make the pot as sweet as you'd like." It was Donn's voice, but with a slight east-end accent, as though he were someone who'd worked his way up from the streets here in England and not an Irish Republican.

"I'm not interested in your 'pot,' be it sweet, bitter, or sour." The other man's accent was pure British boarding school, the vowels alternately elongated and clipped, the consonants sharp and distinct. "And it seems to me I have three criminals worthy of capture, not one. Why should I accept a single man when I could have all of you?"

"With all due respect, sir, there's only the one of you, and there's the two of us."

"I don't believe there's any respect due to you, so I shall not offer it. Instead, I offer you an ultimatum. Put down your weapons and surrender to the queen's justice, or I will bind you with the spell that gives pain and nightmares rather than one which simply restricts your movements."

It's time to make our appearance, Etta thought. *Before they start tossing magic and bullets about.*

I'll lead, shall I? Mal stepped forward, with a shield spell nearly complete on his one hand and a blast of power partially formed on the other. He entered the room first and Sorcha felt the blast of power release, and then the shield pulse into life. Then she was in the room, too. The lines of the shield stretched between Donn and Kevin O'Malley lying prone on one side, and Mage-Captain Lucien Blake on the other with Ronan at his feet. Donn and O'Malley would have been stunned by Mal's spell, while Ronan still slept under the influence of the sleep-net.

Blake had a pistol and his own spell at the ready, and he leveled the pistol at Mal, Sorcha, and Etta as they entered. "That kind of shield can only withstand three or perhaps four direct hits. This weapon holds six rounds." He held the unfinished threads of the spell far too close to Ronan's prone form, and Sorcha's heart seized with fear. Blake saw her reaction, and deliberately extended the hand toward Ronan.

"Bluster all you like," Etta said. "I'm here for what is mine."

The duchess marched through the room, ignoring everything but the black bag that sat on a shelf behind Blake. Sorcha watched her and trembled. If he hurt Ronan, she would never forgive herself.

Etta stopped beside the shield. "You recognize me?" He nodded. "Then hand the Wells over and we won't hurt you."

"To hurt me, you must drop this shield. I need do nothing to have this man in my power."

Sorcha couldn't help it. The words burst out before she even knew she was going to speak. "Like you had Rebecca in your power?"

He froze, and the threads of the spell he held tangled. Whether that was a welcome development or an unfortunate one, she couldn't determine yet. He stared at Sorcha. His eyes were brilliant blue and cold as a Highland winter. "I don't know how you discovered that name, *Seeress*, but you are very much mistaken." He nearly spat the words, particularly her title. Did he understand how much the name chafed?

She clutched her skirts to hide the shaking of her hands, but she suspected everyone in the room could feel her fear, infusing the magical energy that swirled around them. "I Saw how much you hurt her. You've been hurting people for a long time, but I know why."

His cold anger lit to furious rage, all the more sinister because he kept it tightly controlled. It burned like a gas jet, so hot and concentrated it blazed as blue as his eyes. "Do not presume to comprehend anything about me."

"I told you, I've Seen you. I Saw what they did to you, how they beat you until you broke, and then taught you that hurting others give you power."

"I hurt no one unnecessarily." His voice was still even-toned, but there was a vibration underneath, as though his fury had become a physical thing, impossible to contain. The spell threads pulsed with extra energy. Either they would tangle and fall apart, or burst and possibly hurt both him and Ronan.

She placed her hand against the shield and met his searing blue gaze. "Why was hurting Rebecca necessary?"

Another spike of heat somehow cascaded between them, though nothing could have gotten through the shield. There was self-disgust there now, not just rage. "It is none of your business, but that harpy never let a man hurt her in her life. She used me, and had the temerity to pretend tragic heart-break when I chose to disentangle myself from her clutches."

The truth of his words cast a beam of unwanted illumina-tion, confirmed by her suddenly helpful intuition. Memories of the visions cascaded through her mind, filtered through this new knowledge. He did not enjoy violence and pain. They were tools he'd learned to wield, but with precision and restraint, not malicious abandon.

Sorcha hunched inward against the sudden urge to vomit. How could she have been so wrong?

"I...I'm sorry."

Etta pulled Sorcha away from the barrier. "I have no idea

what you two are talking about, but what I care about is my property, which you had no writ or warrant to seize."

"I was under direct orders from the queen." He spoke to Etta but still watched Sorcha.

"The queen isn't above the law. Your actions were theft, no matter who gave you the order."

Blake's head swiveled in a slow, deliberate motion toward Etta. "They are too powerful to be in private hands." He stared her down, his eyes again cold. But he'd relaxed back into his defensive pose as he shifted his attention away. The spell he held did not reshape. In fact, it began to unravel.

Sorcha had distracted him from his threat to Ronan, even if she'd been very, very wrong about him. He wasn't afraid, and he wasn't cruel, and his words were not a justification of his actions, only a statement of fact.

Etta might have been born in a one-room cabin in the Appalachians, but she stared back at Blake with all the hauteur and power of a woman born to lead. "I plan to utilize them for the public good. I am currently discussing terms with Parliament on a fair contract for their use."

A flicker of surprise crossed Blake's face, betrayed by the barest twitch of an eyebrow, the slightest tilt of his head. "You're lying. You'd say anything to reclaim them."

"I might, but I don't have to. Amelia lied to you." He flinched, but not in surprise now. In anger. He was more than willing to believe the queen's sorceress had been playing him false. Perhaps because he'd already suspected it. How hard had he been forced to argue to bring the Wells here to the Tower?

Even so, he asked, "What did Lady Falcestershire lie about?"

"She and the queen have coveted these since she first suspected we had them last year. But there is no law that forbids my clan from holding those items."

"No? My understanding is that the act in question states all Wells are to be under the protection of the army and to be used only at the direction of the Prime Minister and with the agreement of Parliament."

"It doesn't state 'all Wells.' It refers by name to the ones already held by the Crown at the time the act was passed. Parliament's intention was to take the right to use them away from the King." She continued to stare at him. "If the law were on Amelia's side, she'd have taken them by legal means. Don't you suppose?"

"Perhaps, but the spirit of the law is that only the Government may have custody."

"And the letter of the law allows my clan to have them. You are sworn to uphold the letter of the law, are you not?"

Blake scowled. "If these are spoils of war from France, then they do not belong to your clan. I was told the first duchess acquired them during the war with Napoleon."

"I already told you, Amelia lied. She had no idea how we got them. But I can assure you that Lilias made them. She outlined the process meticulously in her journals."

Blake's eyes widened. "Dark God."

"I'm not going to share that knowledge, and the journals are warded so only the current duchess can read them. I'm half-tempted to destroy those particular entries, anyway. But that's irrelevant at the moment. Those Wells have sat quietly at Fay House since Lilias created them fifty years ago."

"Why would she make such things if not as a weapon?"

"That may have been her intention when she made the first one, the little one. But after what happened when she used it..." Etta's voice trailed off. "She never wanted anything like that to happen again. She made the bigger ones because someone is draining magical power from England, and she couldn't stop it. She couldn't even find anyone to believe her and help her uncover what was going wrong. But the drain is much more powerful now, and the proof far more difficult to ignore. I've had a meeting with the Home Secretary, the Defence Secretary, and the Prime Minister, and all agreed that the situation has grown dire. I mentioned that I had a...temporary solution that had briefly gone astray. No one admitted outright to having taken my property, but it was strongly suggested that—should I find the objects once again in my possession—we could discuss terms for their use."

"It is very easy to check your story. This room is equipped with a telephone. It rings in the barracks, and their line goes directly to the Ministry of Defence."

"Please call. We'll wait." Etta settled into a relaxed pose, and Blake backed away and lifted a telephone receiver from the wall, never taking his eyes off them. He spoke to someone on the other end of the line, then waited.

Ronan's body lay near Blake's feet in a position that would leave him with sore muscles and stiff joints, but otherwise, he seemed intact. He had no obvious bruises or injuries that she could see from here. She longed to go to him, but she dared not breech Mal's shield. When she glanced back at Blake, intending to check that he was still in the same place, she stopped, arrested. He watched her with an intensity that made her hot and cold at once.

This man had lived outside of her property for nearly a year, had entered her house more than once, had invaded her privacy and her sanctuary. And yet he'd never taken advantage of his presence in the house. When she and Ronan had cast the reconstruction spell, they'd seen him searching, but never taking anything until the Wells, and never seeking to harm anyone except when it was necessary to escape detection. He avoided her rooms. He had a mission, and he carried it out, no deviations, embellishments, or extraneous action.

She'd seen so many images of his life, so many snippets of

his childhood and early adulthood. She'd assumed she knew him, understood him. She didn't understand at all.

He must have seen her, walking the property or in the village. He'd recognized her just now. So she met his gaze and waited.

The phone rang. He blinked, then lifted the earpiece from the cradle. He listened for another minute, thanked the caller, and hung up. Then he uncocked the pistol, holstered it, and closed his hands into fists to show he wasn't preparing any spells.

"It seems you are correct. I have been ordered to remand these items to your custody pending an official edict for their use."

Mal took his cue from Etta, who dipped her head in a single nod of acquiescence. He dispelled the shield, and Sorcha ran to Ronan.

"That man is a criminal," Blake said, and Sorcha's head snapped up. "I will give you the Wells, but he stays with me."

Sorcha stood over Ronan's body. "I don't think so. You stole from me, and you would have ripped my wards to pieces if he hadn't helped me. He has defended me and helped me recover what was not yours to take. You can't have him."

Etta stepped beside Sorcha. "Do you have any evidence that this man has committed a crime? Other than the word of this other man, who was actually in the act of committing a crime?"

Blake's expression didn't alter, but he did glance at Donn before shifting his attention back to Etta. "I do not personally hold evidence against him, but his compatriot here claims he's a known smuggler who has been remarkably capable at eluding the authorities, and worse, a Fenian."

Ronan paid very well to elude the authorities. He'd told her that not a single port in England was run by an honest man. But Sorcha felt no compulsion to share that information with Lucien Blake. He might be an honorable man, but his definition of honor was more rigid than hers.

"That man is the Fenian." Sorcha pointed at Donn. "They both are. I heard him using a London accent with you, but he's as Irish as they come. His name is Michael McCauley, and the Republicans call him Donn. I wouldn't believe a word he tells you."

Etta sent a warning message into Sorcha's mind to stop while she was ahead. Out loud, she said, "That one comes with us. I don't care what you do with the others."

Blake watched Etta for another long moment, then Sorcha. His eyes were intensely blue, but no longer with burning rage or cold control. No, now they were bright, and as warm as a painting she'd once seen of ocean water in the tropics. Then he handed the bag to Etta. "Retrieve him. Leave the others." He marched to the door and waited for them.

Etta used the link to ask Evie to meet them at the carriage. Mal hoisted Ronan over his shoulder. Sorcha followed the duchess and her husband from the little room, and Blake followed her. He escorted them up the steps and out of the White Tower, then across the grounds to the public entrance.

Sorcha moved toward the line of waiting carriages, angling for the one which bore the Clan Fay badge. Blake grasped her arm and stopped her. She twisted in shock and her magic tingled at the contact. "What?"

"You deserve better than that scoundrel."

"Says the man who repeatedly entered my home and disrupted my life." She shifted her arm away. He didn't follow.

"I am sorry for the necessity. I didn't wish for you to be harmed by my actions. I attempted to lessen the impact of my presence in your life."

"That doesn't excuse what you did, or make it better."

"No, and for that, I must beg your forgiveness, though I do not expect to receive it." His expression held sincerity and honesty, two things she absolutely did not want to identify about Mage-Captain Lucien Blake. She needed him to be a villain now, not a misguided hero.

"You won't." Sorcha stepped away, but this time he wrapped his hand all the way around her wrist and squeezed. Not hard enough to hurt, but enough to assure that she realized he had the power to keep her. Her magic flared again, and its instant connection with his was both startling and frightening.

"How did you know to seek visions of me? I kept myself warded all of the time."

"I didn't seek them. They came to me." She tried to jostle her arm free. "Please unhand me, sir."

He didn't.

"I swear to you, I would have stopped them if I could."

His gloved fingers closed tighter over the soft wool of her sleeve, and he frowned and blinked rapidly in bafflement at her explanation. But he changed the subject rather than pursue it. "No matter what the duchess says, that man is trouble. Stay far away from him."

"I don't take orders from thieves." Sorcha wrenched her arm from his grasp and marched across the street. Etta still stood beside the carriage, waiting for her.

"What did he want?"

"Nothing important. Let's go."

She climbed up and settled into a seat beside Evie, but as they drove away she peered out the window. He stood at the gate, observing their departure. Until the carriage took them around a corner toward Seward House and he disappeared from view, Sorcha could not look away.

~

THEY REMOVED THE SLEEPING SPELL FROM RONAN, BUT THE effects would take a while to wear off, so they settled him into a bed and sought food. "What happens next?" Evie asked over a sumptuous feast provided by the Seward House cook. Everyone was starving after using so much magic. Evie sat on Sorcha's left, and Mal and Etta were across the table. Mal's father had gone to his club and not yet returned.

"I think it's time for me to go back to Skye," Sorcha said. "Although I suppose I'll be leaving the Wells here?"

Etta gestured with her fork. "The Wells need to stay here. I don't relish constructing an agreement that I can swallow to use them for the common good, but no matter what terms we come to, they'll need to be in London. But I don't see why you can't stay here, too."

Her mouthful of wine went down wrong, and Sorcha coughed. Evie patted her on the back, and Sorcha wiped at her watering eyes. Then she said, "But I'm the Keeper of the House."

"I can hear the capital letters when you say that." Etta rubbed at her eyebrow for a moment, closed in on herself like a hedgehog, rolled up to protect her sensitive middle. Then she dropped her hand and squared her shoulders, a decision made. "I read in her journals how Lilias made her sister take that oath, to protect Fay House, and each daughter after her until you. But it was wrong of her to do that."

The suggestion that Lilias had erred made Sorcha gasp. "The house needs to be protected. My line can't inherit the title, but we have the magic, so she thought it was best that we serve the clan in that way."

"I don't think it's best." Etta leaned closer, her dark eyes flashing. "I consider it slavery. You were a child when she made you swear the oath. I would have you make a decision now, as an adult."

Sorcha took another deep gulp of wine, this time for fortitude. Something fluttered wildly in her belly, and it seemed to be dancing in time to her erratic heartbeat. "Are you...displeased with me, after what's happened?"

Etta scoffed. "Of course not. I'm angry with myself for letting you stay up there alone so long. No one person, no matter how skilled in magic or how strong, should be expected to shoulder that responsibility alone."

"Lilias didn't trust anyone else."

"Lilias was paranoid. Trust me on that. She went through terrible experiences in the war against Napoleon, and they colored her view of the world. She became very...rigid and unbending. She lived in fear and acted accordingly. She forced my great-great grandmother to run away to America so she could marry the man she loved." Etta's usually open, pleasant expression hardened. "She enslaved your family line with an oath and mine with a geas. That geas killed my mother, and it drives me even now."

Sorcha gasped. "She did what?"

Etta nodded. "She summoned my mother in a vision and placed a geas on her. She wanted to be certain someone would continue fighting the magic drain in the future. But my mother's magic was too different, and the geas killed her, then passed to me."

"Great Goddess. I had no idea."

"So what I'm saying is that you should not feel bound by the oath you swore to her. If you want to leave Fay House and follow Ronan, you can do that. There are plenty of Fay family members who can watch the place. Some would even choose the solitude, though I'd like to see us open a new branch of the school there. But either way, living so far removed from other people doesn't suit you."

Something squeezed in Sorcha's chest. Etta was giving her permission to follow her heart. But would Ronan want her to come with him? In Portree, he'd not been able to tell her he would stay. When she'd told him she loved him, he hadn't been able to give her back the words. "I…I don't know what to do."

"I could also use your help here, as I said. I'm going to need someone to be in charge of the Wells, and I've promised the Home Secretary that I will begin forming a spell to find the source of the magic drain. Your intuition and visions will be an asset."

"I have to think about it. I've never considered a future not tied to Fay House."

"Take as much time as you need. You can still help with the spell while you're deciding. Don't rush back to Skye because you believe you need to. You don't."

That should have been a proposal of freedom, an offer to leap free from the chains of her oath and fly. Instead, the foundation beneath her crumbled away, and she feared she would not fly, but fall.

20

Ronan woke in the dark with a pounding headache. What had he been doing? Had there been whiskey involved?

He rubbed his temples and rolled. A tiny shaft of light pierced a crack in the drapes at the window, revealing the dim outlines of an unfamiliar room. The single piece of visible furniture was much more refined than in the places he usually woke after a night of over-indulgence. And he hadn't indulged heavily in a long time.

The pillow under his head was stuffed with soft feathers, the mattress equally plush and pliable as he shifted. He didn't have the hollow queasiness in his stomach that accompanied a hangover, just pain in his temples, so he didn't think he'd gotten drunk and blacked out.

A soft sound came from beside him. Someone was sharing the bed with him, someone who had a distinctive cloud of pale hair.

Sorcha. She was here. And alive.

The memories flooded back, of Donn disappearing, of Evie saying that whatever he'd planned must be starting, of running to the White Tower and the door that Kildunnen's contact had spoken of. Then, nothing.

He stroked Sorcha's hair, grateful that he could touch her, could revel in her softness and the heat of her magic tingling through her skin. After a moment, she woke, and shifted.

"You're awake. Thank the goddess." She started to rise, but he nestled beside her and drew her close.

"What happened?" he asked. The headache wasn't as bad lying flat, especially not with Sorcha tucked against him. She lifted a hand to his temple, and her magic flowed into him.

"You were placed under a sleeping spell. We took the talisman off you yesterday when we returned, but the spell didn't wear off right away, and we couldn't wake you." She did something as she rubbed him, perhaps a delving or a minor healing, because the headache eased and then ceased. "We think it was Kevin O'Malley who put the spell on you since a talisman was used. He carried you to the basement, where Donn was waiting. So was Lucien Blake. By the time Etta, Mal, and I arrived, Donn was trying to bargain with Blake. He offered to hand you over in exchange for the Wells."

"Did he, now?"

She slid her fingers down the side of his face and shifted so she could press her lips to his. It was a gentle kiss, filled with affection instead of passion, and that baffled him. Passion he understood. He desired her, and she desired him. But affection and passion had rarely shared space in his life before.

"He did. That's when we decided to move. Mal knocked out Donn and O'Malley and tossed up a shield so Blake couldn't attack us. Etta was resplendent. She never appeared more like a duchess than last night. She demanded he give her the Wells back, and she told him she'd already made arrangements to use them on behalf of England. He investigated her story, and was forced to let them go."

"Why did he let me go? If Donn was offering me for a trade, he must have told him who I am."

"He did. And Blake didn't want to release you. But I wasn't going to let him keep you. I said your accuser was the real villain, and Etta insisted you be freed. So Blake let us all go."

"What happened to Donn and O'Malley?"

"Fina didn't come after us. Evie said she waited outside the White Tower and was still there when Evie left to meet us at the carriage. That made Evie mad because she wanted to attack, but Etta told her not to. We heard from certain channels last night that Donn and O'Malley both escaped custody, so I'm guessing she helped them flee."

"Unfortunate. It would have made our lives easier if Donn was in jail."

"Agreed. Etta is going to open Skye House here in town today and take the Wells there. It has more protections than most fortresses, and it's more difficult to enter than the Tower since it doesn't attract tourists."

"Good idea. Will you return to Skye?"

Sorcha shook her head. Given her current position against his shoulder, that meant she nuzzled his neck. "She's already sent my cousin Rob and his wife Eleanor with a group of students to guard the house. She asked me last night if I would like to shift my focus and join her here in London. She's started to raise awareness about the magic drain, and she needs people she can trust here with her."

Ronan pulled back. There wasn't enough light to discern her features clearly, and he couldn't help but wonder how she had reacted to such a request. She'd already told him about the vow she took to protect the Fay ancestral home and all its secrets. That vow was why she'd come hundreds of miles south, in search of what she'd lost.

"What of your oath?"

"She says that times are changing. The house is important and needs to be protected, but that's something we can all take turns doing. She wants to build a new school between the estate and the village, where they can send advanced students. There's so much space, and the magic is more concentrated there. They'll be able to practice, and we'll be able to fill Fay House with people again."

"So even if you did go back, it wouldn't be the same."

She blinked, then settled back against her own pillow. "Yes. It wouldn't be the same." But neither of them were talking about the presence of students in her grounds, or more family members filling the house. They both meant that they would never again be alone at Fay House.

He supposed that was true of all relationships. Those heady first days settled into the tedium of life, and couldn't be reclaimed. But there was something especially sad about losing that with Sorcha, because while he could have imagined going to her on her island, he had no place here in London. In fact, it was probably best that he leave the city soon. No matter the duchess's lies on his behalf, Lucien Blake was not a fool. He would be watching, waiting for Ronan to betray himself.

Sorcha's choice would determine their future. And it was best that she choose London. She deserved every chance at happiness and fulfillment, and he had seen the way she worked with her cousins, as though they were the pieces of a steam engine fitting together perfectly and marshalling forces none of them could have handled alone.

"It's a grand idea." He couldn't touch her, though he longed to. "You'll do well with Etta, and she'll appreciate your talents in ways few others would."

"I don't disagree, but I haven't decided anything yet. My whole life has flipped upside down in the last week. I'm not sure what I want anymore."

He couldn't stand not being able to see her, so he crafted a quick magelight and tossed it over the bed. She blinked against the flare of brightness, and he levered himself over her. He knew what he wanted and what he needed to do. But he could not deny himself one last time with her.

"What I want is you," he murmured, and he pressed his lips to hers. She opened for him, surrendering to his passion the way she had on the floor of the Fay House casting chamber. She responded to him when he brushed kisses down her throat and over her breasts, but she didn't demand. Instead, she drove him to sweet madness with her little moans and gasps. She didn't want to have to choose anything right now, and he didn't mind choosing this for both of them.

"I need to be in you, my Sorcha, *a solas, a chroi,* so deep in you that neither of us can tell where I end and you begin."

Her breath caught as he slid two fingers inside her, the heat and slickness of her making his mouth water. He told himself he was using his non-dominant hand because it was the one that had been closest at the time, and not because it wasn't the one he'd used to make Bella cum.

Sorcha was the only one in his bed, and this was the last time he would ever make love to her. He pushed away all other distractions and focused on the woman who was everything he could never keep. He wanted to taste her again, but the need to join with her, to experience the oneness only melding their bodies could bring, drove him.

Someone had removed his clothes when they put him to bed, and he wore only a nightshirt. He stripped it off, and she wriggled out of her nightrail and tossed it to the side of the bed. Then he stopped and drank the sight of her. Nothing would ever be so lovely to him as this woman, her skin bathed with magelight and her hair a pale cloud against the pillows. Her dusky-rose nipples were peaked and tight, and he bent to stroke them with his thumbs. She writhed and her hips bucked, seeking him.

"Yes, *a chuisle.* Soon." He stroked her thighs, loving the way the pale, silky hair sprinkling her soft skin tickled his palms. She lifted her hips again, entreating him without words. His rigid cock rubbed absently against her bent knee, and the little shocks of pleasure fanned sparks in his belly and brain.

He licked his thumb, then parted the glistening folds of her sex to find the little bundle of nerves at its peak. She moaned as he stroked it, finally asking him, finally choosing.

"Ronan, please. Now!"

The slick slide into her tight heat was as exquisite as the first time—and as devastating as a mortal wound. Because this was the last time, the last joining. She'd told him she loved him when she drove them both to madness two nights before, and this was the only way he could answer her. Every thrust proclaimed it, every moan was secretly his heart's cry.

A chuisle, a chroí, a solas. Tá tú go h-álainn. A anamchara. Táim i ngrá leat. Go síoraí. Is tú mo ghrá.

My pulse, my heart, my light. You're so beautiful. My soulmate. I'm in love with you. Forever. I love you.

But he couldn't speak those words, could not ever let her know his truth, or she would never let him go. So he said them with his body, shouted them with his cock, until she broke and shuddered around him, crying his name into his mouth as he melded his lips to hers. His balls tightened and pleasure swamped him, the convulsions of his body breaking their kiss as his seed flooded her and his hips jerked hard against her cleft. She trembled again, an aftershock of pleasure as he spent himself inside her.

They lay in a stupor, after, and Ronan tried to find the

will to heave away, to say what must be said. Her sweat-slick body still cradled him with its lush softness, and he couldn't speak the words.

But then she chuckled. "I suppose this is a good argument for why I might choose to leave Skye."

That gave him the shove he needed. She couldn't stay with him. It was better for them both if he left—if he stayed an island, surrounded by saltwater and never letting anyone swim too close. It tore at him that he was making her be the same, but it had to be done. His cock slipped out of her and he rolled away, sitting so that she had to look up at him.

"Don't let me be part of your decisions. I've heard what you've said to me, Sorcha Fay, and what you believe. But love does not appear in a week. It's a slow, steady thing, and what we feel now is not slow or steady. It's hot and quick, and before we know it, it will be gone."

She watched him with a wary gaze, her body still replete with pleasure. "You don't really believe that."

No, he didn't, and that was the baffling thing. But unlike Sorcha, Ronan was an excellent liar. And for the first time in his life, he was going to be the one to leave. Because if he stayed, Sorcha would choose him. And that would ruin her life. He would ruin her chance to stand beside the duchess in society, her chance to shine and show the world her incredible gifts. She couldn't be tied to an Irish criminal whose own father had disowned him and labeled him a bastard.

"I believe it because it's true. You'll see. In a few days, you'll be busy with the duchess and helping her fix English magic, and you won't even notice that I'm gone."

She sat up then, her eyes wide and expression bleak. "You're leaving?"

"Aye. Today. Blake knows who I am, no matter what you or Etta said. He let me go because it was expedient in the moment, and I'm sure he figures he can guess where I'll be when he gets around to bringing me in. Now that Donn has escaped, he's going to be eager to question me. I hate to protect that gobshite, but I'd be giving myself away, too."

That much, at least, was the truth.

"I'll go with you, then. No matter what you believe, I love you, Ronan McCarrick." And didn't that love flay him straight to the bone? Didn't it leave his heart bare and bleeding? But she would regret going with him, as soon as she appreciated what it meant. She would become the mistress of a smuggler, of a thief, conman, spy, and murderer. They would never be able to settle in one place, would move at the whims of the leaders of his Cause. And he couldn't do that to her.

"You believe you do, but it will pass. I belong alone. I'm not a man worthy of love."

"You are. You just don't believe it." She shifted as though to stand.

"I'm not!" He shouted it, and she flinched back. Her hair was a wild tangle around her head, and the cool bluish mage-light transformed her into an ancient goddess, pale as the moon and with eyes like the morning sky. And damn it, for whatever the love of a broken man was worth, it was hers.

But if he wanted to save her, he would have to break her, too.

"I'm not a good man, *a solas*." He stared into those eyes that both revealed her brilliant soul and reflected his dark and bitter one. "You never asked me what I did, to elicit the information from Isabella."

She recoiled, and that open, honest love was shuttered by pain and doubt. "We haven't had much time to talk."

"No, we haven't. And I made sure we didn't. Because I didn't want you to know." The hand that had been inside of Bella closed into a fist. What he'd actually done wouldn't be enough to drive Sorcha away. She'd excuse it, justify it, even as he had in the moment. So he lifted that hand, took her chin, and forced her to face him as he lied. "I fucked her against a tree in the park." He deliberately used her way of pronouncing it so she would understand exactly what he meant.

She jerked away, and he let her go. He tried to ignore the trembling of her limbs, tried not to bleed from the raw wound he'd clawed through their hearts. Swallowed the bile and acid that rose in his gullet as he forced out more lies, more words like brands that would sear and burn and destroy them both.

"She wrapped her legs around me, and I lifted her against a trunk and sank my cock in her. Then I fucked her until she came. After that, she was more than happy to tell me everything." He broke their locked gazes and stood. "That's the kind of man I am. I knew it would hurt you, and I did it anyway. Because this," he pointed to the bed, "is as far as we'll ever go. We've had a good time, and I've made you cum, and you've given me some good rides. Now it's time for us both to move on."

He strode naked to the wardrobe and found his clothes. Someone had washed and pressed his things. She didn't say anything, didn't protest, as he dressed and found his boots. At the door, he pivoted and gazed back at her. He couldn't deny his heart this one final chance to drink her in. Gorgeous, even when wracked with pain. His love, his light. His Sorcha. But no more.

"Good-bye," he said, and slipped out the door.

21

At first, Sorcha feared she would weep for hours, but she hadn't cried at all. Every fragment of her body and soul hurt—a ceaseless burning agony that radiated from beneath her breastbone and filled her with pain, yet left her emptier than she'd ever been.

After that, she'd been hollow and numb, as though a vital piece of herself, the element that made her feel things, had left along with Ronan. She'd moved through her day like one of the clockwork automatons she'd seen on her only other trip to London, in an engineering exhibition that her cousins had dragged her to.

When she'd seen the nearly life-sized clockwork butler that ran on a track like a human train with a tray to carry drinks, she'd wanted to run straight back to Scotland where things were not made of cogs and pulleys and metal. Where things made sense.

But now she empathized with the machine. It was, after all, only a construct, fulfilling the function for which it was built. Her body was no different. Her heart pumped blood, her lungs took in air, her mouth swallowed food that her intestines converted to energy. If she had once believed that man was more than this—that people could have deeper connections with each other and the world—then she'd been a fool.

Etta came to her room when she did not appear for breakfast. Sorcha sat at a desk, writing letters to Mrs. Mackinstrie and the others at Fay House, as well as Cousin Rob and the other Fays that Etta had sent to guard the property. As Keeper of the House, there were things she knew that would need to be passed on. Not all of them could be written, but the mundane day-to-day things were safe to commit to paper.

"Sorcha, what's happened?"

Sorcha placed her pen beside the letter, the motion languid, as though she had to push her hand through syrup. "Ronan is gone. He…didn't want to stay anymore. He said things would be difficult for him, now that Mage Captain Blake knows he's here."

Etta leaned against the writing desk. "I thought as much when he came to me and asked for his fee."

She should have been appalled that he'd still wanted money after everything that had happened, but he was first and always a revolutionary, and it wasn't greed that drove him. The Fay coffers were deep, and he would use them to help his Cause.

"It's for the best. I want to help you with your spell, and to stand with you as we fight whoever is stealing magic from this island. He only cares about Ireland, not England or Scotland. He doesn't want the same things I do."

Etta reached out a tentative hand, and Sorcha took it, accepting the squeeze. Etta tried to send positive magic along with the contact, but it fell into the deep well of Sorcha's emptiness and made not a ripple in the numb expanse within her.

"If you've decided, it's time to go to Skye House. Mal tells me Lilias had a casting chamber built there. We can use that as a staging area for the spell."

"Yes, she did. It's not as elaborate or large as the one actually on the Isle, but Skye House has a creditable chamber. I haven't seen it since the last time I was here when I was a girl. When Lilias died, the second duchess closed the house and only a small staff lives there now to maintain it."

"Horatia and Beatrice weren't equal to the task that Lilias set for them. But I am."

Sorcha forced a smile because it was what Etta expected, but she couldn't look her cousin in the face while she did it. "It will be all over society by nightfall that you've opened the house and are planning to stay, not visit and go to the occasional ball and soiree."

"I already told the leaders of the country last night that we recovered the Wells and I would be visiting my solicitors to draft an agreement for their use. They were appropriately apologetic about what happened, but secretly seething. They don't like needing me, and I don't intend that they become complacent with our arrangement. London should be aware there's a new Duchess of Fay, and I'm not going away."

At Skye House, Etta, Sorcha, and Mal helped the small staff open long disused rooms. The servants were all Scots, and they didn't even blink when the duchess scrubbed and polished right beside them. Sorcha shook dust covers, wiped tables and chairs, aired mattresses and made beds with fresh linen. Mal hauled furniture around and tinkered with the dumbwaiter that had been a brand-new installation before the house was closed.

In the afternoon, Sorcha washed with tepid water in a basin and came down for tea still in her dirty frock.

That was a mistake. Etta had callers.

Amelia Upton, Queen's Sorceress and Dowager Countess of Falcestershire, sat in the newly-clean parlor wearing an exquisite calling gown, her hair piled in artless profusion that must have taken her maid hours to place just-so.

At her side was Mage-Captain Blake. He watched Sorcha from the moment she entered the room, and his eyes saw far more than she wanted to reveal. While Etta and Amelia sparred over the theft of the Wells, and Etta made pointed threats to go public with the queen's plan to imprison her and strip her of her powers a year ago, Sorcha tried to sit perfectly still and not fidget under Blake's gaze.

Finally, Etta revealed her trump card. Amelia turned white when she learned that Etta had secured the backing of the Home Secretary and the Prime Minister, who both agreed that the Wells would be best put to use fueling British magic until the army could assist Clan Fay in discovering the source of the drain and then deal with whoever had caused it.

At last, Blake broke eye contact. To Etta, he was all composure and business. "To that end, Your Grace, I've been assigned as your liaison with the Home Office. I'm to stay with you and monitor the Wells. It is my belief that the criminal and revolutionary Michael McCauley, known as Donn, will attempt to take them again."

Etta argued for form's sake, but Sorcha could tell that she knew she wouldn't win. The duchess had brought in the English government, and there was no way she'd be able to escape bureaucratic oversight now. But they also had the full might of the Empire behind them, should they need to use it. It was a trade-off Etta had understood she was making before she went to visit the Prime Minister.

As Ronan had known what Lady Wiltshire would want when he had gone to her at the park. And he'd done what she asked.

The pain was not as deep, this time, as when he'd first slapped the truth in her face. Yes, he'd done it. Yes, he'd fucked another woman only hours after rising from Sorcha's bed. But he'd had a reason. *Sorcha* was his reason. He'd been trying to do what was best for her, had sought only to recover what had been stolen. It hurt, but she understood why he'd made the choice.

It wasn't quite forgiveness, but perhaps, in time, she would be able to accept what he had done. What she could never forgive was that he'd used that as an excuse to run.

"Sorcha?" Etta said her name, in a tone that meant she'd already tried to draw her attention at least once.

"I'm sorry. I'm very tired, and I wasn't attending."

"Mage-Captain Blake has offered to assist us with the spell I spoke of this morning. He says he once tried something similar on one of his missions."

Sorcha didn't want to acknowledge him, didn't want to fall into his trance again, but as he was the subject of the conversation, she had no choice.

His eyes were so blue, and she hated them for not being stormy grey. "I look forward to working with you," she murmured, and she wondered that everyone in the room did not call her out for the lie.

Amelia stood, and both Blake and Mal stood with her, the motion more instinct than actual respect from both of them. Sorcha was shocked that Blake wore a hint of a smirk at the sorceress's discomfort. Perhaps he'd learned enough about her now to dislike her as much as they did.

"If you'll not accept my help, I'll be going. But Her Majesty will not be happy that I've been excluded."

"I will send reports to Her Majesty," Blake said. "She will be kept informed."

Amelia huffed and left the room. The butler, McGroarty—an ancient Scotsman who'd been in charge of this house since Sorcha was a wean—closed the door behind her with a decisive click.

"Well," Etta said, and malicious humor filled her voice. "I thought she'd never leave."

Blake cleared his throat. "Shall we proceed with the spell, Duchess?"

Etta stood and gestured for everyone to follow her. Sorcha took the caboose position in their little train, wishing she could stop and let them move on without her. But Blake kept slowing when she did, which made Etta and Mal slow, and eventually Blake held out his arm for her.

She took it reluctantly. The moment they touched, magic shocked through her. They both stopped, there in the middle of the hall, and stared at each other. Blake was a light mage, as she was. It was a rare affinity, and she'd never met another before.

She opened her Sight and was bombarded with the scents and flavor of cinnamon and coffee. His magic was robust and brawny, sun-based and attuned to fire, whereas she was most comfortable with moonlight and air. Within their shared affinity, he was her opposite, and yet the similarity at the core of their magic drew them together.

Before she could stop it, they were linked, and she experienced his thoughts as he did hers. *You are too bright for that Irish bastard.*

He must have seen something of their argument, or perhaps felt her numbness.

And you are too aware of your strength to strike so cruelly.

Shame and embarrassment washed through the link, and he withdrew. She disentangled her magic and pulled away her hand. "Perhaps it's best that we not do that again," she said softly.

Etta and Mal were watching them from a few feet farther along the hall. Etta didn't ask, only stared at Sorcha a moment longer, and then continued to the casting chamber.

In the hallway, Sorcha paused and watched Blake. He eyed her warily, now, and with a mixture of confusion and curiosity. Perhaps he wanted to explore the connection as much as he feared it. She couldn't even be afraid of it, because as powerful as the link had been, it had not filled the emptiness that Ronan had left behind.

She paced away, assuming he would follow. He did.

"When you came into my house, you used something of either myself, Le Fay, or the duchess to enter the vault. How did you acquire it?"

He seemed surprised that she knew, or had guessed, but he answered. "Her Grace has been visiting London frequently to attend society functions. It was simplicity to arrange a mishap with a maid and a hatpin."

"Ah. I suppose she staunched the flow of blood with a handkerchief, and Etta didn't think to ask for the cloth. She won't fall for that again."

"Perhaps not. But once was enough for my purposes."

"Why didn't you simply attack me? You avoided me, and my staff."

"You were not in my orders. I was told to maintain secrecy, and that time was not an issue unless it appeared your family would use the Wells. I had actually intended to wait longer after it was necessary to harm your servant, but the dowager countess heard a rumor that Her Grace had begun to hint at the problem of a magical drain to members of both houses of Parliament, and had implied that she had a solution."

She paused outside the door. "But that means you were already aware she wanted to use the Wells to help."

Blake's expression shuttered with anger. "I did not. I was only informed that I needed to move as soon as possible. It was only after you…reacquired your property that I was told how Lady Falcestershire determined our new timeline."

"So she lied to you the whole time."

"Indeed. I…had not expected that of someone so high in the queen's service."

Sorcha snorted, but it was bitterness, not humor, that filled her voice when she spoke. "Perhaps next time you will ask more questions of your compatriots."

"She was not my compatriot. She was my commanding officer, however temporarily. It was my duty to follow her orders."

"Even flawed and illegal orders?"

"Sometimes action must be taken that is outside of written laws, to protect the greater good."

"A nice principle. Be careful how you apply it." Etta had come back to the doorway. Although her accent had rounded in the last year into something almost Scottish, she'd reverted now to the high, quick, nasal accent of American Appalachia. Etta was upset. "For example, we may need to bend the rules of magic you were taught in order to cast this spell. Will you be able to do that?"

His chin dipped in a curt, single nod.

"Then come." She strode away into the big room.

Skye House's casting chamber was not as large as the room of the same function at Fay House, but it was still larger than many ballrooms. The floor was a masterpiece, with different types of polished crystals, metal, wood, horn, and bone worked into elaborate symbols and patterns.

Etta directed them each to a place on the floor and had Blake demonstrate the type of spell he'd used before. Then they dissected the weaving, and each made suggestions on how to alter it to suit their purpose. Sorcha couldn't help wishing that Ronan was here. His tracking spell gave her insight enough to add to the conversation, but he was the one who would have been able to contribute the most to this effort.

It didn't matter. Ronan was gone, and she would never see him again.

She finished crafting an addition to the spell and tried to ignore the fact that it fairly pulsed with grief.

Etta tested the pattern, and said, "That's interesting. Is this what you used to track the Wells from Skye?"

"As far as I can remember it."

Blake leaned close to the weaving, examining the pattern of interwoven threads that formed a cluster of symbols and shapes.

"This is not your design?" he asked.

"No. I'm not even sure it was Ronan's. He mentioned that Evie had helped him craft a tracking spell once. Where is she now?"

"Investigating something else for me," Etta explained. "She'll be back later. I wasn't expecting us to dive right in this afternoon."

Blake shifted a few of the threads. "This spell requires you to have an understanding of what it is that you seek. I assume it performed admirably in your search, but we don't know who or what is draining magic."

"No, but we do know that it's going somewhere. I'd hoped we'd be able to modify it to seek that magic, to sense places where energy isn't flowing as it should."

"We'll try that and see what happens," Etta said, over-riding Blake's attempt to object.

They linked hands around the spell, Etta to Sorcha to Blake to Mal and back to Etta. The duchess controlled the merge, her pine and tilled-earth scent filling Sorcha's magical awareness. But the scent and the taste of cinnamon and coffee refused to be ignored. Even when they dropped their hands, she could still sense the warmth from Blake's. None of them wore gloves, as fabric impeded the ability to weave the strands of power, and her magic had gone incandescent when it encountered his.

He didn't press her, didn't take advantage of the connection that even now gave her access to his thoughts and feelings, and he to hers. They weren't controlling the link, and Etta hadn't taken the merge deeper than surface magic. But she and Blake had tumbled past the surface again, almost accidentally.

I won't hurt you. I don't pretend to comprehend this, but I have no desire to take more from you than I already have.

I believe you. And she did.

He spent the next half hour arguing with Etta about how to shift the spell, making what should have been a simple process take much longer. Etta prevailed, and once he finally accepted their plan, he casually cast a mechanically-perfect net that incorporated all of their ideas and acted exactly as they'd planned.

Sorcha was stunned at the precision and deftness of his casting. She had already recognized that he was a formidable mage, based on what he'd done at Fay House. But this was the first time she'd seen him casting. It was breathtakingly meticulous and exact.

But although the spell worked, Blake had been correct in one of his objections. They didn't have enough information to narrow their search, and this spell only highlighted how bad things were. It showed that magic was being pulled from everywhere, even the casting chamber that was meant to enhance and funnel power. There wasn't a single flow of magic in the mile that the spell could search that didn't have at least a tiny portion of its energy being redirected. They tried to follow the path, but there were too many streams. It was like standing at the mouth of a massive river delta and trying to follow a single drop of water as it swept from the main body of the river into the sea.

"That was a spectacular failure," Etta admitted once they'd dispelled the weave.

"Yes, but it has had one positive effect," Mal said. "Mr. Blake now understands how dire this threat really is."

Blake gave a curt nod. His voice was low, his tone sharp but steady. "I've inspected the analysis you compiled from military records showing mage aptitude scores over the last hundred years, and the steep decline makes a compelling argument. But there could be other causes. This, though... this is proof. I will tell my superiors as much when I send my report."

They'd broken the larger link, but Sorcha and Blake were still lightly connected, and his grudging respect and growing admiration filled their merge. Oh, he'd balked and blustered, especially when Etta showed him how he could better cast a particular symbol-shape more efficiently with the particular mix of magical energies in the room. But then he'd tried it, and the symbol flared to life, and Sorcha had experienced his surprise and almost wonder.

How long has it been since magic felt wonderful? she'd asked. He hadn't answered, but she didn't need him to. Now, she said, *We aren't monsters or liars, Mage-Captain Blake. And we do know what we're doing.*

He gave the tiniest flinch, and then actually smiled at her. *Perhaps you do. Most of the time. And my name is Lucien.*

She shouldn't accept the familiarity, should maintain as much distance between them as possible, but that would make her a hypocrite. *Very well. Lucien.*

"Let's take a break," Etta said, "and have Tea, and then we'll try something else."

RONAN KNOCKED BACK ANOTHER TANKARD OF ALE THAT tasted only a mite better than piss and dropped the mug back onto the table. It clattered as it tipped and fell, empty. He almost called for another, but he was already more than tipsy, and this was not the sort of place to get sloshed and keel over. He'd reached an uneasy truce with Bart after a few angry telegrams were exchanged, and for the moment his captain believed that Donn was responsible for Ronan missing the rendezvous. Which was true in most respects, but was completely false when Ronan examined his own motivations. He'd missed the shipment because Sorcha had been more important to him in the moment, and he had to accept the consequences of his choices.

Tomorrow he would board a train and meet Bart and the ship in Liverpool. This place would suffice to bide his time, but he didn't trust a single patron sharing the smoke-filled air.

Especially not once the vestibule door opened and Donn walked in. He sauntered to Ronan and took the empty chair at his small table.

"I got word that you were here, drowning your sorrows."

"I'm not sure why you cared to come. You were willing to sell me out to Blake."

"Yes, I was! I would sell anyone or anything, including me own ma, to free Ireland from the English. Any of us would. And the fact that you wouldn't makes me wonder why you're even fecking here." He leaned closer. "I had a telegram from Liverpool. You were supposed to be there for a shipment yesterday."

"I know. I made a choice to prioritize my mission. The money I received from the duchess is enough to pay for ten times as many weapons."

"But those were already paid for, boyo. And now they're off to bleeding Africa."

"I could have taken the express train if you hadn't knocked me out and tried to use me as a bargaining chip." But Ronan's skin flushed with heat. Maybe anger, maybe shame. Was Donn right? Was he not committed enough to the Cause? "I want Ireland to be free as much as you or any other person."

"Do ya now?" Donn pushed the tankard toward him. "I didn't mean for it to be you. It was supposed to be the girl. She's a distraction for you, and it would have removed that distraction from your life."

"At the expense of hers?"

"The fog-breathers wouldn't be killing her. She's a cousin to the bloody Duchess of Fay. And it's her property they stole. I'd have made it look like she hired ruffians to help her steal it back, and then they double-crossed her. By the time she woke from the sleeping spell and told her story, we'd be long gone, and all of that power would be ours."

"They wouldn't let us keep it."

"No, and so we'd have to spirit the things away, quick-like. Maybe to France, or maybe on a steamer to America. The Fenian lads in Boston could mind the prize for us while we debate on how best to use it."

"Boston isn't a bad idea. There's so much wild magic in America, no one would notice the extra."

"Ah, so there you have it. We'll send them to Boston. I'll even let you be the shepherd across the waters, now things have gotten so hot for you here."

"There's a problem with that mission."

"Yes, there is, isn't there? We don't have the power in our hands. But we could."

Ronan stared at him. "Are you asking me to…" he couldn't finish the sentence.

Donn's smile was too-broad, too slick, and Ronan imagined it dripped with oil. "Ireland needs that power, Ronan m'boyo. I'm going to claim it, one way or another. Much easier to have you waltz in there, play nice with your ladyfriend for a touch, then dance right back to me with the prize. I wouldn't have near as lovely a time with her."

Despite the veiled threat of those last words, Ronan hesitated. It would devastate Sorcha if he stole the very thing he'd helped her recover. Or partially helped, since he'd slept through the most important action.

To take that victory and smear it with betrayal would be far, far worse than if he'd walked away in Skye. But by the time they found the Wells missing, it had been too late for him. He'd already been inside her body, had already discovered pleasure and connection beyond anything he'd ever known.

Was he willing to betray that? To forsake everything they'd shared, for Ireland to be free?

No, he wasn't.

But he was willing to do it to stop Donn from doing it instead. If Donn went, he would 'accidentally' kill her. And Ronan would never allow that to happen.

"As you say." His grin wasn't forced, because he'd known Donn too long not to commit to his role. He played the part, and would do as he must. "Easy as lying."

2 2

Every window on Skye House's first floor glowed into the night. Ronan contemplated walking up to the front door and asking to come in, but though he assumed he'd be allowed through, he couldn't stand to see the pain in Sorcha's eyes again.

And if he saw her, he might not be able to go through with this.

He walked around the house, testing the wards. They were properly grounded to keystones, and Etta and Sorcha's magic ran through the renewed matrices, a mix of the duchess's deep woods and Sorcha's night-blooming flowers. He approached cautiously, and the spells did not react to his presence.

He hadn't expected them to, but it was far too much of a relief to realize that Socha hadn't been angry enough to forbid him entry.

The mews and carriage house in the rear of the property were dark. The ducal carriage had been kept there for a while, but there would have been no horses on the premises for years. He'd overheard Mal ask his father to lend them a team the morning of the trip to the Tower, so those beasts might still be here. Ronan had gotten friendly with the groom that came with the team. Even if he were seen entering this way, the man wouldn't think much of it.

It took only moments to cast his lock-picking spell on the door. It hadn't been specifically warded against magical intrusion, and the lock opened with a satisfactory click.

Ronan kept his steps light and nearly silent as he moved through the mews. The place was dark, the only sounds the shuffling and breathing of the horses. Lanterns were a risk in a stable, with straw bedding ready to ignite from an untended flame.

That worked to Ronan's advantage, and he slipped through into the back garden of Skye House.

From here, it was simplicity to cross to the cellar door. The scullery and kitchen entrance would be cleaner, but also manned by staff. This one would only be used for coal deliveries. Its lock was warded against magic, but he'd been breaking into warded houses for nearly half of his life. He had plenty of tricks to overcome these sorts of wards, and a few minutes later he raised the hatch and descended into the cellars.

The rest of this would be much trickier. He didn't know the layout of the house, or where the Wells were being kept. The magic currents in the area revealed activity on the floors above, but it was more the potential for magic than actual spellcasting. Evie had told him the duchess wanted to locate where English magic was going, and she'd been working on different kinds of weaves to achieve that purpose. The disturbances must be Sorcha and Etta, experimenting with variations to determine what worked.

Good. They would be distracted, focused on the threads of their own spell, and not paying too much attention to a few minor workings done elsewhere in the house.

He skulked through the cellars and storerooms to a stair-well. It opened in the servant's quarters, but no one saw him go through a narrow hall to the hidden servant's stair. There must not be many people currently on staff, because he didn't encounter another soul even after he exited on the second floor and cast his tracking spell.

The Wells hadn't been put in a new null vault, probably because all of the players now knew what house held them. Shielding was pointless. But it would have made Ronan's task much more difficult, as he would have been forced to search every room in the place. As it was, he was able to follow the spell to a particular room on the third floor. Curiously, the door was unlocked, and the room itself was not a vault like the one in Fay House back on Skye. This was more like someone's study or private library. There was a…presence in the room. He couldn't describe the sensation better than that. He'd never actually encountered a ghost, but it would be his luck to find one here.

The Wells were out of the black bag and sitting in a large copper bowl. Runes and Ogham tree script were etched into the bowl, and symbols were formed with inlays of different metals. The bowl kept the Wells inactive, their power contained within their cylindrical forms. He'd planned to cast his own dampening spell on them, but this was convenient. He put the bowl and the two cylinders into a rough canvas sack and slung it over his shoulder.

He retraced his steps as far as the servant's stair when a discreet cough sounded behind him.

Evie stood a few paces away, wearing boy's clothing and tightly pinned braids.

"Where do you think you're going with those?"

"Donn found me after I left Sorcha. He threatened her, said he would come for these himself and wouldn't it be a shame if the lovely lass died protecting them?" Ice formed in the pit of his stomach. "I won't let him kill her."

"If he wants her to die, he'll do it anyway, and you know that."

"He only wants me under his control. I'm doing what he wants, and as long as that continues, she'll be safe."

Evie sighed and rubbed the back of her neck. "What has become of you, Ro? Even in the darkest days, you wouldn't have done something like this. We don't betray our own, and Sorcha is *yours*, body and soul."

"She's not mine. I let her go."

"You don't get to decide that, *dheartháir*. She does. All you've decided is that you won't be hers in return."

"Dark God take you, Evie. I am doing this for her."

"And now you've perfected lying to yourself, as well as to others. Well done."

"Don't talk to me about lying to myself. You're good at it, too."

She flinched, but otherwise her expression of exasperated concern didn't change. "Maybe I am. Maybe I do. But I'm not hurting the woman I love because of it."

Ronan pressed his open palms to his thighs, then raised both hands with fingers splayed, an indication that he was ready to cast a spell if necessary. "I'm doing what I must. Are you going to try to stop me?"

Evie held her hands in a mirror to his gesture, and then closed them into fists. "No, I'm not. You're better at offensive spells anyway."

"I truly am sorry that I have to hurt you both. I'd give anything to change the way this entire adventure has gone."

"You can't change what's passed, but you can choose what you do next. Don't make an even bigger mistake."

He stared at her for another moment, taking in the familiar elfin features: her brilliant red hair and eyes the color of an Irish field. Her magical scent and flavor—chocolate and rosemary—drifted to him on the power currents in the room, along with the heat and energy of a living flame.

"I won't try to stop you, but I'm running straight to Sorcha and the duchess. They'll have you before you're out of the house."

Ronan understood her meaning. If he wanted to do this, he was going to have to prevent her from going to the others. So he did, tossing a barrier around her that would dissipate in an hour, two at most. She didn't fight it as it settled, but she sank to the floor so that she'd be in a more comfortable position during her wait.

"I love you, Evelyn Finn, and I'm sorry." He pushed open the door to the servant's stair, not yet able to break eye contact. Just loud enough for her to hear, he added, "I love her, too." Then he went through the door and pulled it shut.

Etta had dinner brought to them in the Casting Chamber, but Sorcha was exhausted and barely ate. Lucien sat apart from them, as he'd been all afternoon and evening. His contributions had been at times brilliant and insightful, and at others obstructive and close-minded.

The casting chamber door flung open and banged against the wall. Sorcha started and dropped her fork against her plate with a clatter.

"What's wrong, Evie?" Etta pushed back her chair and rose. Mal had already done the same, and Lucien moved a moment later. Sorcha remained seated. Her intuition had already told her it was something to do with Ronan, and she didn't want to know more than that.

"Ronan took the Wells."

"He what?" Etta asked in disbelief.

Lucien rounded the table toward her.

"Leave the girl alone, Blake," Mal said. "She'll tell us what she knows without you forcing it out of her."

"She's one of his compatriots. She'll cover for him."

"Lucien," Sorcha murmured. "Please. Everyone in this room wants those Wells kept safe and used for the good of the whole kingdom. If she wanted to cover for him, she wouldn't have said anything to us at all. Let her speak, and we'll determine the next course of action."

Lucien's gaze pierced through Sorcha, and if she hadn't been so exhausted it might have been harder to withstand it. But she was numb, and empty, and there was nothing for him to see but an echoing void. He jerked a nod in her direction and grabbed the nearest chair, shoving it toward Evie. She sat, and he took the chair beside her, next to Sorcha.

"I saw him upstairs," Evie said. "Unfortunately, he's good in a brawl, and he taught me all my tricks. He put a barrier on me, and it just wore off."

Lucien bristled, and Sorcha put a hand on his arm. Their light magic tried to tangle again, and she didn't have the strength to stop it. He did, but he chose not to. *I don't believe her*, he thought.

You should. She's more dismayed and feels much more betrayed than you. He is like a brother to her, and he took something that we all worked very hard to keep safe.

He's your lover. Why would he do that?

He's not my lover. Not anymore.

Evie had continued to talk while their thoughts flitted back and forth. Now, she said, "He justified it because Donn found him and threatened to kill Sorcha and steal them himself."

"That's an empty threat," Etta said. "Ronan is almost the only person in the world who could have come into the house to take those Wells right now. When I activated the wards today, I had hoped he would change his mind and come back, so I left them open to him. Anyone else needs to be allowed through, and everyone who works here is loyal to Clan Fay, either by blood, oath, or long service."

"So Donn tricked him, or took advantage of his despair to play on his fears," Evie said.

"Despair? What was he upset about?" Mal's voice held an overt tone of skepticism.

Evie inclined her heat toward Sorcha. Mal said, "Oh." Etta patted her husband's arm.

"His emotional state is only tangentially relevant," Lucien said. "Will he take the Wells to Mr. McCauley?"

Evie pressed her lips together, and started a sentence three times before she admitted she didn't know. "I suppose that's his intention, but he has to realize that Donn isn't going to use them for anything good. I'm sure Ronan would like to utilize them much as we intend to, except to bolster Irish magic instead of English, but that's a quiet, long-term, peaceful purpose. Donn likes overt, quick, and violent."

"I'll find him," Sorcha said, surprising herself. "I won't let him give them over to Donn."

"It may be too late for that," Lucien warned, his voice echoing within her thoughts. There, where only she could hear, he added, *And you're exhausted. You probably couldn't even grasp a tiny strand of magic right now.*

That was true, and not only of her. They were all tired. Evie wasn't as exhausted, but she'd already admitted her talents weren't going to be much use. Ronan had picked his time wisely.

Maybe not, but my intuition still works. Out loud she said, "If someone will bring me a map of London, I'll try to ascertain where he is."

~

RONAN MADE IT ONLY TWO STREETS AWAY BEFORE HE identified his shadows. One was O'Malley. The other was a middling mage from Boston who'd come back to the land of his forefathers after he'd made much trouble with the American coppers. Ronan only knew him as "The Yank."

Donn didn't trust him, it seemed. And Ronan had more than ample cause not to trust Donn.

He kept his pace steady, but opened his Sight and started prepping a spell surreptitiously in front of him. Both men were behind, O'Malley directly and the Yank across the street, so the Yank wouldn't be able to see the net forming even if he had his Sight open, too. He might sense a shift in the power levels on the street, though, which meant Ronan had to work fast and time this perfectly.

He finished the weaving but did not breathe the activation words. Once he did that, the Yank would feel a burst of magic, and see a quick net that then inverted, hiding Ronan and the threads of power from Sight. Ronan would have to move very fast and very quietly to escape from the two without leaving an obvious trail.

He waited until Fitzroy Square and triggered the spell. Then he made a dash for Grafton Street and the pub there. He timed it so that he entered on the heels of another patron. He'd come here once several years ago to meet a contact, and recalled a roof garden seating area. He crept up the steps as quietly as he could.

Several patrons graced the rooftop tonight, but none noticed him beneath the glamour. He went to the edge and peered over. O'Malley and the Yank stood together not too far from the square. They appeared to be having an argument about where he'd gone, because the Yank kept gesturing up Grafton Mews, an alley that ran under the pub, and O'Malley back toward Fitzroy Square. Eventually, they admitted defeat and went back to the square.

Ronan used a sweep's handholds cut into a chimney to climb to the nearby rooftop and dashed down it until he reached the men. As he watched, they hailed a cab in the square. Cursing, he made his way back to the street and dropped the glamour to hire his own cab. There was no telling where they would go, but he guessed they would head for where Donn was meant to meet him. He gave the cabbie an address near the rendezvous and settled in for the drive.

~

"HE'S BEEN ACTIVE," SORCHA SAID. "HE MUST HAVE TAKEN A cab here," she pointed at Fitzroy Square, "because he traveled too quickly from here to here," she stabbed a finger at a place near Shoreditch called St. Matthias. "But now he's moving again. He's coming back to us."

Lucien's gaze was skeptical, but Evie's eyes were full of hope. Etta took the map. "Exactly where is he now?"

Sorcha pointed to where City Road crossed St. John Street and became Pentonville Road. "Almost here."

"There are still many places he could be going, but that's a bit far north and west for him to be headed to a ship." Mal had argued that he believed Ronan would want to take the Wells off of English soil and smuggle them to Ireland as soon as possible. Sorcha agreed, in theory, but doubted such a thing would prove possible. Donn was too wily and canny an opponent.

"He's coming back," she said again. "That isn't a guess, or my wishes clouding my judgment. I'm down to the dregs of my passive magic, but what's left is telling me clearly. He's coming here, and he still has the Wells."

"I wonder why he changed his mind?" Etta asked.

"Donn," Evie said. "He must have shown his hand too soon. Ronan may be heartbroken, but he's not blind. Donn doesn't grasp human emotion. He either overestimates people's reactions, or vastly underestimates what it can motivate others to do. He probably tried to have his goons jump Ronan, or maybe had them shadow him. But Ronan is too savvy for that. He taught me how to read a street when I was thirteen. He can walk through Covent Garden Flower Market and tell you exactly how many pickpockets, con artists, and thieves are among the masses. He will spot anyone following him."

"It's pointless to speculate," Lucien said. "If he's coming here, then I shall wait for him to arrive. He will have much to tell us about this night's work."

Ronan contemplated slipping back into the house like before and putting the Wells back, but Donn's plans were much, much worse than he'd suspected and he needed to warn the others. And apologize to Evie and Sorcha.

His gut cramped, shame washing over him in waves of hot and cold.

He marched to the front door and rung the bell.

An ancient and grizzled fellow opened the door. His formal attire marked him as the butler, and his accent when he spoke revealed him as a Highland Scot. The first duchess must have imported him when she had this house built in the late 1820s, because he was old enough to have been a footman at the time.

"The duchess will want to see me," Ronan said in answer to the butler's query about his name. "She probably already knows I'm here."

It wasn't the duchess that came tripping down the grand staircase. It was Evie. She ran across the front hall, said, "Excuse me, MacGroarty," nudged the butler aside and leapt forward. Her fist made a thick smacking sound as it connected with his jaw. She'd added an extra magical oomph to the blow, and his head jerked back as pain burst over his cheek and arced down his neck.

Evie flapped the hand and then cradled it against her chest with the other. "Damn you've got a hard jaw."

"I told you not to hit a man in the face. Go for the soft parts." He rubbed at the point of impact and checked his teeth with his tongue. Nothing loose. While he was distracted, she took his advice and planted another hit in his belly. He stumbled back against the door and tried to draw in air, but she'd managed to hit in the vicinity of his diaphragm and it took five wheezing attempts before he managed to gasp in a breath.

"There. One for me and one for Sorcha, since she's too tired to hit you."

That drew his attention. He coughed, and rasped, "What's wrong?"

"She's actually been doing something productive all day, instead of betraying the only people who care about her and generally making an arse of herself."

"I brought them back."

"Yes, I know. I see you still have the bag. If you didn't, I would have let the mage-captain upstairs take you off to the Clink."

"I'm sorry. I did it all arseways."

"You certainly did. Now march up those steps and give the duchess back her property and throw yourself at Sorcha's feet. If I were her, I'd tell you to go lick the Dark God's balls, but she may take you back."

Evie pointed at the staircase. Ronan took her hand and squeezed it. "I'm not here for that. I'd still ruin her life if she chose me."

"Dry your arse, Ronan McCarrick, and put your bollocks back where they belong. The woman loves you, and you love her. You ought to let her decide for herself what would ruin her life and what would make her happy."

"Like I did for you?"

"Aye, and I'm sorry that what I needed was not something you could give. But you *can* give her what she needs, and you very much need what she can give."

And that was the moment when Ronan admitted he'd been a coward after all. He hadn't run from a selfless desire to save Sorcha from social ruin. He'd learned to lie to himself, as Evie had accused. He'd run because he was afraid if he asked to stay, Sorcha would choose to leave.

And he was still afraid of that.

"Maybe I do need it. But what if she doesn't want to give it?"

"Then you accept that and move on, as you've always done. But it's not much of a risk. She loves you, you gobshite." She prodded him with her free hand.

He reluctantly ascended the stairs. Even if Sorcha loved him, he'd made a hash of things, and he still couldn't see himself as a good enough man for her. Perhaps what he offered tonight would be the first step on a new road for him. The right choice made for the right reasons. His first ever.

Evie led him to a large, beautiful casting chamber, where Etta, Mal, Sorcha, and Mage-Captain Blake sat around an oval table with the remnants of a meal before them. Blake shifted, starting to rise, with an expression of black fury on his face. Sorcha tapped his arm, and they gazed at each other. Something passed between them, and Ronan's hands shook.

He hadn't even been gone a whole day. Had she moved on so quickly? But then Sorcha removed her hand and stared at the table. She was pale and wan, and he'd never seen her so drained or empty of life. Gods, he was an idiot. She was still hurting. She wasn't flirting with the uptight

British bastard, she was protecting Ronan's worthless Irish hide.

Ronan put the canvas bag in an open area of the table.

"Before you say anything, yes, I know that I am a fool, and I will have to pay the price for what I've done. But hear what I have to say, and what I propose we do, before you make any decisions."

Etta gestured for him to continue, but it was Sorcha he wanted to reach. And Sorcha who still would not look at him. He shifted his weight to a different leg and kept talking. He explained how he'd eluded the two men set to jump him, and how he'd hidden at the rendezvous point and overheard Donn's plans for the Wells.

"He wants to be Guy Fawkes. Only, instead of demolishing Parliament, those Wells will obliterate the entire city and everything within five miles."

"Gods above," Mal said.

"I'll not be party to that. I want Ireland to be free, but I'll not murder millions of innocent people to do it."

Sorcha finally lifted her head, and he made his last offer to her, though it was technically to the bloody army man who'd started this whole affair. Ronan dared not ask how he'd come to be in this room, but it was as well he was here.

"Donn needs to be taken. As long as he is in charge of a cell, many, many people will be in danger. Even without the Wells, he's determined to cause mass casualties and damage. He'll find a way."

"Tell me where he is, and I'll have a whole battalion there in an hour." Blake shifted restlessly. Whatever Sorcha had done to keep him restrained, he didn't like it.

"He won't be where I last saw him. Now that he realizes I slipped his net, he'll abandon all of the places I know. But we still have people in common. There are ways for me to pass a message to him. I can tell him that I thought I was being followed by government men, and that's why I spooked and didn't show at the meeting place."

He took Evie's hand in his. "If you come with me, he'll believe that we're both back on the path. We'll say that you assumed the Scots would be with us, but they've bent over for the English, and it's time to part ways for good."

"So you'll draw him out, and then we capture him." Blake's tone was harsh and disbelieving. Ronan met the man's gaze for the first time, and he was startled by how much the mage-captain's eyes matched Sorcha's.

"Yes. Him and his crew. And keep a better watch once you have them this time, eh?"

Blake pushed back his chair and stood. "Are you implying that I let them go?"

"Not at all," Ronan drawled. The other implication was that Blake was incompetent. Which probably wasn't true, but he'd underestimated Donn and Fina. So had Ronan. Which was why he added, "Donn's a slippery bastard. He'll be hard to catch, and harder to keep."

THEY SPENT THE NEXT HOUR ARGUING THE PARTICULARS, BUT eventually settled on a plan. Sorcha went to bed, and Etta sent Ronan to a different chamber to sleep. When he woke in the morning, he contemplated seeking her, but it was better not to push. Nothing had changed between them.

After breakfast, he and the duchess decamped to the parlor.

"I don't pretend to comprehend everything," she said, "but I know that you're an Irish Republican, and that you are actively seeking Irish independence. I want to help you, but I want to do it through legal means."

"What do you mean?"

"The last Home Rule bill failed because it was a mess, and they couldn't elicit enough votes to pass it. I've spent most of this season courting MPs and lords so that they will back me when I take up my seat next session. I've gathered a large base, and I believe, in a year or so, I can pass a better bill. If you and your fellows can be patient."

They'd never had much support in Lords, and no man in Parliament would take on the Irish question without a hefty incentive. But Ronan appreciated enough about this American duchess to believe that she would champion Ireland because she considered it the right thing to do.

"There are many who believe the only way England will let us go is with bloodshed. That the Irish ruling themselves will set a dangerous precedent for the colonies and protectorates."

"The precedent is already set and has been for a hundred years. America is doing fine on its own. All I need to do is find a way to present the issue so that it seems to benefit England. The drain is a way to do that. Ireland isn't as badly affected, and I'm hoping your leaders will agree that you can use that to bargain for independence."

"Won't the English try to take our magic by force?"

"They might. But it will mean bloodshed, and the Prime Minister is the type who prefers to avoid conflict. I believe he'd encourage Parliament to accept the bargain."

"I'll present your ideas. I can't guarantee how well they'll be accepted." He swallowed. "There are those who fear Home Rule would be even worse than what we have now. That it will give us a false belief that we control our own destinies, when we're actually still slaves to the English."

"That's fair, and might even be true. If Home Rule isn't want your people want, then I'll help you fight for something else. But I'm on your side, and there are other ways to free your Isle."

Ronan went to the writing desk and started drafting letters. Some were to the members of the Supreme Council that he knew, others were messages to Bart and his other captains. He'd started a fresh missive when MacGroarty opened the door and ushered in a visitor.

Ronan didn't need to hear the butler's accented introduction of, "Viscount Ashtondell," for a ball of ice to form in his belly. Across the room, the duchess stood to greet the old man.

"Lord Ashtondell. Has your committee come to an agreement on the paperwork my solicitor sent over?"

He entered the room without even glancing at Ronan and sat beside the duchess. His father answered in the affirmative and explained that they'd introduced a late bill to amend the earlier laws about Wells and allow for private citizens to own them while leaving the use in the hands of the government.

Etta argued a few points, and Ronan simply stared at his sire. He'd long since dropped the pen he'd held, though it had left a large splotch on his letter while he'd clutched it upright. Who was this man?

Admittedly, he hadn't seen his sire in some ten years, but the viscount had changed so much. He no longer affected the fussy trappings of wealth that he'd clung to even when financial straits were dire. Instead, he wore a sober suit of modest cut and fabric. Not the cheapest, but certainly not the most expensive. His hair had gone completely grey, like a chunk of granite with flecks of white.

And he was being polite to Etta. He'd never seen his sire be polite to a woman without his tongue pressed firmly to his cheek. There had always been at least a hint of condescension, if not outright mockery.

But he treated the duchess as though he actually respected her.

Their negotiations came to a close, and his father glanced

toward the door, to where Ronan sat at the writing desk. The older man stilled, his mouth dropping open in a comical O.

Ronan nodded. *Yes,* he thought, *it's me. Your son.*

Then his autocratic, overbearing, emotionless sire burst into tears.

2 4

Of all the things Ronan had expected to happen when he encountered his father again for the first time in twenty years, he'd never entertained the notion that the old man would weep. Rage, scream, be coldly polite, dismissive, or outright pretend he didn't know who Ronan was? One of those options had seemed most likely. But not tears. Not remorse.

The viscount stood and crossed the room, wiping his eyes and getting himself under control. Etta stood and made an excuse to leave the room that Ronan barely heard. He held himself rigid in his chair, and his father hung back, a few feet away.

"I thought you were dead." The words were strained, his voice still broken from crying. "After O'Connor died, I stopped getting reports on your progress from Radley. I tried to find you, but the servants at his house said you'd gone to Dublin. I managed to locate a school you sometimes attended, but by then you were gone. I found your mother on a ship's passenger list to America, and when I discovered that she'd died there in a typhoid outbreak, I feared you died, too."

Ronan's muscles twinged with the strain of holding himself still. He couldn't speak. He was very, very angry. His father had kept tabs on him at Radley? Had followed his progress, but had not bothered to speak to him?

"I'm sorry you weren't able to finish school. I'd have paid for the last year, but O'Connor didn't make provisions in his will to allow for it, and I'd promised your mother I would have no direct contact with you."

At that, Ronan finally spoke. "You promised Ma what?"

His father peered at him out of the same grey eyes. "When she left, she told me you weren't mine, and that I had no claim on you. I was angry, and I used that to divorce her, even though I knew it wasn't true. Afterward, I regretted it and asked her to come back. But she preferred her freedom, and I owed her father a great deal of money. He forgave my debt and bought back the land that had been her settlement, and in exchange, I was never to speak to you again."

Ronan's vision darkened at the edges as his entire world shifted on its foundations. Snatches of half-remembered arguments came back to him, his parents screaming at each other. His mother had been as vocal as his father, her temper quicker and fiercer. And he remembered other things now, too: memories of his father that he'd long assumed were only wishful fantasies.

But no, they really had gone fishing on the estate, and his father had taught him how to ride and hunt. A confused cascade of images, even some with his older brothers, filled his head. "Why did you agree to that? Why would you let me go?"

"They were supposed to take care of you. Things had gotten very tight, and I almost had to withdraw Edmund from Cambridge. With the debt forgiven and the money from the sale, I could afford to pay for him to finish. And I had a good run on my investments after I married again. That's what paid for your school after your grandfather died and your uncles refused to take in their shrew of a sister." He sighed. "I would have taken you back, then, but she was obstinate. I'd already married Patricia, and she said she would not allow you to be brought up in a house with a step-mother who would never love you as she could."

"She did love me, in her way," Ronan said, his voice almost a whisper. "But neither of you had the right to make those choices for me. You should have asked me what I wanted."

"You're right," his father said, shocking him again. "I should have. We should have." No other explanations or justifications, merely an acknowledgment of fault. And that, more than anything else, convinced Ronan he spoke the truth. Because even though he now remembered good things about his childhood, he remembered bad things, too. How his parents had used him as a weapon in their arguments, and how his father could be devastatingly cruel.

But it seemed that time—and grief—had changed him.

"Why don't you live with your current wife?"

"Patricia's mother isn't well. She and your sister spend most of their time in New York with her."

"My sister," Ronan murmured.

"Yes. Adelia." His father's chin rose and he looked pleased and proud, and the wistfulness struck Ronan like a gut punch. "I'll have to cable for her to come on the next steamer to meet you. She's sixteen now, and loves to drive me mad when they visit."

"I...I would like to meet her." And he would. Very much. "But I don't imagine George or Edmund will be happy to see me."

His father waved that away. "I'm not very happy with

either of them at the moment. And Edmund decamped for India six months ago in any case. He's taking up a diplomatic post that his wife's father arranged. I hope it teaches him that he's not actually the center of the universe."

That surprised a chuckle from Ronan. "I'm afraid he might be a touch old for that lesson at forty."

"Why not? It took me until Patricia married me, and I was forty-five then."

"So she's responsible for this…change in you?"

"She would have loved you, no matter what your mother said. I should have fought harder. Tricia told me, and I was too stubborn to listen. And then you were dead, or I believed you were, and she helped me through the grief."

"I heard…" Ronan swallowed, uncertain how to say this without offending the old man. "I heard that you're having trouble."

"Yes, well. I may have speculated too freely the last few years, and the estates weren't able to offset the difference. Land isn't worth as much anymore. Your brothers didn't help. I had to cut off both of their allowances when they refused to curtail their spending. Not that it's entirely George's fault. He married a worthless fribble of a woman who believes she deserves to dress like a queen." He chuck-led. "Not that she actually wants to dress like our queen. She would be devastated if she couldn't have her choice of the most expensive patterns and colors."

Ronan forced a laugh, then came back to the point. "I may be able to help. I'm not exactly destitute."

His father stared at him for a moment and then shook his head. "No. I won't take anything from you, after what I did to you. You don't owe me anything."

"I know I don't. I wouldn't offer it to you if I thought you expected it from me."

That made his father chortle, a real, full belly laugh that

filled the room. So many memories were attached to that whooping sound, things Ronan had dismissed as a boy's foolish imagination. "Why does that not surprise me? You were always twice as obstinate as either your mother or I." Then he came forward and held out his hand. Ronan took it and was pulled to his feet. The next thing he knew, he was in his father's arms.

"I'm glad that you're doing well. I am so glad. But you don't have to do anything. It will be lean for a few years, while I restructure my investments. But I've stopped listening to the people who encouraged me down the wrong paths." His father loosened his hold. They were exactly the same height. The last time they'd been this close, Ronan had been over a foot shorter.

"The duchess's father-in-law is the most non-magical person I've ever met, but he has a gift for making money that's not far shy of wizardry. He advised me on things to do, and I'm taking that advice."

"Well, then. What happens next?"

"I don't know." His father patted his shoulder and let him go. They both took a tiny step back, but not too far. "I'd like to take you to my club, introduce you to my friends. What do you do for a living?"

"I'm in shipping. I have a half-dozen vessels—some steam and some sail."

"Good for you."

"I'm also a mage." At that, his father actually guffawed.

"Are you really? We haven't had a mage in the family in generations. But your mother's great-aunt was a witch, so I suppose it comes from the McCarricks." He grinned. "Wait until your sister finds out. She keeps hoping she'll develop a talent, but she's almost too old now."

"I still want to help you, if I can. Even if it's to examine your books and help you find better investments."

"That kind of help I will gladly accept. When can you begin?"

Ronan thought of the plan they had in the works for tonight, and the woman upstairs who was not speaking to him, and the mage-captain who knew too much about him and his past. But for the first time, Ronan thought there might actually be a future here. With Donn captured and almost certainly on his way to the gallows, there would be a void of power in London's Circle. He could give them a new direction, supporting the duchess and fighting for power in Parliament.

It would be a new course for him, and maybe…maybe he and Sorcha could be together in that life.

"I am helping the duchess with something right now, and it's going to take a few days to wrap up our business. Let's say Monday week?"

His father clapped a hand on his back. "Done. Come round to the house. We'll go over the books, and then I'll take you to my club. It won't be enough time for Tricia and Delia to arrive, but I'll have them here as soon as can be."

Ronan wrapped his arms around his father and held him close. Everything had changed. He had a father, and a step-mother, and a sister. And soon, if she forgave him for being a coward and hurting her, he would beg the woman he loved to become his wife.

But first, he had to catch a madman.

Sorcha paced the shop room one more time, furious at everyone in her life, but especially Ronan and Lucien Blake. The two men had not had a single polite conversation, had torn apart the other's ideas, and had deliberately mocked and provoked each other while they laid their trap for Donn.

But when Sorcha attempted to take a position in the trap, they stood shoulder-to-shoulder and insisted that she remain on the periphery, acting more as a witness than anything else. She'd argued, and pled, to no avail. And when Ronan had asked to speak to her privately this morning, she'd put him off. She was too angry to listen to whatever he wanted to say. Angry first that he'd run, and second that even though he'd returned, he hadn't come to her last night to make amends.

She'd sat in her bed, exhausted but unable to sleep, waiting for him to come and tell her he was wrong, that being together was the most important thing. What did she care what society thought? Etta had already done more in her forthright American way to fulfill Lilias's dreams for the clan than anyone else had managed since the first duchess's death. Sorcha had no intention of changing to fit the restrictive societal mold.

And if Ronan wanted to fight for Irish independence, who better to assist him than a brash, outspoken, American duchess who had already managed to convince the Prime Minister and Home Secretary to pay attention to her concerns?

The last Home Rule bill had failed, but perhaps the next, sponsored by the Duchess of Fay, would succeed.

Sorcha reached one end of the shop and started back toward the grimy front window.

Ronan and Evie were inside the warehouse across the street, waiting for Donn. Lucien, Etta, Mal, and a large group of soldiers dressed in rough clothing lined the streets surrounding the warehouse and perched on rooftops. Lucien would not allow his quarry to escape.

She longed to leave this silly little shop, with its assortment of dry goods and shoddy fabrics, march to the warehouse, and demand to be included. But her talents truly did not mesh with their plans, and if she broke cover now, she might ruin everything.

~

EVIE MADE A TINY GESTURE WITH HER LEFT HAND. THEY'D linked again but were keeping the contact light, so Ronan had been watching for that signal. Something had triggered one of the tiny alarm wards she'd placed around the warehouse. And despite the number of vermin in the vicinity, Ronan had no doubt that the culprit was larger than a rat.

Donn and Fina stepped into the light of a hanging lantern. The place hadn't been converted for gas or electricity yet, and if no one renovated the dilapidated structure soon, might never be.

Evie and Ronan both held up closed fists, as did the witch. But Ronan was absolutely certain that the woman's Sight was open and that she had a few spells ready just in case. As did they.

"So you've both seen the light, eh?" Donn said. "Your allies prove untrustworthy?"

"They've bent and let the English take them up the arse," Evie said, an echo of Ronan's teasing comment the night before.

"Can't trust a Scot," Ronan added, though at the moment he even trusted the bloody English officer more than the Irishman before him. At least he could trust Blake to act for whatever he perceived to be the good of the British Empire. He would probably try to arrest him once this was finished. "They bluster about hating the English, but when it comes time to act?" He hoped Sorcha would forgive him for those lies.

"Aye, well, then where's the goods?"

Evie patted her satchel. "They're here." She took a half-step forward. "I'll bring them with us."

Fina made a gesture in Evie's direction, possibly a trigger for her passive magic. Sorcha had noted that the witch had been trained by someone who used such magical crutches. "She's lying. There's nothing of power in that bag."

Rather than angering, Donn grinned. "I didn't think there would be." He pulled Evie into a rough embrace. "These two are too smart for that."

Ronan tensed, but when the blow came, he could do nothing to stop it. Evie raised her hand and slashed him with a blade of magical fire. Because of their link, Ronan couldn't block or deflect it. It raked across his chest, slicing through to the bone, and then over his side. The stink of burnt flesh cut through the magical aromas of the room.

Evie's thoughts matched his cry of agony. *I can't stop it, Ro! He put something on me—*

The link severed, and Ronan collapsed. He watched through a haze of pain as Evie cast a barrier around the three of them, and Fina shot off projectiles of magic at Etta, Mal, Blake, and the army mages. They escaped into the darkness, and Ronan's vision dimmed. He struggled to remain conscious, to fight back and go after Evie, but he lost the battle and fell into the dark.

THE SHOPKEEPER CALLED SORCHA FROM HIS COUNTER. HE WAS a retired regimental of some kind, and he had agreed that they might use his space. But he wouldn't have imagined a furious, pacing female invading his store.

Sorcha made her feet move away from the window.

"You'll only make yourself sick, worrying and waiting. It's the worst part of any campaign. The fighting is awful, but it's quick and brutal and done, and then there's more waiting and worrying."

"I'd prefer that there not be a fight, nor a wait." That she'd prefer not to worry went without saying.

One of the mage-officers came to the front of the store. He was dressed as a shop-assistant and had a small stone that had been spelled so that he alone could hear words spoken into its mates. "Mr. McCauley has arrived. I'm to stay with you until he and his co-conspirators are captured."

Damn. This wouldn't have been Ronan's decision. Ronan didn't want her confronting Donn, but he would not have assigned her a nanny. No, this was Lucien's doing.

"I am perfectly safe here, sir."

Even as the words left her mouth, the floorboards shook and she stumbled back onto a dry goods case, scattering the contents all around and cracking her head on the edge of a shelf.

The soldier stumbled, too, and grabbed for her while the ground tilted and vibrated. He managed to grasp her shoulders, and they helped steady each other until the shocks subsided.

He let her go, his face flushed with embarrassment at the contact. "Are you well, ma'am?"

"Yes, fine." Her head hurt, but that was insignificant now. "We need to go help. People could be hurt."

"I'm supposed to keep you safe—"

"Then come with me. I am going to help if I can." She dashed to the door and the mage-officer called after her. He would follow.

On the street, bricks and debris had fallen into the street from the sides of buildings, and people were picking themselves up from where they'd tumbled. One man stumbled past with a gash on his forehead, and a woman limped on the arm of a soldier, but no one seemed seriously injured.

At the warehouse door, she met Etta and Mal. Mal carried Ronan, who lay limply in Mal's arms. A subtle spell helped offset part of Ronan's weight, and memory tore through her as she recognized a variation on the spell she and Ronan had used to transport the new keystones on Skye. What had happened to him?

Sorcha threw herself at Ronan, putting her hands on his shoulders and shoving her magic into him, searching for signs of life. His shirt and trousers were bright red and glistening with blood.

His magic flickered weakly against hers. Badly injured, but still alive. Thank the goddess.

"We will bring him to Skye House," Etta said. "Blake is sending for one of the mage-surgeons to meet us there."

Mal stepped onto the bed of a nearby wagon. They'd meant to use it to transport the unconscious bodies of Donn and his minions, but it would be better for Ronan now than the cramped interior of the carriage.

Sorcha climbed on and sat beside him. "Damn you, Ronan McCarrick. You weren't supposed to get yourself injured before I could yell at you again." She swiped sweaty locks of hair back from his face. His eyelashes fluttered, revealing the grey eyes that had captured her heart from that first night on the beach.

"Yell...all you...like." He took a shallow breath, and winced. "I'm...listening."

His magic was all apples now, with no more traces of salt. Sorcha wrapped hers around him, hoping that her power might give him the extra energy to survive.

You're off your head. I can't shout at you now. She stroked his face, brushing over the purple swelling on his jaw where Evie had punched him the night before. She placed her lips, very lightly, on the spot.

The cart jerked and started moving. *Stay with me. We'll have you back at Skye House soon, and someone will be there to take care of you.* Why did she have to have such a useless talent? What good was the ability to see glimpses of the future, and scry, and cast a good ward, when the man she loved lay bleeding beside her?

His thoughts came to her, a muddle of Irish, the language he'd said his mother used when he was a boy.

A chuisle, a chroí, a solas. Tá tú go h-álainn. A anamchara. Táim i ngrá leat. Go síoraí. Is tú mo ghrá.

She could only translate pieces of the Irish, but enough to recognize what that last phrase meant. She grazed lips with hers. *I am yours, forever. I will light your way for as long as you can swim to me.* 'S tusa gràdh mo bheatha. *There will never be another for me.*

He lapsed back into unconsciousness, and she held him tight as the cart jolted and lurched across London.

2 5

The mage-surgeon stabilized Ronan and closed the worst of the injuries. He cautioned that it would take several weeks recuperation for everything to heal, since the surgeon did not want to use too much of Ronan's magical energy or his physical strength for the spell.

It was only after the surgeon left that Etta sat beside the bed and took Sorcha's hand.

"Sorcha, love, I have to tell you something."

Sorcha could barely tug her gaze away from Ronan, but she did it. "What?"

"You've not noticed that Evie isn't here."

Sorcha glanced around the room, then back to Etta. "No, I hadn't. I assumed she was still with Lucien, or Mal, helping to track Donn and the others.

"She's not. She's…well, there's no easy way to say it. Donn took her. I've received a message from a Lady Wiltbury, who is downstairs in my parlor. He has agreed to trade her for the Wells."

Sorcha stood so fast her chair tipped back and crashed against the wall. "She's here?"

Etta grabbed for her as she made a dash for the door. "Wait, love. Yes, she's here. She requested to speak with you specifically, and I told her to wait. You need to change."

Blood stained her dress in spatters and splotches, and her hands were red to the wrists. "No. She can see me as I am. He's mine, and she'll never have him again."

The woman in the parlor wore a very fashionable evening gown, and Sorcha wondered what entertainment she had put off to make this visit. She sat rigidly upright on one of the settees that had, until recently, been covered by a dust cloth. Although she held herself with a forceful dignity, the fingers of her right hand moved restlessly in her skirts. She was aware that she sat in the home of a duchess, and said duchess now knew all of her dirty secrets.

Sorcha didn't much care what Lady Wiltbury felt at the moment, and a vicious surge of pleasure filled her as the woman blanched upon seeing Sorcha enter the room. "Great goddess," she cried. "Is that...Rory's blood?"

"Yes. This is what Donn did to him." Sorcha forced her hands—drying blood flaking off of her fingers—into the woman's face. "And you have the gall to come here and broker that bastard's bargains for him?"

The lady sank back against the sofa, curling in on herself as far as her corset would allow. "I swear to you, I didn't know Rory had been hurt. Is he...alive?"

Sorcha stared at her, her body almost trembling from how much she wanted to spit in this woman's face rather than tell her anything else about Ronan. But she managed to say, "Yes. Now, what do you want with me?"

Lady Wiltbury had been cringing away from Sorcha's hands, but relaxed and straightened with the news that Ronan hadn't died. "I was given a message and told to deliver it. That's all I know."

"Why do you have a message for me?"

"I had one message for the duchess, and one for you. I already told Her Grace the other message. The one for you is this: If you surrender yourself in exchange for the girl, *he* will accept just one of the big items."

"Does *he* say how long we have to decide?"

"I am to come back tomorrow, and you must tell me your decision then."

"Where will you meet him?"

"He will meet me. I've no idea where, or when, except that it will be after calling hours."

"Does he have a spell on you right now? Tracking you? Listening in?"

Lady Wiltbury trembled. "Probably."

"I will remove it if you will tell me what Ro—what *Rory* means to you."

The woman nodded with almost pathetic swiftness. Sorcha opened her Sight and searched for any hint of magical threads. She found a few and teased them out, carefully checking to make sure none had been tied into a major organ or blood vessel. She'd read an account from the Napoleonic War that mages on both sides of the conflict used to do that to their spies, so that if they were caught and someone tried to remove the spells, the person would die, unable to be forced to share their secrets.

But this spell was not so diabolical. Sorcha unraveled it, and said, "It's done. Now, tell me."

Lady Wiltbury spilled a tale of debauchery, corruption, and seduction, in which neither she nor Ronan had been innocent. She called him Rory Donnelly, but otherwise her knowledge of him and his personality was accurate.

"And when he recently made contact with you, you demanded that he resume his...previous relationship with you?"

The lady frowned prettily. "I may have mentioned that I missed his particular skills. But if you mean, did we go to bed together again, no. It was quite disappointing, even if his fingers were as nimble as ever."

"His fingers?"

One haughty eyebrow rose. "Yes. He's very skilled at pleasuring a woman with his hands. I mourned that we did not have time for me to return the favor, because I would have loved to reacquaint myself with that exquisite cock. But the timing was not right. He promised to visit me the next time he was in town, but I suppose with this whole business that will be ages and ages."

Sorcha fought to keep her expression neutral and her reaction hidden. Lady Wiltbury had taken her surprised question about fingers as proof of Sorcha's innocence, or perhaps only her naïveté, but it had been pure shock. Ronan had lied to her. He hadn't done any of the things he'd thrown at her when he ran.

Why had he done it? To hurt her? To make her recoil from him? Had he been so afraid of her love that he had to break it, to prove that he could?

Except that he hadn't broken it. She still loved him, the damned Irish idiot. And she wasn't going to let him run away again. She'd been afraid that she wasn't important to him, that he saw her as a casual fuck and nothing more. She'd been afraid that he didn't care.

But if he hadn't cared, he wouldn't have felt the need to lie. He wouldn't have gone to any trouble at all. He would simply have left.

And when he'd been lying there, bleeding in the cart, he'd said he loved her.

"You won't be seeing Mr. Donnelly again," Sorcha said. "He nearly died, and might still." That was very unlikely, but his injuries were serious, and anything was possible. "When you call tomorrow, send someone around to the kitchen. I will be waiting there with my message for Donn. I can't speak for the duchess, but he already guessed that I would wish to make my own choice. I will inform you tomorrow what that is."

~

RONAN WOKE IN THE MIDDLE OF THE NIGHT. SORCHA HADN'T planned on telling him about Donn's bargain, but the first thing he did, after pulling her close and murmuring in Irish that he loved her, was ask if Evie had gotten free.

She'd been forced to admit that Evie was still with Donn, and about the proposed trade. She didn't mention the modification that her life would stand in for one of the Wells. She hadn't spoken of that to anyone.

Nor did she confront him with the truth of what had happened between him and Isabella in Hyde Park. Now was not the time for recriminations or accusations. He'd lied from some twisted sense of honor, or perhaps simply from fear. It didn't matter anymore why. He loved her. He'd said the words, and that was enough.

He'd made the choice to run because no one had ever loved him enough to fight for him before. No one had ever loved him enough to stay. Even Evie had left to fulfill her own dreams and choose her own destiny. That choice had cut him deeply, but now his pain was much, much worse. Evie had gone to that warehouse for him, and he hadn't been able to save her.

All of those lost loves had changed something inside of him. Had made him suspect that he wasn't worthy to be loved. And so, when she made him confront the truth of her love, he'd fallen back into fear.

His claims at the time were also true, in part. He did want what was best for her. He simply didn't believe that he could be her best choice.

She would have to prove it to him now. Would have to do what he physically couldn't. He struggled to stay awake, attempted to fight the weakness that dragged him back into oblivion. He wanted to go after Evie, or at least to help plan a rescue. But he'd been through too much, and the sorcerous healing had drained him. He fell back to sleep, and she laid a very light sleeping spell on him to keep him that way. He'd be easy to wake if necessary, but would sleep through the pain and any minor disturbances.

Etta and Mal wanted to mount a full-scale rescue, this time with the overt presence of the army and the police. But Lucien's military superiors did not want to incite trouble in the streets of London with a massive manhunt, and though the police would happily take credit for his capture, the Bobbies had little interest committing their officers to searching for an Irishman who had yet to be linked to a specific crime in their city.

After the disappointing meeting, Sorcha followed Lucien upstairs to the sitting room where they'd been keeping the Wells. He sat next to the bowl that muted their power. "All this trouble because the first duchess had to hoard power."

"She had good reasons, and we'll be able to use them in the way she intended."

"Good intentions often lead to disastrous consequences. A young woman is going to die because of these."

"Maybe." She touched his arm, and the spark of shared magic shimmered between them, as it always did. It no longer frightened her, but felt comfortable, almost familiar. She thought they might learn to be friends, someday, or even partners in magic. That was why she'd come to him with her plan.

"I don't think Evie has to die. What if we brought Donn something that looks and feels like a Power Well, but is really something else?"

"You want to set another trap?"

"Yes, but this time I'm going to be there. It will be you and me, with no one to spook him into rash action. And we'll have what he believes are the Wells there where he can see them. That was the problem last time. Fina sensed that Ronan wasn't holding them. He told me she shouted to Donn that they hadn't really brought them, and that was when he grabbed Evie and made her rake Ronan with a scything spell."

"Yes, but how are we going to create something that will fool her?"

"A recursive spell-loop."

Lucien whistled. "That could work, but they're highly unstable."

"I know. I'd want to take advantage of that fact."

"Hera's tits! You want to deliberately destabilize a loop in a populated area?" His mouth dropped open in an uncharacteristic display of shock.

"I'll build it so that it creates a concussive blast that renders people unconscious, but doesn't break any walls or do any other damage."

"Have you done this before?"

"Once." Heat rose in her cheeks. "Accidentally, when I was a teenager."

He relaxed after hearing she had experience with the spell, but his eyes narrowed slightly when she said it had been an accident. "How widespread is the effect?"

"About three hundred yards."

"That's quite a distance."

"Do you suppose we can encourage him to meet us in a park? That will lessen the casualties."

"Perhaps." Lucien settled back in his chair. "What makes you assume he'll deal with us at all? Didn't he make his offer to the duchess?"

"He made an alternate offer to me. He'll trade Evie for one Well and me."

"One Well is still enough to do considerable damage."

"Yes, but we'll not be bringing that to him."

"What does he want with you?" Lucien looked troubled, and not a little worried for her.

"Revenge on Ronan. I sense he still carries some affection for Evie, and he would prefer not to kill her if he doesn't have to. But he's furious with Ronan for double-crossing him, he and wants to hurt him. Hurting me accomplishes that."

"Did the messenger tell you all this, or do you just…feel it?" She applauded his effort to accept her intuition has a viable source of information, even though he couldn't keep some of the skepticism from his voice.

"Both. But I think he'll be excited to have me in his grasp, and perhaps not as observant as he might otherwise be. I'll say that I've gone behind Ronan's back and brought you with me, which will make him assume that I've betrayed Ronan in the bargain. He'll be so pleased that he'll relinquish Evie to you without much of a fight. Then you can shield her, and I'll destabilize the loop."

"What about you? Won't you be shielded?"

"Not possible. I'll be unconscious along with everyone else. I trust you to take care of the rest." When she'd conceived the idea, her intuition told her that he was the only one who could assist her. When she considered Etta or Mal, the outcome wasn't as certain.

"It's a mad plan, and much of it rests on your intuition about this man."

"My intuition has never failed me before, as long as I

listened to it, and not to my head or someone else reasoning the feelings away."

"Very well, I'll do it. It's our best chance to catch him and save that girl's life."

"Then let's rest. Tomorrow is going to be a busy day."

IN THE MORNING, SORCHA MET LADY WILTBURY'S MAID outside the kitchen door. Sorcha handed her a note. In it was a place and time for the exchange. It was one of the more open areas of Hyde Park, and with the steady rain that had begun falling around dawn, it would be deserted for much of the day.

Sorcha crafted the loop and set it in an empty jar, wrapped in an illusion spell to appear like one of the Wells. She placed the jar in a knapsack and then went to say goodbye to Ronan. He was still asleep, with the spell still in place, so she sat by his bed and told him what she planned to do.

"I'm sorry you're not awake for me to say goodbye properly, but in case things go wrong, you should understand that I love you, and I forgive you. If I make it through this, I won't let you run again. But first I have to procure Evie for you." She kissed him, savoring the heat and the flavor of him, pure apple, with not a single hint of salt. "*Tha gaol agam ort,*" she whispered, and left.

RONAN SWAM UP FROM DREAMS OF BLOOD AND LOSS TO Sorcha's voice. She was talking about a spell-loop, and Hyde Park, and the Serpentine, and how no one would be on

Rotten Row at this time of day in this much rain. Then she said she loved him, and she would retrieve Evie.

He struggled to wake, but something was shrouding his senses, making it difficult to open his eyes. She kissed him, and he longed to kiss her back, to open his mouth and draw her tongue inside, but he couldn't move. Then she was gone. He fought harder against the soothing blanket that wanted him to drift back into sleep. It could have been minutes or hours later when he finally succeeded in opening his eyes.

He tried to sit, but pain screamed through his abdomen where Evie's enforced spell had sliced him open. He gently probed at his belly and found no open wounds, but everything was tender and swollen, only partially healed. It hurt to take a deep breath, but he did it, and then let out that breath in a roar.

Moments later, a maid popped in. He told her to fetch the duchess immediately.

Etta and Mal arrived together, and Ronan told them a portion of what Sorcha had said, omitting the location of the meeting.

"Great Mother, we have to go after her. She's going to get herself killed."

"I will go after her," Ronan insisted. "All I need is for one of you to pour energy into the healing spell the surgeon left on my wounds. It's going to take a lot out of me physically, but I can collapse later."

"You're not going anywhere," Mal said. "Even with both of us together, we wouldn't be able to return you to fighting trim."

"Good luck finding her, then. She told me where she was going. And no, I'm not going to tell you. If you want to come with me, fine, but I'm not going to let you two hare off without me."

The door opened again and McGroarty the butler stepped in. "Pardon me, Your Grace, but Mage-Captain Blake is no longer in the house. One of the kitchen maids saw him and Miss Sorcha leaving three-quarters of an hour ago through the back garden."

Ronan forced himself onto the pillows and to the hells with the pain. "That pompous arse will make things worse. Help me out of this bed, damn it!"

Etta and Mal shared a 'married' glance, and then they linked hands.

"Very well," Etta said, "but we'll go after her linked and shielded. I don't want anyone severing the merge like that witch did to you and Evie at the warehouse."

She put her and Mal's linked hands on Ronan's belly, and they fed power into the healing spells until they glowed even without the use of his Sight. The pain in his abdomen subsided to a manageable pang. Both of them let go and stumbled back. Etta caught herself on the bedside table, and Mal pressed a hand to the wall. He should have been dismayed at what they'd sacrificed for him, but he couldn't regret anything that brought him to Sorcha faster.

He pushed to his feet, and barely wobbled. He wasn't wearing anything, but the duchess was more interested in the state of his wound than the rest of him.

She leaned against the bed and pressed lightly on the still-pink scar. "You'll do for now, but anything too strenuous, and you'll rip this new flesh open." Her voice lacked its usual American enthusiasm, and her hand on his flesh trembled with weariness.

Ronan pulled away from her and went to rustle in the wardrobe for clothes.

"That was a lot of energy we spent on you," Mal said as Ronan shoved his legs into a pair of trousers. "Even with the three of us linked, we'll barely rate what one of us could do at full strength."

"It will have to be enough," Ronan growled, and finished dressing as quickly as he could.

2 6

Rotten Row was nearly empty when Sorcha and Lucien arrived. A few grooms had horses on the path, but most had chosen to remain indoors on this saft, soggy morning. The air was thick with fog and rain fell steadily. The two of them had cast minor wards to deflect the rain on the ride over, but even with the magical assistance they were both well on their way to being soaked as they walked farther into Hyde Park.

Lucien had chosen the spot along the Serpentine with care, placing them at a point in the park with the most open space nearby. Sorcha was confident that her spell would destabilize as it had when she was a girl, but she approved of his caution anyway. The last thing she wanted was to hurt someone while trying to save Evie.

They reached the meeting location and waited. Both of them kept their Sight open to stay alert for spells. Sorcha watched to the west, Lucien to the east. He had his arms folded over his chest, and his index finger made a soft sound, just audible above the constant patter of raindrops, as he tapped against the magic-dampening cuffs he had in his interior coat pocket.

She shifted and one boot squelched in a muddy patch. The odd tang of rain mixed with dust scented the air, along with the more subtle brine and fish scents of the water. So much water would inhibit everyone's ability to cast spells today, a fact Sorcha welcomed.

Two riders came down Rotten Row, and then halted and dismounted. One rider held the horses while the other ducked under the railing toward the Serpentine.

Lucien made a tiny hand gesture that meant the figures were illusions. As the one illusory person approached, the threads became more and more visible. Then they unraveled, revealing Donn, Fina, and Evie. Evie wore a wide necklet—almost a collar—that was the focal point of a spell net that covered her from neck to waist. It restricted her movements and her magic.

"I see you brought a friend to the party," Donn said. "Have you also brought what you promised?"

Sorcha held the jar in front of her face. Her illusion was much better than the other witch's and would withstand a great deal more scrutiny. Raindrops beaded on the surface and dripped onto her hands. "I have. He's here to take Evie back. I'll go with you, as promised."

She let the jar return to her side. Donn's gaze followed it, then returned to her face. His lips formed a terrible rictus of avarice, and if she had actually intended to let him take her, that alone would have changed her mind. "It's your show, birdie," he said. "What shall we do?" His words were a taunt, a reminder that he held the real power here. He only assumed he did.

"I'll stand here," she said. "He'll come to you and take Evie. Then he'll continue on, to the Row. I'll be here with the Well."

"Well and good, then." He nudged Evie, and she stumbled

forward, slipping on the grass, and unable to catch herself because of the necklet. Lucien dashed over and lifted her into his arms. He continued walking, his pace measured and steady, toward the Row.

Now was when the double-cross would come. Someone was still with the horses, perhaps several someones. If they had offensive magic ready, they might be able to put it in play before Lucien could shield himself and Evie, and before Sorcha could destabilize the loop. But the rain still fell in steady sheets, and spells would lose power quickly passing through so many droplets of water.

A shout sounded from the east, in a different direction than Donn's men and horses.

An answering call came from the illusory groom, and the illusion fell away, revealing three men and many more horses than had been apparent. Coming from the opposite direction was a small group of riders. She identified them without being able to see a single face. Ronan, Etta, and Mal.

Donn cursed, and the witch started drawing down threads to make a quick, offensive weave. Lucien stopped, cast the shield, and shouted for Sorcha. She had already begun unraveling the pieces of the loop that kept it spinning, bleeding power into the air and giving it the feel of one of the Wells. But she had to hurry. Already Ronan and the others might be close enough to be caught in the loop's concussive effect.

A spell flew toward her. She couldn't spare the attention to deflect it, and it knocked her hood back. But the rain had done its work, and instead of blasting into her, it landed like a weak punch. It hurt, but did no damage.

She tied the loosened ends together in the formation she remembered from childhood, and then stared into the all-too-sane eyes of Donn, who now loomed over her. He reached to take what he believed was the Well from her grasp, and she breathed the word to activate the loop.

Energy pulsed through her body, and then Sorcha knew only darkness.

~

THERE WERE RIDERS ON THE PATH AHEAD, AND A CLUSTER OF people by the water. From this distance, Ronan couldn't determine facial features, but Sorcha's blond head and delectably curvy shape was unmistakable.

We'd better not be too late, he thought to the others, and he heeled his horse from the jarring canter into an outright gallop. Etta matched him for speed, maintaining the shield that she'd insisted on casting once they reached the park and he revealed their destination. Mal rode between them and several paces behind, guarding their rear.

Ronan could distinguish the others, now. Blake had someone in his arms—probably Evie. Donn was too close to Sorcha—and stepping closer. Blake raised a shield, and the witch Fina pulled down threads of power for a spell. The riders were revealed as illusory when three men walked out of the illusion field, and each raised their hands with weavings ready to toss against Etta, Mal, and himself.

Then something shifted. A pulse of light washed over everyone, followed by a trembling bass rumble that roiled in his stomach, and finally a blast of force that was partially deflected by Etta's shield. But she was tired, and the shield collapsed, and their horses reared in panic.

Bright pain flared along his chest and belly, and something pushed at him. Then he was sliding off the back of the horse. He landed with a jarring crash onto the path.

Beside the Serpentine's edge, Sorcha crumpled to the ground. Donn fell beside her, as did Fina and the men on

Rotten Row. The rest of the illusions vanished, and one more rider, holding the reins of the real horses, toppled. The horses went down, too, but with more grace than their human companions.

Ronan pushed to his feet and stumbled toward the river, clutching at his side. Etta had managed to keep her seat and rode up behind him. Mal was on foot, and he had taken Ronan's horse's reins as well as his own. Ronan dropped to the ground beside Sorcha and gathered her in his arms. His wound screamed at him, but it didn't seem to have broken open, so he ignored it.

"She should be fine."

Ronan snarled at Blake. The mage-captain had set Evie on her feet and was removing a magical suppression collar from her neck.

"What were you thinking, bringing her here? And what in the hells happened?"

"She cast an unstable loop, and destabilized it on purpose."

"Ah," Etta said, dismounting. "Very risky, but it seems to have paid off."

"Except that she's unconscious." Ronan felt the need to state the obvious. No one else appeared to have noticed.

"That was the risk," Blake agreed. "She would have to remain unshielded to make sure the others were affected. Now I can take them all into custody. Duchess, Lord Malcolm, will you assist me in placing suppression and restraint fields around these people? I have three sets of magical restraints, but that won't be enough."

"Of course." Etta and Mal followed Blake. Evie knelt beside Ronan.

"I'm sure she'll be fine. She understood what she was doing. She stared down Donn and let the thing go off in his face. It was magnificent. If you try to run away from her again, I'm going to break your legs to stop you."

"I'm not going to run. She told me why she did it. She came to rescue you for me, because I was too weak to come on my own. She did it because I love you, and she would do anything to protect the people I love. Except she forgot to include herself."

He lifted her and hefted her onto his lap, cradling her head on his shoulder.

"She didn't forget. But she loves you, too. Sometimes that means compromise."

"When did you become so wise about love?"

"Since I started to encounter actual examples of it in my daily life." She gestured toward the duchess and her husband. "Those two are stupid in love with each other, and the headmistress and her husband are still happy after over fifteen years."

"Love aside, it isn't going to be an easy road for us." He thought of his father, and his siblings, and his Cause. He thought of Lucien Blake's knowledge of his past, of the problems Sorcha would face adjusting to life in a city with millions of residents. No, it wasn't going to be easy.

"Loving never is." The words came from the vicinity of his neck, murmured in a voice that was the sound of his own heartbeat.

"No, and you've started us off with a difficult display, haven't you?" His words were only half teasing, but he softened them with a kiss. Sorcha responded eagerly, and if they'd been anywhere but the middle of Hyde Park in the rain, he would have let that response grow. Instead, he broke the kiss and nuzzled her nose.

"I had to do it," she insisted. "It was the only way to secure Evie and capture Donn without risking the Wells."

"I know. And you did well. But allow me to be angry that

you had to put yourself in danger to do it." He kissed her again, hard and fast. "How do you expect me to live in a world of darkness when I've discovered the light?"

She lifted her hand. It shook, but it steadied when it landed on his cheek. "Or me, when I've come through your storms and found that I don't need to run away from the rain?"

"What rain?" he asked. "You're my sun." He stroked her face, the face of his light, his love. He murmured to her in Irish, calling her his pulse, his breath, his life. "I love you, but I'm still afraid I'm not enough," he whispered.

"I can't See every future, but I know this. All I need is you, beside me. Look in my eyes. No matter what the world throws at us, our love will withstand it. You don't need to be in the dark anymore."

She glowed with radiance, and her magic woke along his nerve endings, swamping him with mulberry and thyme, filling him with so much brilliance that he finally believed, with Sorcha, that his life could be different. That he could choose the right path, and leave his old self behind.

He took her mouth again, and followed her into the light.

EPILOGUE

SIX MONTHS LATER

"DAMN." SORCHA RUBBED HER TEMPLES AGAINST THE throbbing ache. She'd spent several hours with Ronan, Etta, various members of Clan Fay and the Army, as well as other mages and witches, casting a spell that was meant to find the source of the drain.

After several failed attempts over the last few months, Ronan and Evie had created a new version, implementing elements of his reconstruction spell with the assistance of Sorcha, Etta, Lucien, and Mal's sister and brother-in-law, Viola and Ian. That was the version they'd cast with with the assistance of half the magically-talented people in London. They'd finally gotten a result, but judging from the dumbfounded expressions around their circle, no one was sure what to do with the information.

Later, when it was only family, Sorcha paged through books from the library with very little success. Ronan sat beside her, reading a letter from his sister Adelia that had come on an express ship from America. She would be in London in two days. Sorcha was very nervous to meet her, although the meeting with his father a few days ago had gone well.

"We're going to need to hire a historical scholar," Etta said, her voice scratchy with weariness, "because I know absolutely nothing about King William and Queen Mary, except that there's a college named for them in Virginia."

"Does anyone in the family study that period in history?" Sorcha asked.

"I don't know," Mal said. "Olivia likes to dig old things up, but her last letter was all about some town in Italy where she's found proof of a conspiracy by Magisterium leaders to spread the black death to leaders of a local coven that worshipped Demeter. That's hundreds of years before the Glorious Revolution."

Ronan cleared his throat. "Speaking of the Magisterium, I'm acquainted with a professor named Alexander Reilly. He used to teach at Trinity College, but he's here in London because he just published a book about the history of the Magisterium and Academy conflicts and he's giving lectures in town. Since the Glorious Revolution was precipitated by that conflict, he might be able to help us."

"Send him a telegram. We'll bring him on board." Ronan slipped away to call the local telegraph office. Etta had gotten a telephone installed in Skye House to have more convenient and reliable communication with her new allies in the government. She'd even taken up her seat in Parliament before the session closed for the season.

"I don't know enough to tell if I'm overlooking something." Sorcha pushed the books away. "But if we have to try again, I'll go mad."

"Me, too," Mal agreed.

Ronan came back inside. "The telegraph office is sending off the message. We should hear back soon."

"What sort of friend is this Alexander Reilly?" Etta asked.

That was code for, 'is he a republican?', but the question was derailed by a feminine voice shouting, "Not Dr. Alexander Reilly?" The voice was attached to a woman of average height who'd entered the library. The last time Sorcha had seen her, she'd had dark hair and eyebrows, with a hint of warm red highlights. Now Olivia Seward's hair was pure silver, almost iridescent, the same color as the streak that marked all the magical members of Clan Fay.

But until that moment, Olivia had never displayed more than a minuscule talent, not even worthy of training.

Malcolm was on his feet, taking his sister into a hard embrace. "Liv! What in the hells happened to you?"

"Oh, this?" She pulled away from her brother and patted at her hair. "That's why Gran brought me back from the Continent. A week ago, I woke from a dream and it was like this."

"What kind of dream?" Sorcha stood behind Mal, and Olivia's features relaxed when she saw her.

"Oh, thank the goddess. I was afraid you'd be in Scotland. You're the only one I know who has visions all the time."

"So it was a vision, then?" Sorcha had suspected as much. She could sense Olivia's magical talent, and it wasn't much different from the last time they'd seen each other, over three years ago. But vision gifts did not require massive amounts of magic.

"More than one! I keep having them. Sometimes a dozen in a day. We came back as quickly as we could, but I need you to help me make them stop."

"That is unusual, but it may be a result of the delayed onset. It can be frightening to witness things and then have them come to pass. But don't worry. I can teach you techniques to deal with them, and to help interpret what you don't understand."

"No, that's not it. I mean, I'll take all the help I can, but it's not the future I'm seeing. It's the past."

That was more unusual still. The only time Sorcha had ever seen the past was when she'd had the visions of Lucien Blake's life. And she still hadn't figured out why she'd had those.

Etta walked to her sister-in-law. "Can you control what you See?"

Olivia stared at her, and Mal took Etta's hand. "Liv, this is Etta, my wife."

"Oh. I wasn't sure. You only said she was American in your letters." Her blank expression shifted to warmth. "I'm pleased to meet you, and I'm dying to talk with you about this clod here." She punched her brother on the arm. "But to answer your question, I can only control them a little. I was able to move around in one, and one time I recognized what I was seeing and the vision focused on the segment that I knew."

"If you can control it at all, with practice you'll be able to control it at will." Sorcha took Olivia's hand and pulled her to a sofa. "Seeing through time is a rare gift, and very valuable."

"That's why I came home. I knew you could help me."

Mal sat on his sister's other side and put his arm around her. She leaned into him gratefully. "I wish this had started years ago. I was always so jealous of you and Viola, getting all of Mother's attention." She glanced around the room. "Is she here?"

"No." Mal's hand stroked up and down his sister's arm in a soothing motion. "She's at home. Why didn't you telegraph when this started?"

"I thought about it, but even though we started home

right away, I kept hoping it would stop. And then I decided it was better not to worry you until I saw you."

"How did you know to come to Skye House?" Sorcha asked.

"One of Gran's friends met us at the station and mentioned that the Duchess was in town and hosting a big gathering of witches and mages. And honestly, I wanted Mal here more than Mother."

He squeezed her tightly and kissed the top of her head with its shocking hair. "You'll not feel that way when you see her. She's thawed in the last year. Having new magical grand-babies and an outspoken daughter-in-law has done wonders for her personality."

Etta perched on the arm of the sofa. "Why did you shout about this Dr. Reilly when you came in? Is there some reason why we shouldn't work with him? We're embarking on a rather sensitive project, and if you are familiar with him..." The sentence trailed off, but her voice rose in inquiry.

"Oh, him." Olivia's face flushed. "He's a scandal-monger. Have you read any of his journal articles? Absolutely libelous, if the people in question weren't hundreds of years dead."

"You've read many historical journals on your travels?" Mal asked. "I'd have imagined your actual explorations would be much more exciting. Gran said you were always digging at some site or spending hours with moldy manu-scripts and folios."

"They were, without doubt. Much more exciting." She grinned at him. "But how else was I to discover which were the best places for publication?"

"Places for publication?" Mal peered at his little sister like she'd removed her head and started tossing it around the room. "You're publishing in scholarly journals now?"

"Yes, naturally," Olivia said, in the way of little sisters whose brothers are being unforgivably obtuse. Then she frowned. "Except that snake Reilly keeps submitting articles on the same topics, and his are so sensational they always choose *his* to publish. His methods are specious at best. He's an *anthropologist*." She put so much venom into the word that she might have said he was a follower of the Dark God. "That basically means he can concoct whatever he wants and pretend it's science. He's driving me mad!"

A footman entered the library and handed a slip of paper to Ronan. He read the message and chuckled. "Well, he'll be able to drive you mad in person, *colleen*. He's on his way here now."

Thank you so much for reading *A Theft of Magic*. I hope you enjoyed it.

- Want to know when my next book is coming out? Sign up for my newsletter at http://eepurl.com/bY89o1, like my Facebook page at https://www.facebook.com/caramckinnonauthor/, follow me on Twitter at https://twitter.com/cara_mckinnon, or sign up for release messages on BookBub at https://www.bookbub.com/profile/cara-mckinnon.
- Reviews help readers find books. Good or bad, I appreciate every one.
- *A Theft of Magic* is the second book in the Fay of Skye series. Book one is *Essential Magic*. Book three is *Memories of Magic*. *Secret Magic* and *Blood Magic* are forthcoming.

Her visions will save English magic...
If his teachings—and his love—can keep her alive.

Olivia Seward never developed the magic of her elder siblings, but now she's plagued by visions of the past. Etta, Duchess of Fay, asks her to use those visions to discover the source of the drain on English magic. Unfortunately, the visions draw too deeply from Olivia, leaving her weak and vulnerable.

Savitendra Reilly, a half-Indian, half-Irish historian, is hired by the duchess to research the origins of the Aegis Spell, but it is the magic of his birthplace that Olivia needs to learn to control her visions.

The only problem: Savit is an ascetic, performing magic by honing his mind and ignoring the needs of the flesh. Olivia is a hedonist, and accesses her power through pleasure. And every time they do magic together, Savit's desire for her grows.

If he succumbs to their mutual passion, he believes won't be able to protect her from the ravages of her unpredictable gift. But Olivia is convinced the only way to access the truth of the past is to immerse themselves in each other–sharing bodies, minds, hearts, and souls.

In the dream, the woman's intense, dark gaze met Olivia's. But no ephemeral figment created by Olivia's sleeping mind could hold such intelligence—such anger—in her eyes.

Whatever this was, it wasn't a dream.

Olivia's ghostlike perspective, floating around and through the people around her, changed abruptly. The woman pinned her into position, gave her substance in this not-quite-real place. When Olivia wrenched her gaze away from those piercing eyes, she observed the collar gripping the woman's neck, its copper surface worked with Greek letters and Devanāgarī script. Matching cuffs surrounded her wrists, and her hands curled into tight fists.

This was a sorceress, bound for trial. From her dress and that of the two mages beside her, Liv judged the period as late sixteenth or early seventeenth century, the same period as the remains she'd been cataloguing earlier in the day. Olivia had recently taken over supervision of a dig at the site of a mass witch burial in southwestern France, near the Atlantic coast. Most of the actual digging had stopped for the season, but she was attempting to organize the mess the previous foreman had left behind.

She recognized the pattern on the collar and cuffs. When she'd seen them this afternoon, fire had tarnished and warped the magical suppressants, fusing them to the woman's skeleton.

Olivia had noted the presence of the metal in a detached way before, wondering why they'd felt it necessary to restrain the woman until the moment of death. The magic in the pieces was still strong enough to buzz against even her weak talent. None of the other bodies had any evidence of wariness on the part of the magistrates.

But now she had no doubt why they'd feared to remove her bindings. Liv looked again into the woman's eyes, and three hundred years disappeared. The woman could see her, as though Olivia stood in the courtroom and was on the side of the accusers. The sorceress's dark eyes smoldered with hatred, but there was confusion, too. She couldn't speak—the collar would prevent that—but Liv understood.

I will tell your story, Olivia promised. The woman blinked, and Liv added, *You will not be forgotten.*

Some sort of link must have been forged between them, because a surge of magic came up from the woman. *My name is Izarra Balere.* The words weren't in English, but the meaning was clear anyway.

I see you Izarra Balere. I will remember you.

Memories poured into Olivia then: of the woman's life, her husband and children who had already been taken and put to death, her sister who had fled to the West Indies. The many people Izarra had put on boats, never joining them, always coming back for more, until she was captured and brought before the court.

And then there was pain. So much torture and suffering that Liv started screaming, and though she tried, she could not wake.

Agony lasted an eternity, the way time in a dream can seem like a lifetime and yet be only a moment.

Then another presence entered the not-dream. He was

warm, and solid, and somehow both calming and energizing, like a cup of milk mixed with spices.

He drew her out of the morass of misery and deposited her back into her unconscious body. As her other senses returned, she saw a luscious male form, strong and lean. She had no firsthand experience with spirit bodies, only a vague knowledge from magical studies courses, but if his was any reflection of his actual flesh, she would very much like to see him again when she was awake and aware.

Then he was gone, and she opened her eyes.

To find out more about *Memories of Magic*, click here.

ACKNOWLEDGMENTS

Once again my editor, Anna LaVoie of Literally Yours Editing, has proved her mettle. With every book we work on together, I appreciate her talent and insight more and more. Thanks also to my copyeditor, Symantha Reagor, for putting up with my comma errors.

Special thanks to the ladies of my group blog tour who helped me launch *Essential Magic* and are on board for this book, too: J.L. Gribble, Jennifer Loring, Andi Adams, A.J. Culey, Jessica Knauss, and Sheri Queen. They are all fantastic authors, and you should check out their work!

As always, I would not be the writer I am nor able to produce these books without the teachers and extended community of Seton Hill University's Writing Popular Fiction Program.

To my family and friends who have supported me in this endeavor, thank you forever. My parents, Leroy and Kathy, are always willing to take the kids when I go to conferences and signings. My husband Steve is my rock, and I could not do any of this without him.

And of course, a huge thank you to my readers. You are the reason I write. I hope you love these books as much as I do.

Love at the Edge of Seventeen: A YA Romance Anthology

"Three Jagged Pieces"

COMING SOON

Born to Love Wild: A Paranormal Romance Anthology

"A Change of Heart"

and the historical setting and details are beautifully done. Highly recommended." – Amazon review
- "[A] great romance." – Goodreads review
- "Masterfully written." – Amazon review
- "Cara McKinnon does a masterful job of transporting her readers to magical 19th century Scotland. Her detailed descriptions of historically accurate attire and etiquette helped to fully immerse me in a story that I was unwilling to put down until the very end. Engaging characters, powerful emotions; all with a unique and captivating method used to describe the casting of spells." -Christina Robbins, author of *Seeking Solace*

PRAISE FOR A THEFT OF MAGIC

- "McKinnon hits it out of the park once again with this delightful blend of alternate history, historical fiction, action, and sensuality...an exciting magical romp from start to finish." – J.L. Gribble, author of *Steel Victory*
- "Politics, schemes, and betrayal...twists that I definitely didn't see coming. The sex started early and got steamier as it went." – Dawn from Up Til Dawn Book Reviews for The Romance Reviews
- "The characters are beautifully crafted, the historical details make the world come alive and seem so vividly possible, I almost want to search for the missing magic myself." -Amazon review
- "What a superb fantasy historical! A great read that I shall keep and reread again and again. Her way of blending fantasy and magic with history was great.

I was captivated and enchanted and enthralled by her writing and her stories. I cannot wait to see what else she does. You will absolutely not be disappointed in buying this book or the series." – Goodreads review

ABOUT THE AUTHOR

Cara McKinnon has been writing magical stories since age five, when she penned a gripping tale about a unicorn couple – her first foray into fantasy romance. Cara is a graduate of the Seton Hill University Writing Popular Fiction MFA program, which she recommends to all genre writers. She lives in Western Maryland with her husband, two children, and an oversized lapdog named Jake.

Cara loves to hear from readers. Visit her online or send a message.
caramckinnon.com
cara@caramckinnon.com

www.ingramcontent.com/pod-product-compliance
Lightning Source LLC
Chambersburg PA
CBHW031221120726
47905CB00002B/421